PRINT EDITION

Unreachable Skies Vol. 1 © 2018 by Mirror World Publishing and Karen McCreedy

Edited by: Robert Dowsett

Cover Design by: Justine Dowsett

Published by Mirror World Publishing in August 2018

Mirror World Publishing

Windsor, Ontario, Canada

www.mirrorworldpublishing.com

info@mirrorworldpublishing.com

ISBN: 978-1-987976-48-9

For my wonderful parents, with love.

Unreachable Skies

Vol. 1

By Karen McCreedy

M|W mirror world publishing

With best wishes for a happy Christmas 2019,

One

"The heir is hatching. Vizan must come at once."

Morel had not bothered to knock before he flung open our dwelling door to make his announcement – crass behaviour for a First Herald, I thought, even if he did have urgent news. His sudden appearance had made me spill the herbal drink I'd just mixed, and I took a moment to ladle more from the pot over the fire into the beaker in my paw. It gave me something to do that didn't involve thinking about the problems and complications that Morel's news brought.

As he folded his wings and stepped over the threshold in response to my nod, I voiced the most immediate concern: "Vizan can't come. You know he's ill."

"But he must." Morel's dark mane was sticking up in alarm, and I didn't envy him telling Kalis that Vizan wouldn't be there. "The Fate-seer has to be present at the hatching of a Prime's egg. Especially—"

He snapped his jaw shut on further comment, but it was easy enough to guess what he hadn't said: *Especially now, when the egg had been laid by a female who had had the Sickness.*

I could have told Morel that having a Fate-seer present for a hatching had made no difference to Carma or Lisha or to nines of other females. In every case they had counted themselves fortunate to survive the Sickness, and in every case the eggs they'd laid had produced...I pulled my thoughts from those poor crippled hatchlings, and snapped at Morel to close the door. "The last thing Vizan needs is a cold draught ruffling his fur."

The faint salt tang of an onshore breeze vanished along with the draught as he did as he was bid, but it was clear from the way he wrinkled his snout and flattened his ears that he thought he might catch something by coming further inside.

I had felt that way too seven moons before, on the day I had first become Vizan's apprentice. When he'd ushered me through the door – a Trader's youngling who had expected to spend her life flying from cluster to cluster with goods and provisions – I had half-expected to find decaying piles of sacrificial bones under the table. But the Fate-seer's dwelling was much the same as any other: the wall stones set one on another to spiral upward and inward, a fire glowing in the hearth to one side, a well-scrubbed vinebark table, upholstered sitting-stools, zaxel stems scattered across the floor, and a woven-reed screen in front of the nests. However, only this dwelling had bunches of healing herbs hanging from the roof-stones, and jars of ointments and salves lining the shelves. Only this dwelling had baskets of dried camyl leaves, twists of zenox powder, and handfuls of chalkmoss scattered across the workbench, waiting to be sorted beneath the light that streamed through the see-shell.

It also had a sticky patch on the floor where the herbal mix had just spilled, and I heard Morel's grunt of disgust as he stepped in it.

"Vizan's over here." I ushered Morel around the screen, and saw his nose and whiskers twitch as he caught the scent of the drink I had mixed – a smell which did not quite mask the sickly odour emanating from the Fate-seer's nest. "Now do you see why he can't come?" I crouched low to hold the beaker under Vizan's black-striped snout. His nose barely twitched, but he opened one eye and managed to sip a little of the hot liquid. It was hard to bear the sight of his once-imposing body lying helplessly in a soiled nest. His greying fur was matted, because brushing it made it fall out; he couldn't even summon the energy to tuck his tail around his legs and it hung limply over the edge of the nest. His breathing rattled wetly, with a noise like wave-driven pebbles and, as I placed a paw on his shoulder to help him change position, I could feel the bones beneath the skin.

I looked up to find Morel spiralling a paw across the front of his grey tunic in the age-old gesture of prayer, his ears dipped to the correct angle of respect. "May the Spiral watch over him." He scratched at the thin beard under his chin, clearly unsure what he should do. He was as new to his role as I was to mine: neither of us knew what the protocol was. After a beat or two, Morel set his ears upright.

"If Vizan is not well enough to come, then you must. Kalis is frantic," he said. He rubbed a paw over the brown fur on his snout and I noticed that the skin beneath bore a pattern of red marks.

Vizan coughed and I set the beaker down, wiping his mouth with a cloth. Once I'd tended to him, I raised a paw to point at Morel's sore nose. "Kalis bit you?"

"It's just a nip." Morel gave the marks another rub, then put his paws behind his back as though to keep them as far from his injury as possible. "My own fault. Kalis ordered me to fetch the Fate-seer right away, and I was foolish enough to say that Vizan wasn't well." His claws made a regular 'pitter-pit' sound against the uneven stones of the floor as he wiggled his toes, and I smelled impatience mingled with anxiety. Clearly he had no wish to incur more of the Prime's displeasure by returning without a Fate-seer.

Neither did I. But...

"Kalis won't want me praying over his egg. Vizan was his sire's Fate-seer and his grandsire's. I'm just an apprentice."

"No!" Vizan's voice was little more than a thread, but there was surprising strength in his wrinkled paw as he clutched my arm. "You must go, Zarda. You have the Sight. You are the Fate-seer now. Go! Go with Morel..."

"Vizan..." I hesitated, too afraid to voice the questions that had been gnawing at my thoughts since the Prime's egg was laid: *What if the hatchling is like the others? What might happen if he, too, is crippled?*

It wasn't a question I could have imagined asking a couple of moons ago. The sun shone by day, the Spiral watched over us by night, the moon waxed and waned every fifty-four days, and every drax could fly. Even after the Sickness had taken so many in the growing season, there had been no reason to imagine that the survivors would face the horror of hatching deformed offspring from their late batch of eggs.

Vizan seemed to sense what I couldn't put into words and his grip on my arm tightened. "We Saw him, Zarda," he croaked, "in the Dream-smoke." He coughed, and his next words came in ones and twos, forced out between snatched breaths that rattled in his chest: "The Visions...are never wrong...never." I could see he was trying to set his ears upright to indicate his sincerity, though he was now so feeble they did little more than twitch. "This hatchling...will lead...victory...over the...Koth."

I glanced up at Morel and saw my own doubt reflected in the set of his ears. The mountain-dwelling Koth had raided and pillaged our farms since the Spiral first shone in the sky. It was true that I'd shared Vizan's astonishing Vision, but still I had trouble accepting it as fact.

Vizan must have sensed my doubt. "You Saw it too...we both Saw." He began to cough, and I reached again for the beaker, but he waved a paw toward the door and I read anger in his one open eye. "Put on the badge. Go!"

"Very well – but only if Morel agrees to fetch a healer to look after you."

Vizan rasped something that might have been, "I don't need looking after," but I waited till Morel nodded agreement. "I'll fetch Doran – she's the nearest since Symur died – but not until after I've taken you to Kalis. We can't afford to waste any more time."

It would have to do. At least I could trust Doran to brew the right mixture for Vizan – she had visited often while I nursed him, bringing plants and herbs for his medicines, and helping me to blend and mix them as we talked. She and I had been hatched in the same cluster, spent our first cycle together, and had expected to remain within a few dwellings of each other throughout our lives. Even when the Sight came to me as a half-grown I did not think to be taken to the Fate-seer, since he already had an apprentice far more gifted than I would ever be. But the Sickness came, the apprentice – and his successor – died, and there was no-one else for Vizan to teach. Doran had moved from our hatching-place too, but we had remained friends and I could always rely on her to tell me the latest news from the Expanse.

"She will talk my ears off," muttered Vizan, his voice a strained whisper.

I smoothed his matted mane, something I would never have dared do if he had been well. "You will enjoy hearing all her news."

"She has an egg…" He broke off to cough again.

"Miyak can keep it warm."

I left the beaker where Vizan could reach it and stood up, ushering Morel ahead of me as we moved around the screen to the living space. I saw his snout wrinkle again and I realised that I'd not kept the place as tidy as I would have if Vizan had not been sick. A stack of unlicked bowls sat on the workbench next to a pile of unsorted herbs. A blob of branmeal had dropped onto the table from one of the bowls, and the smell of unwashed tunics rose from the basket beside the screen. I hesitated, wondering whether I might take a moment to clear the worst of the mess away – I could at least put the waste bucket outside – but Morel had already spotted the Fate-seer's silver badge of office and he plucked it from the hook behind the door, holding it out for me to take.

Soft light from the westering sun angled through the see-shell, making the badge, with its intricate spiral pattern of raised dots, sparkle. I spiralled a paw over my chest, seeking strength. I couldn't do this! Yet…if not me, then who?

Morel was hopping from foot to foot, his ears twisting in alarm. "Come on, Zarda, take it! We have to go."

The badge was cool and light in my paw, its circular edge worn near the top, where generations of Fate-seers had held it while they pinned it on. Feeling the weight of their legacy, I hesitated for a heartbeat more before I fastened it to the front of my tunic. As I smoothed the black-and-white striped fabric, I realised that it was stained with grease and kestox syrup, but a glance at Morel's impatient ear-twitching told me there was no time to change. I took a moment to brush my fur, comb my whiskers, and wipe my paws, then set my ears straight and tried to keep my tail still.

"I'm ready." That was untrue. I had been nervous enough on the few occasions that I had been admitted to Kalis' presence, and there had been no need then for me to do more than dip a bow and set my ears and wings to the appropriate angle. Vizan had taken me with him to observe, and Kalis had taken no more notice of me than he had of Vizan's shadow. Now I was being asked to take Vizan's place – not merely to speak, but to watch over Kalis' egg and pray for the hatchling.

Pray? I wasn't even sure I could remember the correct words for the occasion, let alone put them in the right order.

Morel didn't hear the doubt in my voice, though. He half-raised his wings and dipped his ears to acknowledge Vizan, turned, and ducked out through the doorway.

I peered around the screen to give Vizan a last glance, half-hoping that he would sit up and declare that he felt much better, but his eyes were closed again and he rasped a snore. There was nothing for it but to follow Morel outside.

Vizan's dwelling was the central point of the High Council cluster. Not for the first time, I wished that there was enough room on the curving pathway for me to spread my wings and fly over the other dwellings on the isolated mesa. The thought had hardly grazed my mind when the long shadow of a guardflight patrol skimmed overhead. I looked up to see who was on duty, but against the after-zenith sun all I could see was a silhouette with a bow in one paw. From where I stood the trackway spiralled through the cluster, thin soil showing through the moss that covered the rest of the plateau in red tussocks. A delicious aroma of fresh-cooked fish drifted from the next dwelling, where Hapak, the Chief Artisan, lived, reminding me that I hadn't eaten since dawn. My stomachs rumbled a protest, but I'd long since regurgitated and rechewed my breakfast; I would have to stay hungry for a while longer.

An easterly breeze freshened the air with the scent of waterweed; half-heard voices from Hapak's dwelling vied with the hiss-and-rattle of the sea dashing pebbles against the base of the cliffs. The wind was chilly, reminding me that the harvest season was almost over, and I raised the fur on my arms a little, wondering if I might go back inside for a snack and a warmer tunic.

Morel, a few steps ahead of me on the winding path, looked back to check I was following, and slapped his tail on the ground to show his exasperation. "Zarda, we do not have time to admire the view." Without another word, he turned and led the way around the trackway to the *Spirax,* where the Prime dwelt.

The *Spirax* awed me. It always had. The black cone towered over the councillors' dwellings as a mountain dwarfs the foothills around it. Some said it had been built by the God of the Great Spiral himself, descended from the skies; others swore that the Ancestors had been blessed with special powers. No-one had any idea how long it had dominated the landscape, or how long it had taken to construct, for the *Spirax* was not built of stone: it had been carved from the hard black rock of the promontory on which it sat, its tapering sides polished to a shine. When approaching from a distance, it seemed to be one with the sheer cliffs below it; now, as we moved towards it, its surface shone purple under a cloudless blue sky.

"Zarda!" The call was heralded by a clatter of wings, and I turned to find Shaya, the leader of the Hunters, folding her wings and hurrying towards me along the landing path. I always found her rather intimidating, with her sleek brown fur, slender snout and odour of self-confidence. She had the air of someone who wouldn't even need a waste bucket, let alone forget to put it outside. At least she wasn't carrying her spear – she would not have been allowed to land on the plateau if she'd still had that in her paw. "My egg will be hatching in a few days. Would you ask Vizan to attend on it? I—" She stopped, and looked down her snout at the badge I wore.

Her stare was disapproving, the set of her ears disbelieving, and I reached up a paw to touch the badge, reminding myself that Vizan had told me to take it. "I have Vizan's authority—"

"And an urgent summons from Kalis." Morel's ears twisted with impatience, his whiskers quivering as he shifted his weight from foot to foot. "We can't delay, Shaya. I'm sure Zarda will visit your egg as soon as she can."

"It wasn't Zarda I asked for," she said, flicking an ear dismissively. "I'll be on my way. There's a dead floater over the estuary. We need to haul it down before the breeze carries it over the Expanse. We don't want it falling on one of the clusters." As she turned to head for the nearest take-off spot, she added: "It's dangerous work. Not something we leave to the apprentices."

Morel gave me no time to contemplate her point. "Come *on*, Zarda! The egg will have hatched by the time we get there!"

Hurrying through the *Spirax's* eastern entrance in Morel's wake, I switched to night vision as I followed him through the vast Feasting Hall. I glanced up at the concave ceiling, where huge seatach bones had been positioned to look as though they were keeping the roof in place. I had no time though to stop and admire the effect, or to get more than a cursory whiff of the residue of ancient meals which permeated the walls. The rock underfoot was cool and smooth, bare of any floor covering or furniture since the hall was so rarely used. Only when the next Prime succeeded Kalis would the fires be lit in the huge hearths, and stools and tables be brought from storage. At the far end of the hall, an ornate arched doorway, twice my height and wide enough for me to spread my wings had I been allowed to, led to a wide passageway that curved upward. There were torches here. They lined the walls in burnished copper brackets, and oily smoke wisped around our feet as we toiled upward. Narrower corridors to our right – some lit, most dark – led to rooms in the centre of the edifice, and Vizan had once told me that there was a narrower, stepped corridor further in, which wound the opposite way to the sloping passage Morel and I were clambering up. Apart from a murmuring of voices and clattering of pots as we passed the cooking chambers on the lower levels, the sole sound I could hear was the slough of our feet against the polished black floor – that and my breathing, which was, I was must admit, a little laboured by the time we turned into one of the horizontal passages that took us toward the middle of the rock.

I was grateful for the momentary pause outside the nesting chamber door as Morel knocked and waited. Warm from the climb, I pressed a paw against the smooth passageway wall and opened my mouth to draw cool air over my tongue. It refreshed me a little, but did nothing to quell my anxiety.

I didn't hear Kalis' command to enter, but obviously Morel did, for he opened the door with a flourish, dipped his ears as he moved into the room, and stepped to one side to allow me to enter the chamber.

"Lord, I regret to report that Vizan is unwell," he announced. "He sends Zarda as Fate-seer in his place."

I set my wings and ears to the appropriate angle and bowed low, then straightened up and waited for Kalis' command.

"Zarda? The apprentice?" Kalis' voice dripped with disappointment and displeasure, and I had to make a conscious effort to stop my fur standing on end.

The Prime stood beside his nest-mate, Varna, in the middle of the chamber, next to the platform that held the nest – and the egg. Varna, her pale fur bristling with worry, didn't take her eyes from the egg, but Kalis stood straight, his bulky black-furred frame towering over me. His white tunic glowed in the light of the torches that lined the walls, and the crystals in the badge at his throat sparked red in the torchlight.

"What ails Vizan?" he asked, the words bouncing off the walls in a deep rumble. "Is it the Sickness?"

"No, Lord." I took one hesitant step forward. "He's old. He says it is his time."

"Well, it's very inconvenient of him." Kalis' voice became a growl, and I felt that it was not the right moment to point out that Vizan was probably not happy about it either. Kalis grunted, flicked a curt ear, then dismissed Morel with a wave of his paw. The herald bowed and scuttled off, the lay of his ears signalling his relief. "I suppose you will have to do," said Kalis. "You have the Sight, yes?"

"Yes, Lord." I almost added that my gift was very slight compared with Vizan's, that it was not even comparable to the two apprentices who had preceded me. That I had been a poor third choice for Vizan, and had not had time to learn even half of what he had taught his earlier pupils. But they were dead of the

Sickness, and I was not, so I clamped my jaw shut on all of that. Kalis was already annoyed – no need to add to his impatience.

"So tell me, apprentice," he said, indicating the walls and nest with a circling finger, "is everything as it should be?"

Vizan had been responsible for the arrangements in the chamber, so there was no reason for doubt. Was Kalis testing me, or was his question no more than the natural anxiety of any sire about to see his first offspring hatch? Either way, a swift glance around and a brief sniff assured me that all the traditions had been properly observed: sweet-smelling avalox had been woven into the nest, lit torches in ancient copper brackets spiralled up the otherwise-unadorned walls, winding in overhead to the ceiling's central point. A single candle had been lit to mark the time, and a shard of Kalis' own shell, brought from the Egg Vault, had been placed in the nest itself.

I flicked an ear to acknowledge Limar, the nest-nurse, who was sitting on the raised nesting platform, stroking the coarse purple shell and murmuring encouragement to the occupant within, then turned my attention back to Kalis. "It's perfect, Lord," I assured him with a little dip of my head. "All that's necessary now are the traditional prayers."

"You know them?"

I hoped that my doubt wasn't too tangible. "Of course. Vizan is an excellent teacher." I stepped closer to the nest and spiralled a paw across the front of my tunic. *Spiral give me strength!* I thought. Aloud, I said: "Great Spiral, look kindly on this hatchling. Give it the strength, the wisdom, and the stamina to learn well and fly far, as its ancestors have done. Let it be guided by your lights and look to your pattern for understanding and enlightenment. Let it grow to be a good and true leader, as its forebears have before it. So it has always been."

"May it so remain."

No sooner had Kalis and Varna spoken the refrain and spiralled their paws over their tunics than a crack split the egg's shell with a faint tearing sound. Around me, the odour of anticipation and excitement grew stronger.

Limar gave the egg a little pat, her posture and odour exuding self-importance. "That's it," she said, her voice strong but soothing. "Tap a little harder now, you're nearly through."

She could, of course, have ripped the shell apart with her own claws, but that would not encourage the strongest. If the hatchling couldn't break out of its own shell, it would ultimately be too weak to survive: it must prove itself from the start or die.

Tiny cracks crept down the sides of the egg, every minute split greeted with bleats of hope and excitement from Varna. This wasn't her first hatchling, of course – she had produced Limar from her proving-egg with a guardflight mate two cycles ago – but her new pup would be Prime someday, Spiral willing. Unless...

I pushed my doubts aside, remembering the Vision that Vizan and I had shared. This hatchling was destined for great things; there was no way he could be affected by his dam's Sickness in the way that others had been.

Could he?

Silence. Was the hatchling too weak to break out? How long were we supposed to wait before declaring it a cracked shell? What was the protocol for proper disposal? I glanced from egg to candle, candle to egg, sending wordless prayers to the Spiral that the hatching would resume before the flame went out. My feet ached and I wiggled my toes, cringing at the noise my claws made on the cold rock floor. If only tradition allowed for stools in the nesting chamber...

A ripping noise heralded another crack around the top of the eggshell and I forgot my discomfort as I began to murmur the traditional incantations. I stood to one side of the platform, looking over the egg toward its parents, who were holding on to each other as they stood on the far side of the nest, breathing encouragement. As tiny claws appeared and began to break the shell apart from within, Kalis gave a shout of joy and licked Varna, who was snuffling with happiness.

The tiny creature pushed away the entire top of its egg and everyone in the room roared delight at the sight of the white mane on its head and neck. The nest-nurse got to her feet, her ears twitching with excitement. "A male," she exclaimed, as proud as though she had produced him herself.

The hatchling struggled out of the bottom half of the shell into the Nest, his fur still wet, chest heaving from his exertions, and the roars died away. Varna howled, pulled away from Kalis, and backed away, shaking her head. Limar, who had been reaching to pick up the infant, stayed her hand and looked at the Prime, awaiting guidance, but Kalis appeared to be too horror-struck to speak.

It was I who reached down to pick him up. I too was astounded – and not a little afraid. My teacher the Fate-seer had predicted that this infant would be the saviour of his people, a great Prime who would lead the Drax to victory against their greatest enemy. I couldn't understand how this horror could have happened, how all the portents and signs could have been so wrong.

"Zarda." Kalis found his voice at last, sounding the more terrifying for speaking so softly. "Vizan told me that this nestling would be the hero of our people. That he would be the Prime who would finally defeat the Koth and halt their raids forever. Tell me – how is he to become that when he is born deformed?" His paws clenched, and his voice rose to an anguished roar: "He has no wings!"

Two

My own shock rendered me wordless for a heartbeat or two, and I turned the tiny nestling around to examine him from all angles. He smelled perfectly normal, giving off that pungent, wet odour of the newly-hatched. His whiskers twitched and his claws scratched as he wriggled in my grasp, mewing.

"I do not understand either, Lord," I said at length, falling back on a formal style of address for want of anything coherent to say. "The Dream-smoke is sometimes unclear, but never misleading, and I Saw the Vision too – Vizan spoke true, I assure you." I shook my head, and plucked a handful of moss from the nest to clean the infant's pale fur. As I stroked the moss along his back, I felt the bumps near the shoulders, where the wings should have been. Yes – exactly like the other deformed offspring I had seen: the wings had started to form, but they had not developed. The legs and tails of the afflicted hatchlings were longer than on normal drax, but that would not help them fly. It seemed that the Sickness had indeed done more than carry off the males and the nestlings – it had left its legacy in the eggs of the females who had had the illness and recovered. Including, alas, Varna.

The nestling was still mewing and he began to look around, dark grey eyes blinking in the torchlight, his little snout quivering as he sniffed the air. Searching for his mother, of course. The newly-hatched always sought their dam, and always knew who she was, even if there were other females present. Vizan thought that it might be a throwback to a time when every drax had the Sight – assuming that the legends were true. Vizan believed they were, and had wondered if some Sickness had been responsible for leaving only a chosen few with the gift. Not that I had much faith in gifts at that moment, since neither Vizan nor I had Seen that Kalis' heir would be wingless; nor did I have much hope of escaping Kalis' wrath.

"He is strong, Lord," I pointed out, as the nestling squirmed in my shaking paws. "I will consult the Dream-smoke. Perhaps—"

"Perhaps we should just kill him now and be done with it," Kalis growled, his mane bristling. "It would be the merciful way."

"No!" Varna, her initial shock passed, rushed over to take the nestling in her arms. As she gave him his first lick, his nose twitched, catching her scent. Instantly, he stopped mewing and settled against her, one small paw clutching a fistful of her fur. "He is our pup, Kalis. He will need our help and protection. After all, none of us are perfect." As she spoke, she set her ears upright and raised her head to look Kalis in the eyes, and I sensed some unspoken secret pass between them.

Kalis growled low in his throat and for a moment I feared for Varna as well as the hatchling, but whatever she had meant by her last sentence, it stayed his teeth.

No-one moved.

A torch flickered, a pawful of moss dropped from the nesting platform, the hatchling whimpered…and Kalis stepped back, his mane and ears still signalling anger and distress, though his growling ceased.

Varna gave the infant's pale fur another lick and rocked him a little, nodding a dismissal to Limar, who collected the shell-shards and exited with a hasty bow. Her haughty air had vanished and I had no doubt she was glad to get out of the room unbitten.

"What are we to tell everyone?" Kalis waved a paw in the direction of the open door. "The heralds and guardflight have already been sent to spread the news that the egg was hatching. Cluster-criers will be on their way before nightfall; the Councillors and Chiefs will be in the audience chamber by dawn to present their respects and good wishes to this...abomination. What are we supposed to tell them?"

With a brief and silent prayer to the Spiral for protection, I dared to remind him of my presence. "You must tell them the truth."

"Never!" Kalis practically spat the word and I took a step back as he turned on me, his wings partially extended as his temper flared. "To admit that my heir is a useless cripple? That my nest-mate and I cannot escape the consequences of the Sickness any more than any other drax can? Pah! We would have our wings ripped off." He wrung his paws and paced about the chamber, making little detours around Varna and the nestling.

"You would have the sympathy and respect of every drax, Lord," I said. Again I wished that Vizan was not so ill – he would know the right thing to say. Thinking of Vizan made me wonder whether Doran had arrived to look after him yet, and that gave me the inspiration I needed: the Prime's hatchling was already a talking point. "Do what you will, Kalis, rumours will already be spreading." I waved a paw at the empty nest. "Do you think that Limar will not have been asked what the egg bore? Do you think she will not have told? And whoever she tells will tell others. Word will be spreading even now. If you do not acknowledge the truth, the drax will know it anyway, and they will resent your silence. *Then* you will need to fear mockery and wing-tearing. Your people need to feel that they can trust you."

Kalis bared his teeth, and I took another step back, my claws scratching on the stone beneath my feet, but after a couple of heartbeats he turned away, the set of his wings still betraying his anguish. "Take him then," he said, his voice clipped and rough. "Make your announcement and show him from the balcony. And if you should happen to trip up and drop him, I'll not bear any grudge."

"But you should be there too!" It was Varna who pointed out the obvious. "You know the tradition, Kalis."

"Part of that tradition is that we show off his wingspan," Kalis snarled, backing away as Varna moved toward him with the nestling. "So you will forgive me if I do not choose to take any part in it this time."

Torch flames hissed; a pot smashed in a distant chamber, the noise loud in the silence. I counted four heartbeats. Five. It seemed Kalis had said all he wished to, and Varna could think of no suitable reply. I sighed, and ventured into the icy stillness: "May we at least give him a name that the criers might shout it?"

Varna opened her mouth but Kalis spoke first, silencing her. "Dru," he said. "It was to have been Druvo, after my great-grandsire, but since he is half a creature, he shall have half a name. Now get him out of my sight before I change my mind."

Protocol dictated that I allowed Varna to leave first, and while I dithered over whether the dismissal had in fact included me, Morel hurried in through the open door. His ears were still signalling alarm and I thought perhaps it was apprehension at having to deal with Kalis at such a time – till the herald gasped out his message: "Your pardon, Lord, but there has been another attack."

"Where?" Kalis' demeanour barely changed – he still exuded rage and frustration – but the news of the raid seemed to channel his anger, to give it a focus. The Koth might be elusive, but at least he could order some sort of action against them, however futile it might be.

A half-grown drax in the red-and-white striped tunic of a guardflight apprentice emerged from the shadows behind Morel and dropped to one knee, all but prostrating himself in front of Kalis. "The attack was at Far-river farm, Lord." His voice squeaked, his paws shook as he held out a scroll-leaf for Kalis to take. "The initial report, Lord." His whiskers were twitching with nerves.

So were mine. I wasn't even sure if I should still be in the room, but before I could think of a way to make my excuses and leave, Kalis glared in my direction. "I suppose you'd better come along," he growled, as he stomped past the messenger on his way to the door. "Apprentice."

Trailing across the vast oval audience chamber at Kalis' wingtip, I was conscious at every step of the stripes on my tunic, the grumbling of my stomachs, and the rustle of the zaxel stems under my feet. As we skirted around the ancient council table which occupied the middle of the floor, I glanced across at the iridescent slimecrawler shells – each one more than two paw-widths across – which hung from the glossy black walls. To my left, set into the external wall, the biggest see-shell I had ever seen afforded a slightly distorted view of the darkening sky outside. I wondered what sort of giants the *Spirax* builders must have been, to pull a floater with such a carapace out of the sky. On the other side of the table, the faint smell of ashes from the hearth mingled with the scent of crushed zaxel and the lingering odours of the nine councillors who regularly sat around the table to advise the Prime.

I caught a trace of Vizan's scent as I brushed past one of the upholstered stools and fought down a howl. He should be here, not me! It took cycles to train a Fate-seer, what could I possibly say that would be of use to Kalis?

As though to prove my own stupidity, I stumbled as I followed him onto the raised dais where the Throne-stools stood, and put out a paw to grasp one of the stool's arms to prevent myself falling. As I did so, I felt the carved orenvine twist beneath my fingers, and the white fabric of the stool, into which a spiral pattern of red stitches had been worked, appeared to swirl like mist. The threads seemed to fly inward... *a knife flashed, blood spilled.*

Gasping, I pulled away from the stool and stood up. My fur was on end from my ears to my feet; Kalis did not need the Sight to work out what had just happened.

"You had a Vision?"

"Yes, Lord, though I am not sure if I saw past or future. There was..." I hesitated. If the Vision was of the distant past, then telling it to Kalis would not matter, but if I had just glimpsed something recent, hidden – or something yet to come...I decided I would tell a partial truth for now, and consult Vizan later on whether to tell the rest. "I saw a knife, with a finely worked horn handle. There was snow." I shook my head. "The rest was unclear."

Kalis grunted and crossed the dais into the shadows to pull something from a sheath attached to the wall. "Did the knife look like this?"

I moved across the platform to get a closer look, though I didn't need to. The moment he had held it up, I knew it was the same blade I had Seen: a Koth knife, the grey horn handle beautifully wrought with strange, intertwining shapes, the edges still sharp even after cycles of disuse. "Yes, Lord. Exactly like that."

"Then you Saw the past. This is the knife my great-grandsire Druvo took from the Koth he fought in single combat."

I knew the story, though I had never seen the proof of it. As Kalis placed the trophy back in its place between two sconces, I looked again at the blade's serrated edges, and couldn't help but feel that they had not yet finished drawing blood. If only I was more experienced! Or had better control of my Visions. As it was, all I could do was smooth my fur back into place and add what I had Seen to the list of things to ask Vizan when I returned to the Fate-seer's dwelling.

"Come, we have wasted enough time," Kalis growled. He strode back across the dais and I followed him through the arched doorway which led from the chamber to the parapet that jutted from the *Spirax*'s western side. It was the first time I had stepped onto the vantage point, and I had not realised how narrow it was – a single pace from doorway to edge. I swayed a little in the wind that threatened to blow me off my feet and I extended my wings just enough for balance.

"Good evening, Lord. Good evening…Zarda."

With my attention on Kalis, I'd not noticed there was anyone else on the ledge, and I turned to find Fazak, the Keeper of the Records, standing beside me. He must have already been there when Kalis and I arrived in the audience chamber, for no-one was allowed to fly straight to the parapet save the Prime himself.

I made a conscious effort not to raise my hackles as I greeted him. "I am pleased to find you looking so well, Fazak," I lied, politely.

"And I you," he said, giving a little mock bow and dipping his ears. "I'm so sorry to hear that Vizan is unwell, especially..." His hesitation and his glance at Kalis told me that he'd already learned everything there was to know about Dru's hatching. "...in these troubling times," he concluded, gesturing at the view to indicate that his words were not intended to slight the Prime or his offspring.

What troubled me was that Fazak had been on the balcony ahead of Kalis and seemed quite at ease about it. So did Kalis, which was even more worrying. Traditionally, the Prime consulted his Fate-seer for advice before seeking counsel from anyone else. I would make sure I reported this breach of protocol to my teacher when I returned home. 'Good evening, Lord' indeed! Whose parapet was it, anyway?

I could think of nothing to say in reply to his mock sympathy, and settled on dipping an ear in acknowledgement before turning my attention from Fazak to the view inland. Just below and in front of us was the Tusk – the isolated pillar of black rock on which some of our rituals were carried out. Its flat top was bare of anything that evening save a few tufts of firegrass, and the level ground around its base was similarly empty – though there was space enough on the tussocky moss for thousands of drax to gather on important occasions. To right and left the shoreline curved into small bays, and a little way inland from the *Spirax,* where the ground became a gentle slope, avalox bushes marked the boundary of the assembly area, the distinctive green of their branches dulled in the fading light. Beyond the lip of the slope was the edge of the Expanse where most of the dwellings were, and torchlight through see-shells made it easy to pick out the spiral form of the nearest cluster.

In the distance, a flame flared and steadied, and I realised the nightly beacon had been lit on Guardflight Rock, at the centre of the Expanse. Far beyond it, on the horizon, the snow-capped peaks of the western mountains were hazy in the twilight. Towering over them all, the peak of Cloudsend jutted above the clouds, glowing like a hot firelog as it caught the last rays of the sun.

As I watched, the glow faded, but as the sun's light was replaced by that of the Great Spiral overhead, I admired the symmetry of its pattern reflected in the lights from the dwellings on the ground: each cluster of dwellings laid out in a spiral, and all the clusters forming a bigger spiral that stretched across the Expanse.

A colony of tiny glittermoths chittered their high-pitched night calls as they swirled and dipped in the breeze, their upper wings glowing white as they flew west toward the distant hills, where meadows of kerzh-grass and zenox patched the land with hues of red and blue.

It would all have been quite beautiful, but for the smudge of purple smoke that billowed from the foothills to the south-west, thick enough to still be visible even in the fading light.

"Another zaxel farm," said Fazak. He pulled a scroll-leaf from the pocket of his bright green tunic and made a show of consulting it, though I had no doubt he had already committed its contents to heart. It must have taken almost half a day for the guardflight messenger to reach the *Spirax* with the details of the raid, but I didn't doubt for a moment that Fazak would have flown clear to cloud-base height as soon as the smoke was seen so that he might work out which unfortunate drax had been attacked. He must have had the relevant scroll-leaf in his paws for a least a quarter-day – certainly for the entire time we had been preoccupied with the egg and its hatchling – but he read from it as though he hadn't already memorised the contents: "Tenanted by Hamor and his nest-brother Difel. Its last harvest produced the highest yield of any farm." He looked past me to address Kalis. "A most profitable tithe for you, Lord." Then, glaring at me as thought the raid was my fault, he added, "There will be nothing from them for the next cycle."

"Are they hurt?" How typical of Fazak that his sole concern appeared to be the loss of the crop and the tithe. I turned to look at Kalis as I spoke, expecting that he would check the report he'd been given, but it was Fazak who replied:

"I believe there was some mention of Difel being bitten." Fazak rolled up his scroll-leaf and tucked it back into his tunic pocket. "Hamor was unhurt – though apparently he is still not recovered from…whatever it was Vizan was treating him for."

I ignored the faint sneer in his tone. "Fur-clump," I recalled. "A bad case. Vizan said it might take some time to heal. Clearly he was right."

I could – should – have asked how Fazak had received information before Kalis did, but I clamped my mouth shut on further comment as Kalis snapped his jaws, his teeth closing a mere paw-width from my nose. "I did not bring the pair of you out here to discuss remedies for fur-clump. Hamor's farm is the tenth one the Koth have attacked this season. I want ideas! I want answers!"

That was all very well, but what sort of answer could I give? The zaxel farms were constantly vulnerable to attack from the Koth in the mountains, and their outlying positions made them difficult to defend, but the plants simply would not be coaxed into growing anywhere except on those east-facing slopes.

"The attacks must cease soon, Lord," I said. I folded my wings and leaned back against the warm *Spirax* stone so that I could turn more easily from Fazak to Kalis. "The cold season is almost upon us, and the Koth will be forced to remain in their eyries or freeze."

"That does not help us *now*," Kalis growled, folding his arms and glowering at me. His black fur and white mane were stiff with anger. "I have told Taral more than once to send out more patrols and to arm them well, but whenever something like this happens," he said, pointing at the distant smoke, "he manages some excuse – half-trained apprentices, too few of them, bad weather…"

"All of which are undoubtedly true, sire," said Fazak, his ears set at the perfect angle to contradict the sincerity of his words. "Nonetheless, I have taken the liberty of searching the records for any sort of precedent, and I believe I may have the answer." With a flourish, he drew a second scroll-leaf from his tunic and passed it to Kalis with a slight bow. "Copied from the book of Kolas the Great – *'And the Elite Guard were set upon the Spirax, while their brothers in arms went forth to defend the edges of the plain'.*"

"You cannot quote the book of Kolas as a precedent," I said, flicking my ears to emphasise my point. "It's just a legend, a story for nestlings who are still chewing cud from their dams."

27

"But legends are based on truths, surely," said Fazak. He looked up at the unclouded lights of the Great Spiral as he went on: "As the Fate-seer's *apprentice*," he said, putting a lot of emphasis on my lowly status, "you of all drax should know that. Unless you wish to suggest that the legend of the Spiral is no more than a fantasy woven for hatchlings?"

"Of course not." I spiralled a paw across my chest as I glanced upward. "But in blaming Taral, you are ignoring the essential truth of the difficulties he faces – particularly now that the Sickness has taken so many."

The sun had completely set now, and despite the blessing of the Spiral's lights, I blinked to adjust my eyes to the grey shades of night vision. Below, on the Expanse, the lights in the clusters showed all too well the losses we had suffered – there were gaps, too many gaps, in what should have been many perfect spirals of light. The pattern remained unbroken by day, when the white dwelling-stones stood out against the crimson vegetation. Once the sun had set, though...

I returned my attention to Kalis, wondering whether I dared mention the subject of eggs hatching, and decided it would be better to skirt around the subject. "It will take many cycles, sire, for our numbers to be restored."

"Why have they been cut down so cruelly? Surely that is what we should be asking," said Fazak. I didn't like the smell of him, and not just because of the gag-sweet scent of avalox that clung to his fur. "Clearly we have done something to displease the Spiral, or it would not have sent the Sickness." He was hunched over, maintaining an almost permanent bow as he addressed Kalis, ears and wings set to maximum obsequiousness; it was just as well that I'd not had anything to eat, otherwise I might have regurgitated it right over his fawning sycophancy.

"We have performed the rituals and the sacrifices," I said, "just as they have always been done. Vizan maintains that the Spiral is testing us, just as it did when it took the Sight from all but a few."

Fazak snorted. "Now *you* are talking of myths. There is nothing in the Records to indicate that there was a time when all drax had the Sight."

"Oh, and you have read *every* record in *every* tube in *every* archive room, have you, Fazak?" I retorted, my annoyance overcoming my discretion. "How very impressive – it's barely a cycle since you became the Record Keeper."

Fazak opened his mouth, ready to respond to my jibe, but Kalis cleared his throat in what might have been a low growl. Fazak took the hint and clamped his jaw shut, leaving me with the last word for once.

"This bickering is less than helpful. What I require from the pair of you is advice!" With a jerk of his head, Kalis indicated that I should lead the way back through the doorway into the audience chamber.

I blinked back to normal vision as I went inside, as the torches had been lit. The slimecrawler shells glowed pink, though the black walls seemed impervious to the light, and the blade I had seen earlier was still hidden in the shadows. The room at least seemed warm, after standing in the chill breeze on the balcony, and I was grateful that Kalis had decided to continue our conversation indoors.

Fazak followed me, then waited for Kalis to enter the chamber before making a show of closing the shutters.

Kalis stepped across to his Throne-stool and sat down, resting his paws on his knees as he leaned forward. "Since the Sickness seems to have passed, and there is nothing we can do about that anyway, let us concentrate our attention on what we *can* control. The Koth raiders are becoming bolder, their attacks more frequent. Is my Guardflight incompetent? Or have we been more than usually unfortunate this last cycle?"

He was being unfair. The Koth had always raided and the guardflight had always done their utmost to deter them. Unfortunately, the Koth were able to fly higher and faster than any drax, and if they chose to strike fast and hard before retreating to the mountains, there was little any of us could reasonably be expected to do.

"The guardflight are not incompetent, Lord," I said, realising he would be unlikely to take assurance from me. "Vizan believes that Taral is the best Guardflight Chief he has known – and he has known many during his long life. The problem does not lie with Taral, nor with those he commands." I had stepped down

29

from the dais as I spoke, to stand before the Throne-stool, but realised too late that I had put myself at a disadvantage, for Fazak remained on the platform – where he had no right to be – in a superior position.

"The Sickness certainly hit the Guardflight harder than most." The sneer in Fazak's voice was unmistakeable. He had had two good, strong hatchlings in the previous cycle; Taral had not been so fortunate. His sole winged hatchling had died of the Sickness, a second had hatched without wings – or so it was said. I'd not been there for the hatching, and I didn't want to give any credence to the rumours that he had disposed of it. Much better to believe that it had died, along with its unfortunate dam.

"It hit all of us, Fazak." Kalis growled. "Your nest-mate. My sire." He scratched at his beard as though contemplating mention of his wingless hatchling, but settled instead for baring his teeth, clearly ready to snap at the first one to say the wrong thing.

I set my ears to a respectful angle at mention of his sire – Gevar's death still pained all of us – and reminded myself that Vizan would expect me to play my part. Or, rather, his. "It is as the Spiral wills, Lord." The words tumbled out quickly, sounding trite, unconvincing. I could barely remember the point we were debating and seized on the last phrase Fazak had uttered. "Fazak is correct in saying that the guardflight were especially hard-hit. Troop numbers are half what they were in your sire's time, but—"

"All the more reason to consider building a new Elite." Fazak laced his fingers together across the front of his tunic and raised his chin as though to show off the wispy grey beard that he had combed to a point.

"And where would you find the drax for such an Elite?" I asked. "Those who survived the Sickness must replace their own numbers first – the artisans will hatch artisans, the guardflight will hatch guardflight. It will be two hatchings at least, perhaps more, before any second pups can be sent to learn a different discipline. In any case, the numbers are set, and your imaginary Elite Guard are not counted among them. If they ever existed, they died out thousands of cycles ago."

"I would find them in the same way the Fate-seer finds his apprentices," said Fazak. "Vizan selected you in the same way he selected the two pupils who preceded you – because you have the Sight. If you were not able to Foresee, you would be nothing more than a common trader, like your sire before you."

I bristled. "Common? Where would anyone be without traders to take their wares from cluster to cluster, to bring goods to the *Spirax*, to—"

"Be quiet, Zarda!" Kalis' roar would have stilled a raging sea. "Go on, Fazak. Where would you recruit these 'Elite'?"

"I suggest that any second hatchlings who are strong and can be taught to shoot straight would be a start," said Fazak.

"That may have been a good idea once," I said, determined that I would not let Fazak's ridiculous ambitions go unchallenged, "in the days when the clusters were full, and there was rarely a need for anyone to hatch a second egg. But, as I have already pointed out, there are clusters out there which have no weaver, no healer, no cluster-crier left. They will need any and all the spare second hatchlings to replace what has been lost. Surely their need for a complete community is greater than your ambition for an Elite Guard which the drax have never needed outside of myths and nestlings' tales?"

Kalis stood, the torchlight making the red beads on his badge of office spark like tiny flames. I could smell his uncertainty and seized the moment to add one final thought to my argument. I knew it was dangerous to remind him of his hatchling, but perhaps in reminding him again of Dru's destiny I could quash Fazak's ambitions once and for all. With a silent prayer to the Spiral for strength, I cleared my throat and ventured: "There is also the question of the Fate-seer's prophecy for your own hatchling, sire."

"What does that...creature...have to do with Fazak's Elite Guard?" Kalis' white mane bristled and my nostrils filled with the sour odour of wrath. I needed to speak fast if I was not to have my snout bitten.

"The point, Lord," I said, as I backed away a step, "is that in the Dream-smoke, Vizan and I both saw the red tunics of the guardflight alongside the white tunic that Dru will wear as a Prime. There were no others. So, unless Fazak intends for his Elite Guards to wear the same colour as the guardflight—"

"Certainly not!" Fazak snorted.

I ignored his interruption and went on: "—then they will play no part in Dru's victory. I suggest that that is because they are not necessary, and you should dismiss this idea and instead give Taral the backing he needs to rebuild his forces. Let *him* have the pick of the second hatchlings, where they are not needed elsewhere, and allow the Guardflight an additional egg each in the next melt."

Kalis rubbed his beard and set his ears straight. The scent of anger receded, though there was a lingering tang of distress. I dared raise my head a little, though my whiskers quivered and I had to make a conscious effort not to put my paws over my snout. "Very well," he said, his voice a low growl that brooked no argument. "I will allow Taral to remain as Guardflight Chief, for the moment, and the extra hatchlings will be necessary if we are to keep the Koth at bay. Fazak, your idea of an Elite Guard is interesting, but this is not the time to pursue it."

Fazak bowed, his wings and ears set in perfect acquiescence, though he shot me a look that told me he had not given up yet. "Thank you for sparing me a few moments of your valuable time, Lord," he simpered. "I—"

I was spared more of his grovelling by Kalis' impatient bark: "Enough." He gestured toward the door with an impatient wave of his paw, and there was disdain in his voice as he sent us on our way. "You'll both need to be back here before dawn for the ceremony. Don't let me keep you from your preparations."

Three

I hurried straight back to the plateau, where a warm wind ruffled my fur and carried distant calls from somewhere over the northern bay. Not Fishers, I concluded, twisting my ears toward the sound – they would be in their dwellings by now, dining on their latest catch. It had to be the Hunters. The dead floater that Shaya had mentioned earlier was obviously proving difficult to haul down, but I had no sympathy to spare: I had pressing concerns of my own. The Koth attack and the wingless hatchling in the Prime's nest had been dealt with for the moment. As I rushed along the winding path to the Fate-seer's dwelling, my concern was entirely for Vizan, and when I stepped onto the worn entrance-stone, I sent up a brief prayer to the Spiral that I would find him out of his nest and supping on warm stew and hot tea.

It was a foolish prayer, and a vain one. As soon as I stepped inside and saw the set of Doran's ears I knew that Vizan's light had gone to join those above.

"I thought he was asleep when I got here," said Doran, after we had rubbed snouts in greeting and sympathy, "Then I realised I couldn't hear him breathing." Her ears drooped, as mine did, but as she moved to stir the pot that was suspended over the fire she had a brisk, capable demeanour that I couldn't hope to match.

Looking around, I realised that while she waited for me, Doran had turned her own grief to graft. "You tidied up?" The floor had been swept and fresh zaxel scattered across the stone, cleaned bowls were stacked on the shelf near the nest-screen, washed tunics steamed as they hung over stools near the fire. Even the waste bucket had vanished – Doran must have put it outside, ready for collection by the next trader. "You didn't have to do that."

"And you should have asked for help," she chided as she dipped a beaker into the pot. "Here, I made us some avalox tea."

I took the beaker and sat on the nearest stool, next to the hearth. I couldn't bring myself to look behind the screen. Not yet. Doran had made the tea too sour as she always did, but for once I didn't bother to add more syrup to the mix. The bitter tang matched my mood.

"There was nothing I could do," Doran said, filling a beaker for herself and pulled up a stool next to me, "but I felt I ought to stay with him till you came back. When I put the waste bucket outside, I overheard Limar telling Hapak all about it, and I knew I couldn't leave anyway till I heard from you about what happened. Is it true? The hatchling has no wings?"

I nodded, and gave her an abbreviated account of the day's events, while Doran snuffled and gasped and exclaimed in all the right places.

"So even the great and wonderful Varna wasn't immune," she said, when I'd finished. There was derision in her tone – she'd never thought much of Varna – but I could hear a note of trepidation too, and smell her anxiety.

"You're worried about your own egg, aren't you?"

She nodded. "I've been worried about it ever since the wingless started hatching." Getting to her feet, she turned to slam her beaker onto the table, spilling liquid onto the surface she had so recently cleaned. "All the Melt eggs hatched normally. But so many of the late eggs…" She clasped her paws, noticed that she'd spilled tea on her fingers, and plucked a cloth from its hook near the hearth to wipe them. She sat down again, heavily enough that I heard the stool creak beneath her. "I had the Sickness, Zarda. You of all people must know that it's not likely to go well for my hatchling."

I glanced at her drooping ears, her fingers that still clutched the wipe-cloth, her quivering whiskers, and wished I could assure her that her fears were unfounded. I even got as far as opening my mouth to say as much, before I closed my teeth against the glib promise. I'd witnessed too many wingless hatch over the past moon. Doran would not thank me for a lie. "Some of the hatchlings have been absolutely normal," I said. "Fugol's shell-twins…"

Doran snorted and held up a paw. "Don't tell me about Fugol's shell-twins! I've heard enough of his boasting from three clusters away! But Corla *died*, remember? Right after she'd laid the egg. All the healthy hatchlings from the late batch – their dams died. Didn't they?"

I swilled the last of my tea in the bottom of the beaker as though giving the matter some thought, though I knew that what she said was true. I just wished there was some way to give my friend some hope.

I could see none.

Before I could find a way to phrase an answer, Doran sighed, stood up and replaced the cloth on its hook. "It will be as the Spiral wills," she said, and put a paw on my shoulder. "That's what Vizan would have said, isn't it?"

I nodded, looking across the room at the screen that hid his nest, then stood up to put my beaker on the table. I looked down at it, rather than at Doran, as I glided around the question of her egg: "There are more wingless by the day – but if the Spiral has sent the Prime a wingless heir, then there *must* be a reason! We just can't see it yet." I looked over at the screen again, still half-hoping that Vizan would put his snout around it, sniff the air, and declare that he would like some tea too, please. "I'm just an apprentice, Doran. You of all drax should know that I'm not ready to be Fate-seer yet."

She patted my arm. "The Spiral must believe that you are," she said. "Why else would it have taken Vizan?"

I sighed. "You'd best get back to your egg, Doran. I know you're anxious – and there's nothing more you can do here. Thank you for watching over Vizan."

We touched snouts again and I waited on the entrance-stone while she made her way to the cliff edge and jumped off. The updraft bore her upward in a rush, her silhouette clear against the Spiral's lights, and I watched while she circled to gain height. When she turned north-west toward the river basin and her own dwelling, I remained where I was for a long time, looking up at the swirls of light. There was no cloud to disturb the symmetry of the nine curving arms, and only a sliver of moon to compete with the steady glow they emitted. "What have we done?" I breathed, spiralling a paw over my tunic. "How have we offended you, that you send such trials to punish us?"

There was no answer save the wash of the sea against the base of the plateau, and the fresh salt tang of the onshore breeze. No Vision enlightened me; the only voice I could hear was Hapak's nest-mate Nesha, in the next dwelling, her words muffled by the stones. I could guess what she was saying though: a wingless heir, an untried Fate-seer...

I'd wasted enough time. Putting off the moment would not make it any easier. With a last muttered prayer to the Spiral, I went back inside and crossed the room to confront what lay beyond the screen.

Vizan looked peaceful, his eyes closed as though in sleep, his chin resting on the side of the nest. But his wings were half-unfolded in a final death-spasm and his tail had curled up over his back. Already the sickly smell that had lain over the nest had changed to a darker odour; a dozen flisks buzzed around his ears and some of them alighted on his nose.

I swatted them away and dropped to my knees beside the nest. Ignoring the death-smell and the absence of breath or heartbeat, I cradled Vizan's mighty head and stroked his grey muzzle as though I might warm it back to life. "You can't go. You have not finished teaching me. Vizan, I don't know what to do, how to advise – *what* to advise. I can't even control my Visions!" Lowering his head to rest on the edge of the nest, I stopped stroking his muzzle and rested a paw between his ears. "I don't know who to trust."

I suppose I was hoping that the contact between us would trigger a Vision, give me a last piece of advice from Fate-seer to apprentice before Vizan's light was gone forever, but nothing happened, and I could feel that he was cold beneath his fur.

All I could do for him now was howl the ritual death-scream, to let the Spiral know there was a new light on its way.

I should have begun the preparations for Vizan's final journey right away, but I needed to rest. I was tired and upset, and scared, too, of all the duties and responsibilities that had now blown my way. Settling into my nest was out of the question – not with Vizan cold in his own right next to it – so I pulled a clean blanket from the pile on the shelf, wrapped it around me, and curled up in front of the fire.

The day's events flapped about in my head, joined by imaginings of anything and everything that might go wrong with the coming ceremony. Forgetting the ritual chants was the least of my worries. What would happen if the councillors refused to pay respects to the hatchling? Or the cluster-criers howled a protest? Or Kalis changed his mind? Vizan was beyond harm now but I was not. And even if the ceremony went well, what then? I was barely half-trained – would Kalis, would *anyone*, accept me as Fate-seer?

It was no use. A stone floor was no place to try to sleep, not even snuggled in a blanket. Abandoning hope of proper rest, I lit a torch, put more tea on to brew, found the leaves on which I'd scratched my notes regarding ritual chants, and settled myself at the table to study.

I must have dozed, upright and uncomfortable as I was, because the next time I looked at the torch it was burning blue and was almost out. My tea was cold, the fire had dwindled to smoking embers, and if I didn't hurry I would be late for my first ceremony as Fate-seer.

I filled a bowl from the tub outside – half-empty for want of rain – placed it on the scrubbed table, and turned my attention to the tunics that Doran had washed. Those with white stripes could be put away now, till such time as I found an apprentice of my own. The black ones I smoothed with a paw and hung on the hooks behind the door. Vizan's scent still clung to the cloth, and I pushed my snout into the folds and breathed deep, as though I could inhale something of his strength and wisdom.

A door slammed on the next dwelling and I heard Hapak's voice complaining that his water tub was almost empty: "We'll have to get some from the ocean later if it doesn't rain."

He would be getting ready to put on his ceremonial tunic.

So must I.

I spiralled a paw over the soft black fabric of the Fate-seer's ritual tunic – the garment that I had, until now, helped Vizan put on. I had always admired the workmanship of the shell-trimmings, and the neatly-stitched spirals in precious wormspun goldthread, but now that I was about to wear it myself, I felt the weight of it. Generations of Fate-seers had worn that tunic; I hardly felt worthy to follow in their flightpaths.

I took a deep breath. "Great Spiral, help me," I murmured, and for the last time took off the striped tunic that marked me as an apprentice. I splashed water over my neck, snout and ears, washed my paws and feet, and smoothed my fur. My paws shook as I pulled the neck-loop of the clean tunic over my head and wrapped the back panels behind me, tucking them into place beneath my arms and wings. In front of the reflector that hung by the door, I combed my fur, tied the belt around my middle, and adjusted my badge of office, then drew myself up and raised my chin in an effort to pretend I was worthy of the part I was about to play. The tunic was too big for me – loose under the arms and hanging below my knees – but it had been a little small for Vizan and he had always assured me that it was the ritual that mattered, not the size of the tunic or the Fate-seer wearing it. At least I didn't look as terrified as I felt, though doubtless I was oozing anxiety from every hair. That couldn't be helped.

I was the only Fate-seer left.

I would have to do.

And somehow I would have to cope.

Four

The Audience Chamber was much livelier than when I had left it the previous evening. A fire had been lit in the immense hearth, the shutters were open, and the table had been moved to stand beside the wall under the see-shell. It was still dark outside, but torchlight was reflected from the glaze on the beakers and flasks that had been set out, and the aroma of mulled berrywine hung in the air. Morel stood in the middle of the room, barking orders at junior heralds as they scurried about bearing platters of cold meat and bowls of savoury nibbles, but he stepped forward when he saw me and dipped an ear in greeting.

"Zarda." He eyed my sagging tunic and I saw his whiskers twitch, but he made no comment. Instead, he set his ears low and spiralled a paw across his own tunic. "I heard the death-howls. May the Spiral take Vizan to its arms and his light look on us always."

"I still can't believe he's gone." I flattened my own ears to acknowledge Morel's condolences. "I keep expecting him to wake up and ask what I'm doing in his best tunic."

Morel nodded and his grunt was sympathetic, but already his attention had returned to his duties. He snatched a slice of pink groxen meat from a tray that a junior was carrying past, sniffed it, and dropped it back on the tray. "Take it back to the cook and don't return till it's roasted properly."

As the junior scuttled away, I turned to Morel. "Is he old enough to be a herald? He looks to be a half-grown."

"Half-grown and half-trained," said Morel. He wiped his fingers on a cloth that he'd pulled from a pocket and shook his head. "They're all half-trained. The Spiral knows I only completed my own apprenticeship a moon before my sire went to his last nest, I shouldn't be more than a junior myself for another cycle."

I dipped my ears at mention of his sire's passing and spiralled a paw over my tunic. "The Spiral's pattern is sometimes clouded, Morel," I said, repeating one of Vizan's favourite phrases – one he used whenever he had no explanation for an event. He'd been using it a lot since the Sickness struck.

"Personally, I'd like a little more light." Morel turned to sniff at the platters already set out on the table and nudged a couple of them closer together to disguise the gap where the groxen meat should have been placed. He stepped back to give the layout a last visual check, then with a grunt of "It will do," he turned and dipped a bow as Varna entered the chamber, Dru in her arms.

"Everything is ready," he said. "The Sky-heralds are set at nine wingbeats apart to relay the message to the Cluster-criers, and the *Spirorns* will be sounded as the sun appears. That is when you step onto the balcony." Varna nodded and gave her hatchling a lick. The light from the wall-sconces gave her pale fur a golden tinge, and turned the crystal clasp on her cream-and-white checked tunic to yellow sparks. For just a moment, the set of her ears and the droop of her head suggested the depth of her distress, but then the hatchling squirmed in her arms and in cradling him Varna seemed to gain inner strength.

Morel's glance strayed to the infant and I noticed an ear twitch almost imperceptibly – enough to confirm my suspicion that

Morel did not truly approve, but that he was a good enough herald to do as he was bid without question. Certainly he was the picture of correctness as he touched a paw to his chest and said, "I rejoice with every drax at the news of a Lordling," though I noted that his mane was bristling just a little more than was strictly polite. I doubt Varna noticed – she simply flicked an acknowledging ear and turned her attention back to her nestling, stroking his fur and bending her head now and then to give him a lick.

Morel escorted her to the platform and made sure she was settled on her consort stool before returning his attention to me. The zaxel stems on the floor produced a faint, fresh smell as they crunched beneath his feet. "There are nines gathered outside already," he said, "and more on the way." He rubbed his paws together, lowering his voice till I had to strain to hear his words. "What, in the name of the Spiral, are you going to tell them? That poor hatchling should have been dropped into the sea and forgotten. Instead—"

"Instead, he is destined to become a great and successful leader," I said, squashing my own inner doubts and keeping my voice firm, confident. With a glance at Varna for permission, I stepped onto the platform and moved to the doorway that led onto the balcony, blinking my eyes to night vision as I looked out. The sky was as cloudless as it had been at sunset, when I had stood outside with Kalis and Fazak, though the breeze that ruffled my fur blew now from the south, carrying with it a chill from the Great Ice. The sliver of moon sat over the peaks of the high mountains on the western horizon, and with the light from the Great Spiral overhead, there was more than enough illumination to see winged silhouettes flying toward the *Spirax* peninsula from all directions. I took a long, steadying breath, and offered up a brief prayer that Vizan and I had not misinterpreted our vision for the hatchling.

It was quiet outside, save for the constant wash of the sea and the irregular calls of "Landing!" as another cluster-crier arrived on the peninsula's assembly area. With the dawn, that would all change. The fishers and hunters would begin their work, and those drax not already awake would stir and ready themselves for the day ahead. Groxen would honk, melidhs would squawk, the thousand tiny sounds from the wild creatures that usually went unnoticed would begin. As I stood savouring the near-silence of the pre-dawn, I became aware of murmuring from behind me, and as it grew louder, a twist of my ears told me it came from beyond the main chamber door. As soon as Morel opened it, I heard the distinctive bleat of Fazak's voice amid the noise and realised that the councillors had arrived from their dwellings on the plateau – doubtless bickering all the way about the order in which they should line up to present their good wishes. I sighed, checked that my wings were folded neatly, stepped down from the dais, and crossed the chamber to greet them as they entered the room.

"Zarda." Fazak's nod was courteous, just as it had been on the balcony the previous evening, his ears set at the perfect angle of politeness.

I returned the greeting in kind. "Fazak."

I noticed that as well as donning his best tunic, he had again combed his beard to an extravagant point. The style was supposed to be the leading edge of fashion, but I had never seen anyone carry it off successfully. On Fazak's long jaw it looked ridiculous. "You rested well, I trust?" I tried to sound as though I cared.

"I did, thank you. Though some of my fellow councillors have been disturbed to hear," he said as his eyes swivelled toward Varna and his ears twitched as his voice dropped to a whisper, "the news."

I didn't need Vizan's wisdom to guess who had been telling them that news – and muttering about his own misgivings as he did so, no doubt. Well, if he thought to drag me into his slipstream, he could think again. "Still, here they all are," I said, keeping my ears at a jaunty angle, "and I believe that, as Keeper of the Records, you should be first to present your good wishes to Kalis' heir."

Fazak's snout wrinkled with distaste, and his paw spiralled around his tunic as he stared at Varna, as though weighing up his options. He'd put avalox on his fur again, and the cloying odour almost covered the smell of disgust that leaked from him. After a heartbeat or two, he again set his ears to maximum politeness and nodded. "You will excuse me, then. I must complete my preparations."

"As must I," I said, unable to resist reminding him that the important duty of presenting the new hatchling to the rest of the drax fell to me.

With a brief and surely insincere nod of acknowledgement, he took his leave of me and skirted the table of food as he made his way toward the platform where Varna sat with her nestling.

The room had grown crowded. The floor between the table and the platform was a riot of colourful best tunics; some with apprentice stripes, a few with the white trim of juniors. All the same, the scent of doubt hung in the air along with the torch-smoke, and the murmur of conversation was muted, with none of the roars of congratulation and delight I would normally have expected.

I caught a glimpse of Miyak's yellow vlydh-keeper's tunic and amber fur, over near the fireplace beyond a group of traders' apprentices in their pale blue-and-white stripes. I couldn't see the ochre tunic of the Hunters at all, so I sidled a few steps to where Morel stood offering drinks from a tray. "Where is Shaya?"

"Her egg hasn't hatched yet," he said. "She's gone to tend it and get some sleep while Rysel finishes the work on the floater."

I nodded. "Of course." Cutting the tendrils from the carapace was delicate work, best done by someone who had not spent half the night pulling the creature to earth. Even so, I was surprised that Shaya didn't feel able to entrust the work to a different hunter, which would have enabled Rysel to attend the ceremony as her representative. After all, it was no secret that the Prime's egg had hatched.

The rest of the councillors – whatever their private misgivings about the Prime's hatchling – appeared ready to present their good wishes to mother and pup, and each had an apprentice or a junior waiting at their wingtips. Morel and a couple of the junior heralds moved among the throng, bearing cups of steaming avalox tea and hot berrywine on polished bone trays, which caught the flames from the torches and bounced it back to the smooth black walls. I stood by the hearth, cradling a beaker and resisting the urge to tug at my tunic. I was aware of the glances in my direction, heard Vizan's name whispered, though no-one approached me openly to ask why I was wearing the Fate-seer's ritual tunic, and I realised the death-howls had already been followed by news of who they were for.

The candle on the table had almost burned out. Dawn was close. I took a swallow of tea to lubricate my dry throat, drank it too fast, and coughed. Silence fell, and I realised everyone had mistaken my intention, but it was, in any case, time to begin the ceremonies.

I put my beaker down on Morel's tray. With slow, deliberate steps, I walked to the base of the dais where Varna sat and dipped a bow. Turning to face the crowded room, I spiralled a paw over my tunic and began the ritual prayer. "Great Spiral, light our way as we honour the new hatchling of a Draxian Prime." My mind scrabbled to remember the words Vizan had taught me. "Watch over him, keep him safe..." I hesitated. The next words mentioned the hatchling's wings and asked that he would fly high and far. What came after that? "May he travel far, gather wisdom, and grow in strength. As it has always been."

Silence. The sour smell of scepticism. All too obviously, it had not always been so. Zaxel stems rustled, someone coughed. Everyone was looking at everyone else, weighing up the consequences of speaking the refrain – or of not speaking it. No-one would meet my gaze.

Behind me, the stool scraped on the platform as Varna rose to her feet. A brief glance back at the angle of her wings and ears told me all I needed to know, and I raised my voice to repeat the final phrase, louder this time. I heard Varna's growl and didn't have to look around to know she'd bared her teeth; a moment later the room reverberated with the refrain: "May it so remain."

Varna was still growling as she sat down, but I thought it best to ignore the scent of doubt and hostility around me and press on.

I looked across at the Record Keeper. Like it or not, he took precedence at such ceremonies – but what sort of example would he set? Flattened ears? A swishing tail? Outright refusal to present his respects? "Fazak?" I prompted.

As Fazak knelt in front of Varna and the pup, mouthing good wishes, his ears and tail were set at the perfect angle. He looked sincere, he sounded sincere, but with all that avalox cloaking his true scent, I had no idea what actual value his words had. I watched the other councillors, attempting to gauge from their demeanour which were genuine and which were there merely to weigh up the situation.

"I do not trust that drax." I turned to find Taral, the Guardflight Chief, at my shoulder. He must have flown all night to get to the *Spirax* after dealing with the raid at Far-river farm, but there was no sign of effort or fatigue in his upright stance. His scarlet tunic looked immaculate, his bow and quiver of arrows perfectly positioned in the harness strapped across his chest. There was a faint smell of burned zaxel on his grey fur that suggested he had not had time for a proper wash since the previous day, but his curly black mane and beard had been combed. As he watched Fazak, his snout wrinkled with distaste, and I dipped an ear to show my agreement with his words – though I couldn't help but wonder what Taral's own thoughts regarding a wingless heir might be.

"I heard about your own hatchling," I said, setting my ears to show sympathy rather than suspicion. "I am sorry. The Sickness left a terrible legacy."

"Yes." He acknowledged my condolences with a dip of his head. "Misha blamed herself, though I told her it was the Spiral's will and we should not question it. I flew west to deal with a Koth raid two days after the pup hatched, and when I returned Misha had gone, and the nestling with her. I sent out scouts and trackers of course but…" He flattened his ears and his wings drooped. "I believe she went to the ocean."

Or you cut her wings and had her dropped into it, I thought, though to my nose his sorrow smelled genuine enough. Aloud, I said, "I pray that their lights will join the Spiral and shine on us forever."

"Thank you."

I returned my attention to the councillors. Peren, the Chief Trader, was kneeling now, the lay of his ears and bowed head reflecting the genuine sympathy and loyalty I would expect from a drax with a wingless nestling of his own. Unlike Taral, Peren and his nest-mate had kept their handicapped hatchling; their loyalty was hardly going to be tested by a wingless heir.

Taral, too, seemed to be gauging the reactions of those who knelt before the nestling, though I suspected he had different reasons than I to note the names of those who did not appear to be genuine in their good wishes: Sifan the Tally-keeper, whose speckled brown fur stood on end; Hapak the Artisan overseer, with his scarred tail quivering like a branch in a breeze; Broga the Fisher, the oldest drax in the room, who bent her head and set her greying ears to perfection, though her tail moved so wildly she'd have flipped over if she'd been airborne. As soon as she had said her piece, she went to stand with Fazak.

As Miyak moved to take Broga's place, Taral murmured, "Will Kalis be joining us for the rest of the ceremony?"

"No." For a heartbeat I considered telling him all that had happened in the nesting chamber, then I remembered Misha's disappearance and said instead, "It will take him a while to adjust."

Taral grunted. His stance and neutral odour told me nothing, and I wondered how he would react if he knew that Kalis had asked about his competence. Sifan's apprentice – a winged half-grown he had brought from his nest-sister's cluster – was making his pledge, but doing little to disguise his disgust. Marking the name in my memory, I waited till he had moved back before I asked Taral, quietly, about the raid the previous day.

"I sent guards as soon as the alarm was raised," he said, his mane bristling with frustration, "but it was too late. The Koth struck hard and fast, as usual, and had carried off most of the zaxel cobs by the time my flyers arrived. What they couldn't carry, they burned. I sent half the flight after the Koth – though you know how futile that is. The rest of us grabbed bowls and buckets from the nearest cluster and flew to the river to get water to quell the flames."

"It must have smouldered for a long time," I said. "I could still see the smoke at sunset, though Fazak already had your report—"

"*Fazak* had my report?" Taral scratched at his beard, ears twitching. "Interesting. I sent it to Kalis, of course."

His voice was a low rumble, and I kept my voice equally soft as I replied, "He notified Kalis as soon as he received it, but it was pure chance that I happened to be with him."

"Surely you'd have been sent for if you weren't already with the Prime?" Taral was obviously trying to be fair, but I was having none of it.

"I don't know, Taral. Perhaps. But whether I was sent for or not, Fazak should not have been given the report. Not ahead of a Fate-seer."

Taral acknowledged the truth of that with a dip of his ears. "I will talk to Culdo, tell him not to give my messages to anyone but Kalis in future. It was his first time carrying a report. I suppose I should have made it clearer to him that no-one else should have received it. Still, at least there was no-one killed in the raid this time, thank the Spiral."

He broke off, for it was his turn to make the pledge of loyalty to the mewling scrap in Varna's arms. I watched for any hint of insincerity as he knelt, but it seemed to me that his ears, tail and wings were correctly set, and when he returned to my side he had a genuine smell about him. If he did not approve of a wingless heir, he certainly masked it well.

"Tomorrow," he said, "I'm going back to Far-river farm to take another look at the damage. I can't do anything for Hamor and Difel, but perhaps there will be something I can learn, something that may help prevent other attacks." He shook his head and I shared his doubt, but understood his need to examine everything. His next words surprised me. "Would you come with me, Zarda? I'd welcome a fresh perspective, and as Fate-seer perhaps you'll notice something I've missed."

I brushed at my beautiful tunic, feeling less worthy of it than ever. "I am still just an apprentice," I said, "Vizan—"

"—will not be travelling anywhere other than the Deadlands. Will he?" Taral turned toward me and twisted an ear. "The raids worsen moon by moon, cycle by cycle. I need help, Zarda, and I hope that you might See a way to defeat the Koth, or at least anticipate where they will strike next."

"No-one would be happier than I if that happened," I said, "but my visions don't come at my bidding."

"Surely it would do no harm to try?"

He was right, of course. The night's events, and the responsibilities that had suddenly been thrust upon me, were overwhelming, but I couldn't allow them to dictate my response. Vizan, lights rest him, would have urged me to fly west with Taral, and would have been disappointed that I even thought to hesitate. "I'll come with you," I said, "to see if there's anything else that might be done." I returned my attention to the moment. "Right now, though, I must present our new Lordling to the cluster representatives."

The thin whiskers around Taral's mouth twitched and I realised he was trying not to laugh. "Then you had best lick your whiskers first – they have drops of tea on them."

I felt my hackles rise with embarrassment and twisted my head as I licked round my mouth, making a show of checking the view through the see-shell. Outside, the night sky was giving way to shades of purple and mauve, though the moon – distorted by the curve of the shell – still hovered over the mountains. There would be a moment very soon when all our lights were visible in the sky, a moment when the sun's rim peeked over the edge of the ocean – present but not yet high enough to make the Spiral and the moon fade. That would be the moment when the hatchling was presented to the crowd outside.

In the chamber, the councillors and apprentices had formed two loose groups, and as I looked around I felt a chill run right down my tail. Consciously or no, they had banded together with those who shared their opinion on the wingless in general, and Dru in particular. The group around Fazak was the larger of the two, though not by so much as I had feared and he had doubtless hoped. Miyak, still waiting for his own egg to hatch, stood with Peren and Taral. Where Shaya would stand I couldn't guess. The discord was a bad start to Dru's life, but not one I could do anything about. Not without getting myself bitten, anyway, and if Kalis got involved…

I pressed the thought away. I had to deal with the moment; the rest would have to wait. Setting my ears and tail to the correct angle, I turned to address Varna again. "It is time."

As she nodded and stood the room fell silent, save for the scrape of claws on rock and the faint rustling of the zaxel stems underfoot. An overwhelming odour of sympathy mingled with the smoke from the torches, along with a strong scent of doubt, and then, from someone nearby, the sickening smell of loathing.

I spun about and scanned the crowd for the source, for I sensed that whoever felt so strongly about Dru would assuredly wish him harm. I'd not been quick enough – everyone present had already arranged their expressions into bland acceptance, their ears and wings all set to the proper level of respect. I sniffed the air again, but a breeze blew in through the open balcony shutters, making tunics flap and torches gutter, brushing the room with a hint of saltweed and damp moss.

My main stomach felt as though the snacks I'd snatched had grown wings of their own, and I pressed a paw to the front of my tunic as I tried to remember the next part of the ceremony. I had never seen it done and had not started memorising it till Vizan's health worsened a mere nineday ago. With a silent prayer to the Spiral, I hopped up onto the dais next to the Throne-stools. "Wait for the signal," I said to Varna, and stepped through the doorway onto the balcony. The previous evening when I had stood there with Kalis, the assembly area had been empty. Now, beyond the Tusk, nines of cluster-criers were gathered, each in their appointed place on the scarlet moss so that they stood in a spiral formation. Guardflight drifted above them on the breeze, their scarlet tunics blending with the moss, their wings spread in easy glides as they rode the air currents. There were two guardflight at either end of the balcony too, each clutching a *Spirorn*. The iridescent shells that formed their instruments were admired not only for the beautiful sounds they made when blown, but also of course for the way in which their form mimicked the Great Spiral itself. Vizan had told me of a time when there had been scores of such shells washed up on the sands after a bad storm – a gift from the Spiral, it was said. In recent cycles, though, things had changed: the storms brought no more than two or three shells at a time, and Vizan shook his head and said that a change was coming. *"For better or worse, I cannot say, the Smoke keeps it from me,"* he had told me after the last squall brought only a single, broken shell. *"I fear that we have displeased the Great Spiral in some way, but how, I cannot tell."*

I was startled from my thoughts by the *Spirorns* being sounded, the pitch starting low and rising steadily to a sweet, high note that would carry halfway across the Expanse. No drax who heard it would be in any doubt that an Assembly was under way.

As the notes died away, Varna stepped on to the balcony beside me, and at the same moment, the crowd below us took to the air. Their wing-beats, individually as quiet as a drop of water on a pebble, sounded like a great rockslide when such numbers took off together. I flattened my ears against the noise until they levelled out just below the ledge I was standing on, all of them funnelled by the guardflight and the sky-heralds into a flying wedge.

I signalled to the heralds, who held up their paws for silence; the last murmurs of speculation died away and I raised my voice to carry over the susseration of wingbeats. I rehearsed the words one last time in my head, conscious of the councillors and cluster-chiefs in the room behind me just as much as I was aware of the gaze of everyone in the air in front of me. Then, with all the gravitas I could muster, I called the proclamation: "Drax! Rejoice! The Egg has hatched safely and has produced a male!" I paused, waiting for the heralds to repeat my words one to another till they reached those furthest away. The crowd yipped happily, their calls accompanied by a good deal of exaggerated snuffling and even a few backward loops. I waved my paws for silence, which took longer to establish this time. The criers were excited – eager to carry the information back to their clusters to pass on to everyone else. But that had been the good news, the easy bit. How would they react to the rest?

I decided the best thing to do was to continue the ceremony with as much tradition as possible, and hope that it carried us through.

Wind on my fur. The sound of wingbeats. The lights of the Spiral still visible in the crimson dawn. I breathed in the scent of expectation – of hope. Twisting to my right, I took the nestling from Varna, holding him beneath his arms so that he faced away from me and toward the airborne crowd.

"May the Spiral's lights bless our new heir, Dru!" I shouted.

"The Spiral! Dru!" came the returning call – though I heard the hesitation and the questioning note. *Half a name?* they were doubtless wondering, and *Where was Kalis?*

Then a large drax with a shaggy red mane, hovering near the front, pointed as I handed the pup back to his mother and yelled: "He has no wings! The hatchling has no wings!"

The shouts turned to howls, scents curdling toward hostility and disappointment. I stepped right to the edge of the balcony, gripping it hard with toes and claws, and praying to the Spiral I would not fall off and ruin the moment. Spreading my wings, I raised my arms for silence. I had noticed that the gesture worked well when Vizan did it, as many drax had a mistaken idea of a Fate-seer's powers and assumed that a dramatic stance meant that a spell was about to be cast.

Even so, I was a little surprised that the shouts died away so quickly. I had not thought beyond quieting them: now I had to find something to say. I cleared my throat, thinking fast and trying to imagine what Vizan might have said were he standing in my place. Setting my ears upright to emphasise the sincerity of my words, I called: "It is true. Dru has the same affliction as many of your own hatchlings. He is without wings. Nevertheless…" I raised my arms again against the angry murmurs; they did not like being reminded of the Sickness and its results. "Nevertheless, he is Kalis' heir, and Vizan himself has Seen that he will be a great and victorious leader of the Drax. We do not know why this affliction has struck, but I believe that the hatching of this nestling is a sign that we must accept it. The Spiral's pattern is sometimes clouded, but its light will shine through when we least expect it. Now go. Tell your clusters to rejoice, for Kalis has an heir."

They still murmured and muttered as they turned into the wind and began to disperse, but a sniff of the breeze assured me that the anger had gone. Disappointment remained, but I could do nothing about that. I could but hope that Dru's hatching, and acknowledgement as heir, would prevent any more nestling deaths, for there had been rumours that Taral's hatchling was not the only wingless infant to die or disappear. Some, so it was said, had been taken to the Deadlands, or even beyond to the Ambit estuary at the southern edge of the Crimson Forest. Others, the rumours said, had been left in the foothills of the western mountains for the weather or the Koth to take.

"They are not happy," said Varna, bringing my thoughts back to her own offspring, now nestled contentedly in her arms once again. "Kalis was right. Perhaps we—"

"We have done what is right, Varna," I assured her, "though I cannot explain the Vision. I Saw it myself when Vizan took me to the Dream-cave, although…" I closed my eyes for a beat or two, the better to recall what I had Seen. "I did not See him flying. The Smoke gives us glimpses of what will be, and it showed us your pup as a grown drax, holding his arms aloft in triumph, surrounded by dead Koth and guardflight tunics. Vizan and I assumed—"

"We all did, Zarda," she said. "Though perhaps you should visit the cave again? Perhaps the Smoke will reveal more to you, now that Dru has hatched?"

I dropped a small bow of acknowledgement, for it was not a suggestion, politely as it had been phrased. "I would like to wait a few moons, Varna, with your permission. Dru will be on his feet by then, and I would like to take him with me if I can find a way to do so."

"Will that be of help?"

"It might. I can give no guarantees."

She snuffled, and I detected a sarcastic hiss in her tone as she held up her son. "That much is painfully clear, *Fate-seer*," she said, nodding for me to precede her back into the audience chamber. The chiefs and councillors, still divided into two groups, were murmuring among themselves as I re-entered the room, the movements of their ears, tails, and paws telling me which group was which, even without checking their faces or their tunic colours. All the same, every one of them dipped a bow as Varna followed me inside, turning back to their conversations once she had flicked an acknowledging ear.

As I stepped down from the platform, she called me back, and I turned to face her as she settled onto the consort stool. "You may return for Dru in two moons, and if you can find a way for him to travel to the Dream-cave, you may take him with you. Oh, and Zarda?"

"Varna?"

"Thank the Spiral that Kalis did not have you fed to the Koth when the egg hatched."

Five

I'd completed my first ceremony as Fate-seer, and had managed not to make a mess of it. The day was a quarter-sun old by the time I finally got back to Vizan's – no, to *my* dwelling – and I'd have liked nothing better than to rip off the ritual tunic and spend the rest of time huddled in my nest, whimpering.

But the hearth's cold embers, the smell of death, and the buzz of flisks reminded me that there were more important concerns than my own weariness and fear.

I relit the fire, brewed some tea, and warmed up a pan of stew that I found on the hearth – Doran's work, I assumed, as I'd certainly not had time to make any. As usual, Doran had added too much zenox powder, but it didn't matter – grief and exhaustion had taken my appetite. Only the knowledge that I had a long, tiring flight ahead of me made me eat; the taste was irrelevant.

At last, with my bowl licked, beaker empty, and pot soaking, I could put off the moment no longer: I had to tend to Vizan.

The items I needed were all in a single basket under the worktop. The ritual blade was on top and I took care to pick it up by its carved vinewood handle. I'd not wielded the blade before, except to clean it after Vizan had used it, but I knew how sharp its serrated edge was because I'd almost sliced off a finger with it the first time I'd picked it up. *"Try to be more careful in future,"* Vizan had cautioned, as he'd finished binding my paw. *"There's nothing sharper than a seatach-tooth blade, and they never lose their edge."*

Some of my notes, hastily pricked out on scroll-leaves as Vizan spoke of chants and traditions, were curled at the bottom of the basket, but I would not need them for the incantation or the death-ceremony. I had heard and spoken the words too often already as the Sickness took its toll.

"Zarda?" Taral's voice accompanied a firm knock on the door. "We need to leave now if we're to be at the Fate-seer's last nest by sunset."

"Yes, yes – I'll be there in a beat or two."

I was gentle as I removed Vizan's wings and crossed them over his back, as though I might still hurt him if the blade slipped or the cut was rough. I combed his mane and beard, slipped a glowshell into his mouth to help light his way, and stood back. What had I forgotten?

The platter! Of course!

I pulled it from the basket and put it in a carry-pouch, along with a flask of berrywine, and checked that the blade was safely sheathed in my tunic belt.

I couldn't put it off any longer. With a brief prayer to the Spiral that I would be worthy of Vizan's memory and the responsibilities I'd inherited, I opened the door to find Taral on the entrance-stone, flanked by two wing-guards. With their matching heights and black fur, I knew at once that the escort must be Jisco and Veret, shell-brothers who must have been impossible to tell apart before they acquired their battle-scars – a torn ear marked Jisco, while Veret had a thin mauve welt that ran the length of his snout.

Behind them, all the members of the Council stood with their heads bowed, and I smelled nothing but loss and sincerity as they spiralled their paws across their tunics, setting their wings so the tips rested on the ground. Even Shaya had climbed out of her nest to stand with the others, though given her respect for Vizan, I should not have been surprised. "The Spiral will shine brighter," said Taral, "with the addition of Vizan's light."

I remember little about the flight. Always before when we had taken a drax to the Deadlands, Vizan had been flying ahead of me. Seeing his body dangle in the carry-net between Jisco and Veret seemed unreal, like some terrible Vision. I tried to focus on the landscape. We headed north-west, on a curving course which took us first across the northern bay and then over a half-dozen clusters on the perimeter of the Expanse. We flew low enough that I was able to pick out individual drax as they stood outside their dwellings, wings spread in a last salute to Vizan. In the clusters closest to the sea, the Fishers predominated, and there were many deep-blue tunics lining the paths. Farther on, we glided over the cluster where the clay-shapers dwelt next to the Manybend's muddy banks. I glimpsed a patchwork tunic among the copper-coloured ones, and raised a paw as I recognised the long black-striped snout of Swalo the fable-spinner. Should I be waving to a friend? I clasped my paws together, wondering if anyone else had seen and worried that they might think I was not taking my new role seriously enough.

A wingbeat later and the cluster was behind us. We lost the river as it looped north, while we flew over the undulating red stems of the avalox fields that grew between the outer settlements. A line of garish orange marked the boundary between clusters, the distinctive kestox vineleaves swaying in the wind. The dye-makers' cluster was next, and I glanced to my left to look beyond it to the orenvine plantation where Doran and Miyak lived. Its spiral of purple leaves marked the northernmost point of the settlements on the Expanse. From here, the pattern of clusters began to curve around to the south-west, while we flew on. Ahead of us, the river looped again, and our shadows wiped the surface of the water as we flapped across. Stained brown with copper and mud, its progress eastward looked sluggish, almost leisurely, from above, but its appearance was deceptive: there were dangerous currents beneath the surface where it surged over the hidden rocks of Brambletrap Bend. Even here, over six clusters inland from the estuary, it took eight wingbeats to cross as we compensated for the changes in air movements over the water.

A last glide took us over the hummocks of tanglevine that grew on the far bank, then we were over the Deadlands, where stagnant water carried the putrid smell of death and decay. The dull maroon of marsh-reeds was broken by occasional flashes of light on surface water as we glided over still pools and shallow gullies.

As the sun sank lower and our shadows trailed over the reed-and-bramble patchwork below, I saw the lone hillock near the centre of the marsh, where a copse of drumvines grew in a tangled clump. The undersides of their leaves flashed silver as the wind caught them and I flattened my ears against the strange rattle their hollow branches made as they knocked together. Beyond the hillock, a series of low, finger-shaped mounds rose a span or so above the water, and it was on these that the great grey clumps of brambletrap grew. As we flew over the first of them, Taral, at the apex of our flight formation, angled his wings to change course a little more to the north, and I heard a sigh from one of the councillors behind me: "It's a long flight, isn't it?"

I couldn't identify the voice, but I knew Fazak's bleat when I heard it, and it was he who answered, "I don't see why we can't use the brambletrap here. Surely it's all the same?"

It was heartwarming to hear the collective gasps from the other councillors, and the chorus of objections: "You can't put a Fate-seer to rest within earshot of the drumvines!" "Those are for the Guardflight. Always have been, always will be." "You'll be saying next that the Prime's last nest should be next to the mudflats where the mitches bite." "You are the Record Keeper, Fazak, how can you not appreciate tradition?"

"Of course, of course, it was merely an observation."

I hoped that that would be his last word on the matter, and for three or four wingbeats he lapsed into silence. Then, as we began our descent toward the correct clump of brambletrap, he spoke again: "Perhaps on the way back, we can discuss the tradition of the Prime's heir paying a visit to all the clusters on the anniversary of his hatching day?"

The suggestion hung in the air like a dead floater, with a sting to match. There were eighty-one clusters, and it was expected that the anniversary procession would visit several clusters per day, returning to either the *Spirax* or to Guardflight Rock each evening. It would take fifty-four days – a whole moon – no more, no less. But that was the schedule for an airborne heir. How would Dru even begin such a journey when he would never fly?

I shook my head. The only answer I could give, the only one I had, was that the Spiral would show the way. In any case, we had more immediate matters to attend to, and as I watched the Guardflight lower Vizan in his net to the ground, I almost started howling again.

The brambletrap had all but covered the mound on which it grew, and the black soil sucked stickily under my feet as I landed, releasing a stale, fetid smell that seemed utterly appropriate. There was a good deal of muttering and shuffling as everyone landed and found a safe place to stand between the bramble and the marsh, while the guardflight opened the net in which Vizan had been carried, and set his wings at his head and feet. The Great Spiral was becoming visible in a purpling sky that was almost free of cloud.

"Everything's ready, Zarda." Taral's voice was quiet in my ear. I took a steadying breath, pulled the ritual knife from my belt and held it up, its tip pointing at the centre of the Spiral. Everyone stood utterly still. The only movement came from the swaying brambles, the only sound from the marsh glumps, whose twilight croaking had accompanied many a drax to their rest.

I realised I was shaking, and had to take several deep breaths before I was able to begin the chant. Even then my voice quavered – the death-chant was the Fate-seer's duty, how was it possible that it had fallen to me? "Drax will hatch…" I began. I faltered, coughed, began again, and this time I imagined Vizan at my side, encouraging me, but ready to criticise if I did not get it right:

> *"Drax will hatch and drax will die,*
> *Drax will fall and drax will fly.*
> *Take this light from where he rests*
> *Up to his eternal nest."*

"So it has always been," called Taral, his voice harsh, almost a challenge. Perhaps he was remembering the uncertainty in the audience chamber when I had said the prayer for Dru.

This time though the councillors didn't hesitate. "May it so remain," came the echoing chorus.

I dropped to one knee beside Vizan and made the ritual cuts in his chest. Blood oozed around the blade and the smell of raw meat assailed my nostrils. I was panting hard, and I could feel the fur on the back of my neck standing on end, but that didn't matter. What mattered was getting the ceremony right, making sure that Vizan's light was sent to the Spiral with the respect and honour he deserved, and I focussed my thoughts on that as I cut deeper into his chest.

My paws were wet and sticky, and I realised too late that I had forgotten to pull the platter from my carry-pouch. Grateful for the half-light, I fumbled with the straps and withdrew the plate, wondering – rather incongruously – whether the blood would come out when I washed the pouch.

Carefully, reverently, I placed Vizan's heart on the platter, trimmed it, and divided it into nine pieces, then stood and held it aloft. "Will you share this heart?" I asked, looking around the circle of mourners. "And take a little of its wisdom and strength for your own?"

They bowed their heads as they murmured the standard response: "We are honoured to partake."

It was all done correctly, with the pieces passed from right to left and each councillor taking his portion as I spoke the words: "For strength – for loyalty – for honour – for wisdom."

I chewed and swallowed my own share, and prayed silently to the Spiral that if I might have one ninth of Vizan's wisdom, as I had had one ninth of his heart, I might just begin to be worthy of my new role.

It was full dark by the time it was done. The moon's sliver and the Spiral both shone clear, and there was enough light to see easily once I'd switched to night vision. Gently, I placed the wings back on Vizan's chest, folded his paws across them, and stepped back. I'd done my part. All that was left now was for the Guardflight to lift him again in the net, hover over the brambletrap in front of us, and lower him into it.

The wind had dropped, and there was some necessary manoeuvring and the odd grumble as Jisco and Veret found room to take off. They had to run a few steps into the marsh, the splash of their feet providing a wet echo to their frantically beating wings. Then they were airborne and circling around, Vizan in his net held safely between them. A few moments later, a different sound carried to my ears – the scratchy rustle of the bramble stems as they gathered the body and pulled it into the centre of the bush.

My stomachs heaved a little, though perhaps it was my imagination that supplied the faint sucking noises as the plant began to feed.

"He's gone." Taral's voice, a note of disbelief in it that echoed my own feelings.

Vizan, the all-wise, the all-Seeing, Fate-seer to three generations of Primes, had gone to his last nest.

All that was left of his legacy was me.

Hungry, tired, bereft, and afraid, I raised my snout and howled into the night.

Six

I was dismantling Vizan's old nest the next morning when Taral returned. His snout wrinkled as he caught the stench of soiled fur and dried vomit that clung to the reeds I was sweeping up. "I'm going to fly out to the raided farm now," he said. "I'm taking a vlydh with supplies. But if you'd rather stay here to finish...?"

"No, no, this can wait." I set down the broom and brushed at the reeds that had stuck to my tunic. I had put on a clean one before starting work on the nest, but already it looked dusty and worn. Vizan had always looked neat and clean, and I wished yet again that I could be more worthy of him. "I'll just pack some salves and herbs for Difel, it won't take long. Oh, and some more of that rub for Hamor's fur-clump, just in case..."

I scurried from shelf to basket to table, gathering everything I thought might be needed, and adding a few more jars and herb-bags. It had been past moon-zenith when we got back from the Deadlands and I had been so tired that I had crawled into my nest in the ritual tunic. Now I was wondering whether the creases would ever drop out. There was blood on it too, visible as a matted patch of black on black when the light caught it. I should have taken it off right away and put it in a bucket of water, but I had felt as though every hair on my body was crying out for rest and – not for the first or last time – I had not done the sensible thing. This morning I had woken late, eaten in haste, and set to work on the nest. I'd told myself that I needed to be more organised, but I'd forgotten about my promise to Taral to accompany him, and now, as I rushed about the dwelling gathering this and that, I felt flustered and unprepared. Had I thought of everything?

I fumbled with the straps on the carry-pouch, and realised that in my haste I had thrown everything into the pouch I'd used the previous day. The one that was stained with Vizan's blood. I pressed a paw to the rough weave, partly in sorrow, partly perhaps hoping to gain a little of his strength through the contact. I wondered whether there was time to find a clean pouch, but Taral pulled the full one across the table and lifted it.

"You'll need a warmer tunic," he said. "It's trying to snow. I'll put this in the vldyh's pannier."

I didn't have a warm tunic, at least not in the right colour. Vizan had told me to take my old blue Trader's tunics to the dyers, to have them prepared in readiness, but I'd kept putting it off. My expectation – my hope – had been that Vizan would live for many more cycles before I'd need my own black tunics, and having them ready to step into seemed wrong somehow.

Now, I would have to wear one that had belonged to Vizan, or return to my apprentice stripes.

There were three fur-lined tunics neatly rolled up at the bottom of Vizan's storage chest, all of them too big for me. I shook one out and sniffed it, finding the remnants of Vizan's scent clinging to the short coarse hairs of the lining. When I put it on, the lower edge hung below my knees and the sleeves drooped over my paws, but by pulling the straps tight and wrapping another belt around my middle, I managed to keep it from gaping at the back.

I caught sight of myself in the reflector that hung by the door and almost changed my mind about venturing out. I gave myself a firm reminder that I had a duty to be of help to others, and that the tunic's purpose was warmth, not style. Even so, I tugged and pulled at the straps and folds as I walked around the pathway in search of Taral.

"Over here!" He stood in the lee of the *Spirax*, which offered some protection from the freezing south-westerly that flung swirls of sleet into my face as I hurried around the path. The vlydh rested beside him, its six legs bent outward and all four wings folded along its sides. Fearsome as they looked, with their twitching antennae, hooked mandibles, and shoulders that stood higher than a grown drax, vlydhs were gentle creatures, used to carrying large burdens on their long backs. Led along by reed-rope harnesses, they ferried food, arms, vine-trunks, tools, and belongings to wherever they were needed. When they were not being worked, they were content to stay in the branches of the nearest orenvine, munching on the leaves. There were no orenvines on the plateau, but the vlydh next to Taral had a branch from the stores in its mandibles, and I could hear it chewing as I approached.

"I've put your carry-pouch in the pannier." Taral pointed at the woven basket slung from the vlydh's broad back. He looked me up and down and I saw his whiskers twitch with amusement. "You might want to get that taken in," he said, and turned to gather the vlydh's leading-rein before I could think of a suitable retort.

Our flight-path took us into the teeth of the south-westerly and my tunic, big as it was, proved its worth before we had left the peninsula behind us. Sleet stung our noses and dampened our fur, making it harder to fly, and reminding me that I'd not had a full night's sleep for over a nineday – not since before Vizan took to his nest. The sky around us was unusually quiet – no-one was flying anywhere unless they had to – and the clusters we flew over on our way to the centre of the Expanse showed little sign of activity on the ground either. Clearly all the sensible drax were staying indoors.

It was always tiring work, to fly through unpredictable air currents, and I was glad of the rest when we paused on Guardflight Rock to take a drink and a snack of cold groxen tongue. Though it was not as high as the *Spirax* plateau, the view from top of the conical red rock was usually impressive, located as it was in the centre of the spiralling clusters on the Expanse. That morning, the view barely extended beyond the guardflight's own dwellings, which spun out from the base of the rock. At the top, where the Welcome Place occupied most of the available space, lookouts huddled under small hide shelters facing north, east, west and south, but I don't believe they even saw us until Taral barked at them as we landed. Once the vlydh had been tethered to the small orenvine bush that had been planted in the thin topsoil, Taral and I wasted no time in hurrying into the warmth of the Welcome Place.

Inside, it was clear that the shelter was used for storage more than for welcoming visitors. Bows, arrows, and short spears were stacked in neat bundles around the curve of the wall. Spare tunics were neatly rolled in scarlet rows along the shelves, a faint musty smell indicating that some of them had not been used for moons. It would be another cycle and two more hatchings at least before there were enough guardflight to wear them all.

"Thank you." I buried my snout in the beaker of hot tea, brewed sweet the way I liked it, and cast about for something to say. It had always been usual to ask about the host's family, but that had become a sore subject with many drax of late – let alone one whose own nest-mate and hatchling had disappeared. The weather? Hardly. The Guardflight? Numbers down, attacks from the Koth increasing. No, best not mention that.

Taral's dark mane had gone slightly frizzy in the wet, his damp fur giving off a pleasant smell I couldn't quite identify as he pulled up a stool by the fire. I opened my mouth to ask what he'd rubbed on his fur, thought better of it, and gulped more tea instead. As I lowered myself onto the stool opposite him, and bit off a mouthful of the tangy groxen meat from the slice in my paw, it was Taral who broke the silence: "You did well at the ceremony yesterday."

He'd already said as much as we flew back over the Deadlands the previous night, but I didn't mind hearing it again. "I almost forgot the platter."

"No-one noticed, and I doubt that Vizan would have minded. What would he have said about it, do you think?"

"Vizan…" The meat stuck in my throat and I coughed and swallowed, swilling the stubborn morsel down with the last of the tea.

"I'm sorry. I've upset you."

"No." I took a breath, rubbed my whiskers, and sat up a little straighter. "Quite the opposite. You're right, Vizan would have told me to learn from the mistake and get it right in future." I'd been so annoyed with myself for getting it wrong that it hadn't even occurred to me to think of that before.

Taral concentrated on chewing his last bite of meat, and I thought the conversation had stalled, but after a beat or two he took a swallow from his beaker and went on: "Cycles ago, when I was still an apprentice, we were taken to the low mountains in the south." He waved a paw in approximately the right direction. "There's a crag near the coast that we use for training – how to allow for updrafts and downdrafts in the mountains, nightflying through narrow passes, that sort of thing. When we got to the caves where we were to spend the next moon, I realised I'd not packed a firestick. It was a silly, elementary mistake, and the other apprentices were furious with me because it meant we couldn't set a fire on our first night."

He stretched each of his wings in turn, re-folded them and sat forward, cradling his empty beaker in his paws. "My dam, Larta, was Guardflight Chief by then. She asked us all what was the more important thing to worry about – a fire to cook food that we could equally well eat cold, or the Koth?" He sighed, shook his head and stood up. "The answer for me is still the Koth – and I'll not catch any of them sitting in here."

He held out a paw and for a moment I thought he was offering to help me to my feet. Then I realised his intention was to take the beaker from me, and I handed it to him quickly, ducking my head to cover my foolishness and trying not to flick my ears in my embarrassment.

"You're right, of course," I said, as I tugged the straps of my warm tunic a little tighter and rolled up the sleeves. "There are more important things for me to worry about than making a small mistake at a last-nest ritual." I tried to inject a note of humour. "The question is, should I worry more about the wingless, about the Prime's new hatchling, or about the Koth?"

Taral wasn't laughing. "You need to worry, Zarda, about what you don't See."

And without another word, he opened the door and ducked outside.

With a last glance at the fire, I breathed in the tang of warm stone and sweet tea, and followed him out into the rain.

The clouds were low enough that we had to be wary of floaters. Even though there were no tell-tale purple flashes amid the roiling grey, we flew much lower than we would normally have done, almost skimming the tallest orenvines. It was a battle to keep a straight course in the blustery, unpredictable wind that made progress slow, and I guessed that it was well after zenith by the time we flew over the last of the main clusters at the western edge of the Expanse. Beyond them, livestock grazed in fields of kerzh that lay along the banks of Far-river, and further still were the hill slopes that were a gentle precursor to the steeper foothills and mountains beyond. In the warm season, the hills were a patchwork of contrasting colours, making it easy to spot which crops were planted where – the blue of the kerzh grass on the northern slopes, facing the sun; the yellow camylvines on the opposite side in the shade, the pattern broken by the creamy blossoms of the hoxberry orchards and purple stands of orenvine. Now, with most of the crops gathered, and their contours softened by the rain, they looked much alike.

The zaxel farms were based on the higher slopes of the hills south-west of the river. We had flown much further the previous day, when we'd headed north and west to the Deadlands, but with the weather worsening, my wings began to ache with the strain of fighting the wind. I was just beginning to think I would have to ask Taral for another rest-stop when he shouted across to me and pointed. "There," he called, "you can see the damage from here."

Even through the rain, it was easy to see the ashy scar on the hillside ahead of us, the farm's storage pit gaping blackly in the midst of burned and trampled fields. The grey stems that remained after the fat red cobs were cut were themselves harvested in the middle of the freeze and used to strew floors and feed the livestock.

The raiders had made sure that that crop, too, had been destroyed.

The smoke had gone, but the oily smell of burned zaxel lingered. As we glided in over a stream to land near the dwelling in the easternmost field, calling to announce our arrival, the vlydh baulked at the stench and tried to pull away. Fortunately, Taral had a strong grip on the leading-harness, and we alighted safely, though the blackened zaxel stems were sticky under our feet and gave way under our weight with little more than an ashy whisper.

A single orenvine stood, singed but defiantly unburned, at the side of the landing path. Taral tethered the vlydh to it, and as we folded our wings, a young male emerged from the dwelling's doorway to greet us. There was a poultice on his right leg and his mane was scorched. As he turned to greet Taral, I noticed that his mauled left wing had been patched, and I tried to remember who the nearest healer was. Galyn, I thought, from the gatherers' cluster. She had done a good job by the looks of it but, as Fate-seer, I had better and rarer balms to apply.

"Difel," said Taral, "I must apologise again that my flyers were not able to protect you. How are you today? How is Hamor?"

"I'll heal. So will Hamor, though he is very distressed, as you can imagine. You mustn't blame yourself, though, or the guardflight – they can't be everywhere, I know, especially now." He acknowledged me with a nod and went on: "We joined the death-howls as they spread across the Expanse. I hoped they were not for Vizan, but I see you wear the Fate-seer's tunic now." Difel dipped his ears and spiralled a paw across his tunic. "May the Spiral take his light," he said, adding the usual sympathetic noises that soothe a little and help not at all.

Something nudged my foot and I looked down to see a mud-burrower squirming blindly across the path. Harmless as it was, it sent a chill up my wings: I couldn't help but be reminded of how bereft, how helpless I was without Vizan to guide me. Taking care not to step on the burrower, I moved across to the vlydh and reached up to unstrap the pannier. "I heard you were bitten, so I brought a tincture of camyl to speed the healing. I have more salve for your wing, too." Looking about, I added: "I'm afraid the repairs to your farm will be less straightforward."

Difel's ears drooped and his mane bristled in an understandable mixture of depression and anger. "There were three of them," he said, "and they were huge. Ugly beasts, all teeth and claws. They were armed, too – but I managed to wrest one of their weapons from them in the struggle. Come in out of the cold, I'll show you."

We crossed the threshold into a dwelling that bore all the hallmarks of a household suffering illness and shock: unswept floor, an odour of stale food, unlicked platters that had not been cleared from the table. It was just like home.

"You must excuse the mess. My illness has burdened Difel with too much to do, and he's been so busy outside he's not been able to tend to the dwelling very much." The new voice spoke from the shadows behind the screen towards the rear of the dwelling, and Taral and I moved across to find its owner. Huddled in an untidy nest, with a warm blanket wrapped around him, Hamor was a pitiable sight. His fur was tangled and matted, with bald patches of mauve skin showing through. He smelled stale and…yes, scared. The reeds beneath him crackled as he shifted his head, and I noted his shaking paws and watering eyes.

"Hamor, you are no better," I said, placing a paw on his grey snout to gauge his temperature. "I'd hoped that the ointment Vizan left you last time would have helped."

"Oh it did," said Hamor. "Not the fur so much, that's still not growing right, but I felt much better – till the raiders came. It's worse again today, but I'm sure it'll pass."

"Hmm. It will pass a good deal quicker with some more medicine inside you," I said. Turning to Difel, I added, "While I brew it, you should show Taral the weapon you took. Then I will tend to your leg and wing."

Before I could brew anything I needed some clean pots, but there were none. Every container in the dwelling was way beyond licking – the contents had set hard, the crusts betraying their origins: branmeal, stew, soup, tea. I sighed. I would have to venture outside again to fetch water. The sleet was back, threatening to turn to snow, and I shivered despite the too-long tunic that flapped around my knees. There was barely a drop of water in the tub outside the door and I twisted an ear to listen for the flow of the stream we had flown over. The vlydh, I noticed, had squeezed as far into the damaged orenvine as it could, in search of shelter and food, and the sound of its leaf-chewing carried faintly to my ears as I passed. Filling the water-bucket at the nearby stream, I hurried back to the dwelling and set about washing the pots and bowls.

While I worked, I turned an ear to listen as Difel repeated his story to Taral: "It's as I told your flyers the other night – I was covering the store-pit with a layer of zaxel stems to protect the cobs from the weather," he said, "so I was looking down. I didn't see the Koth coming until one of them landed on top of me – that was when my wing got damaged. I tried to give him a kick, but he just seized my leg and bit it. I couldn't fly for help and I couldn't walk – they knew I was no threat. I just had to sit there, watching them transfer a pit-full of cobs into great sacks – like carry-pouches but bigger."

"I don't understand why they didn't use vlydhs," said Hamor, scratching at his chest.

"Vlydhs can't fly as high as the Koth," I reminded him, "just as we can't. And try not to scratch."

Difel was standing by the fire and moved away with a mumbled apology when I approached with a pot full of herbs ready to brew. I carefully set the pot on its hook over the fire and stood over it, stirring the contents.

"*Fwerkian* Koth!" Taral dipped an ear in apology, but his bad language was excusable under the circumstances. He had seated himself at the table, his ears turned to Difel but his eyes on the wicked-looking curved blade he held – the weapon Difel had snatched from his attackers. I heard the rumble of frustration in his voice as he went on: "They attack us whenever they choose – but we have no way to strike back!" With a final growl of annoyance he set down the blade and stood up, pacing about from one end of the table to the other, the rhythm of his claws dulled by the beaten earth floor.

I gave the pot a sniff and lifted the spoon to taste the mixture. "Go on with your story, Difel," I prompted.

Difel settled himself on the stool Taral had vacated and went on: "When they had filled their sacks, they produced firesticks from their tunic pockets. They set light to the stubble and two of them took off. The third went to set light to the cobs left in the store pit, the ones they couldn't carry, and it was then that I saw my chance and rushed at him."

There was enough water left in the bucket I'd filled to pour a beakerful for him, so I passed the drink to him silently and then returned to my pot-stirring.

"I couldn't stop him, of course," said Difel, once he'd taken a good draught of the water, "but I surprised him enough to take his weapon. He hit me with the firestick, though – that was how my mane got singed – and took off after the others."

"You were lucky not to get killed!" Hamor's voice was unsteady, but there was a note of pride behind his admonition.

"It was a brave thing to do," said Taral. He had been leaning against the table as Difel finished his tale, but now he stood up straight and picked up the blade once again. "It's all of a piece," he said, "and the hilt is beautifully carved, like the one on the wall in the Prime's audience chamber. What do you make of it, Zarda?"

I gave the pot another sniff; my brew was not quite ready. "Stir this for a moment, would you, Difel?" I handed him the spoon, and stepped across to take the weapon from Taral…

…and felt it take me into the mountains. There was a horned creature at my feet and a group of Koth around a fire; the blade dripped blood….

"Zarda? Zarda!" Taral had gripped my shoulders and was shaking me, and as I came to myself again, I realised I had dropped the blade. Difel had turned to stare at me, spoon in paw, oblivious to the bubbling pot behind him; even Hamor was sitting up a little straighter in his nest.

I waved a paw, dismissively. "Difel, for the Spiral's sake, tend to that pot! It will be ruined if it boils over!"

He jumped to do as he was bid, and Taral dragged a stool across for me to sit on. "What was it? What did you See?" He retrieved the blade from where I had dropped it on the floor and put it on the table in front of me.

"I got no more than a glimpse," I said. "Just enough to tell me that the blade was carved from the horn of a large mountain beast – it looked similar to a kervhel, but bigger, at least twice the size.

It's a killing blade, for all it looks delicate and brittle." I shook my head and felt my whiskers twitch instinctively as I looked at the curved, serrated edge of the blade. "I'm sorry, Taral, that's all I can tell you – and I'll not touch it again."

Taral nodded, his ears signalling disappointment that I'd not been able to supply more information, but he didn't press me to try again. "I will take it back to Guardflight Rock," he said, as he tucked it into the pannier, which was almost empty now. "It will be interesting to see what the armourers make of it."

I shook my head to clear it of the last faint tendrils of my Vision and got to my feet to rescue my brew. "Difel, you have stirred that enough. Fetch me a fresh beaker to drain the liquid into, would you, and it will be ready for Hamor to drink. Then I will take a look at you."

The sun was sinking towards the mountains by the time we got back to Guardflight Rock, and the news from the orenvine plantation had arrived ahead of us.

Doran's egg had hatched at zenith.

The hatchling had no wings.

Seven

Three days later, with unseasonal snow still falling in patchy showers, Doran came to see me. "Have you heard the rumours?" she asked, brushing snow from the green-and-black squares of her healer's tunic and shaking out her damp fur.

"That the freeze has come early as a punishment from the Great Spiral for allowing a wingless heir to thrive?" I nodded. There had been a council meeting the previous day, and Fazak had repeated the gossip with a relish I could smell from the opposite end of the table. I'd been able to quiet him by pointing out that early snow was not unprecedented, and the meeting had moved on. When the tally-keeper, Sifan, reported that the effect of the Koth raids on this cycle's tithes would be negligible, Kalis' mood had improved, and I'd hoped that he might send out a reminder about previous cold snaps, or even issue a report on Dru's progress, but he'd snarled at the mere suggestion.

I sighed, glanced at the empty stool where Vizan would have sat, and poured two beakers of hot berrywine, handing one to

Doran as she settled herself on a stool by the hearth. "When the first wingless hatched, Vizan said that some such nonsense would surface sooner or later. He said that if there were no wingless to blame, the problems would be Taral's fault for not keeping the Koth at bay, or Sifan's fault for not keeping a proper tally, or the Fate-seer's for getting some ritual or other wrong." I extended a claw and leaned down to turn over one of the burning vinelogs, then settled myself on the stool on the opposite side of the hearth to Doran.

"I suppose we all need someone to blame," she said, nursing her warm beaker. "I know I do."

I'd not seen her since the day her hatchling had emerged. On hearing the news, I'd retrieved my carry-pouch from Taral's vlydh and flown straight from Guardflight Rock to her dwelling. Not that there had been much I could do.

Or say.

"How is Cavel?" I asked. When I'd seen him three days before, he'd been no more than a mewling mite, his fur still wet from Doran's licking.

She sniffed at the berrywine, took a sip, and nodded. "He seems to be thriving." Sadness mingled with pride in her voice. "He's curious, inquisitive, has already managed to climb up onto every shelf in the dwelling..." She paused, her nose twitching. "What *is* that smell?"

"Burnt griddle cakes. Vizan's recipe, my cooking skills. Not a good mix." I'd given the pan to Peren the trader, to take to the metal-shapers for scrap. There'd been no hope of getting it clean. "There's loxcake if you'd like some?"

Doran twitched an ear, considering. "I'd normally say no, but Cavel likes sweet foods. I'll have one, thank you, it should be half-digested by the time I get back."

Setting my beaker down on the floor by my stool, I got up and stepped across to the storage shelves, pulled down the jar, and took off the lid. "He's eating well, then?"

"Oh yes, he's got a good appetite. I seem to spend half my time regurgitating for him." I offered the jar, and she took a cake, gave it a sniff and bit into it. "Miyak would like these," she said, and I held out the jar for her to take another and slide it into her tunic pocket.

"And how is Miyak?" I took a loxcake for myself, noted that there were two left, and put the lid back on the jar. Miyak's anger at the hatching of his wingless offspring had been cold and hard where Kalis' had been hot fury. He'd not said a word as I'd spiralled a paw over Cavel's tiny form and spoken the blessing. Nor had he attended the council meeting, sending Narva from the Dyers' cluster in his stead.

Doran's ears drooped as she answered. "He's still adjusting his expectations. It doesn't help that Geany gave him a healthy, winged youngling." She sighed. "He never spoke of them before, but to hear him talk now, you'd think Geany was a paragon of dwelling-keeping, and Cayan had the biggest wingspan outside the *Spirax*."

I nodded in sympathy. Miyak's first nest-mate, Geany, had fallen victim to a floater; their hatchling, Cayan, had succumbed to the Sickness. Doran, like me, had been a replacement; Doran, like me, felt she had fallen short of expectations.

She popped the last of her loxcake into her mouth, licked her fingers, and chewed. Then, with her tail flicking from side to side in a rare display of agitation, she went on: "He's so desperate for Cavel to fly that he's come up with some wild idea about putting him on a vlydh – says he can make a special harness to strap him on, as though the poor pup is a basket of cargo!"

"Hmm." I savoured the moist crumbs of my own loxcake as I pondered the idea. I doubted that the vlydh would distinguish one kind of cargo from another – it had simply never been necessary before now to entertain the idea of riding on one. "I suppose, if Miyak waits till Cavel's a bit older, and uses an elderly vlydh…" I scraped my stool a little nearer Doran's as I sat down and picked up my beaker. The berrywine was no longer hot, but still warm enough to be drinkable.

Doran barked with laughter. "You can't think it would actually work? What if Cavel fell off? Without wings of his own he'd…" She stopped, her hackles on end at the mere thought of what might happen.

"I'm sure Miyak would make sure he was well strapped on," I said. My mind was racing with the possibilities. If this idea worked, it would solve all sorts of difficulties for Dru – and for

73

other wingless younglings – as well as Cavel. "When was the last time a pannier fell off a vlydh?"

Doran looked surprised by the question. "I don't recall..."

"That's because it's never happened," I said, "at least, not outside of legend. I'm sure Miyak will make sure that Cavel is at least as safe as any pannier."

Doran sighed and drained her beaker. "I thought you'd have more sense." She stood and went to look through the see-shell, staring at the half-frozen droplets that coated its outer layer. "Miyak's got too much time on his hands, that's the problem. With the weather so bad, inter-cluster travel is down, and no-one has hired a vlydh for two days. In any case, the creatures are so confused by this cold spell that Miyak can barely persuade them to leave their vines, let alone move from the plantation."

"Then you needn't worry yet about Cavel being strapped to one." I got to my feet and poured more berrywine into my beaker. "Refill?"

Doran nodded and returned to the hearth, holding out her beaker while I tipped the last of the hot liquid into it.

"What I worry about are the other pups," she said, resettling herself on the stool she'd vacated. "The normal ones. Cavel's too young yet to realise he's different, and at least in the plantation we're not near other dwellings. He can run about outside without anyone pointing or sneering. But I've seen what happens to others, Zarda. Those younglings who have wings taunt those who have none – and their parents are as bad!" She shook her head, ears drooping with distress. "What sort of future will Cavel have? Will any of them have that can't fly?"

As I sat down, I noticed that I had dripped berrywine down the front of my tunic, and brushed at the droplets, smudging them to damp blobs. "I wish Vizan were here," I sighed. "He would know what to do, what we might say to overcome this hostility towards those who are..."

"Crippled?" offered Doran, as I hesitated. I could hear the resentment in her voice as she formed the word.

"I was about to say 'different'," I said, rubbing at a sticky patch on my snout where the berrywine had stuck to the fur. "Which gives me an idea..." I drained the berrywine, rolling the empty beaker between my paws as I went on: "Do you remember when I had my first Vision? My dam was horrified—"

"And your sire was none too pleased, either." Doran's whiskers twitched at the memory. "All that work, teaching you how to be a good trader, and then overnight you're a potential Fate-seer." Her ears twisted a little as she continued: "Of course, at the time, Vizan already had an apprentice."

I nodded. "May the Spiral rest him," I said, running my paw over my tunic. "The point is – I was suddenly seen as being *different*. It was the same with Vizan, and I suppose it was the same with every Fate-seer since the first lights shone in the Spiral, but everyone does more than just regard us as being different." I turned from Doran to watch purple flames lick at the vinelogs in the fire. "Our differences are welcomed as a gift, as something to be embraced."

"Hmm." Doran swirled the remaining contents of her beaker, then took a sip. "I see what you mean. But Fate-seers are different because you have something *more* than a normal drax. The wingless are different because they have *less*."

"Their legs are longer and stronger," I pointed out. "How do we know that that is not a gift? The Spiral's ways are mysterious, they're not for us to judge."

Doran flicked her ears and scratched her snout as she considered what I'd said, then gave a slow nod. "I had not considered that. To be honest, for the past three days I've wished that I could fly high enough to give the Spiral a death-bite." She swirled a paw around the front of her tunic as though to mitigate the blasphemy, but having seen so many struggling with their wingless hatchlings, I had some understanding of her rancour. "Why?" she went on. "Why us? Why now? That's all I've been asking since Cavel hatched."

"And I can't give you an answer," I said.

"No." Doran raised her beaker toward me, and I was surprised to see her ears set forward, a spark of respect in her eyes. "But I doubt that even Vizan could have spoken more wisely, Zarda. Thank you."

"Don't thank me yet," I said. "First, we have to take that message to the rest of the drax. Then we have to pray to the Spiral that they'll listen."

We were fortunate – or blessed, perhaps. As we began to spread the suggestion that the wingless were sent for a purpose, the weather turned.

"You see?" I said, as I flew from cluster to cluster and the wind swung around to the north-east, sweeping the snow-bearing clouds back over the mountains. "The Spiral was angry because we doubted – because we were suspicious – because we were disappointed. Now that we understand that the wingless have a purpose, the snow has gone and the sun has returned."

Some – Fazak prominent among them – still muttered that the strange hatchlings were a curse, but over the course of the next moon, I noticed that their audience dwindled as the weather improved, and fewer drax repeated what they said.

"Even the vlydh are co-operating," said Miyak, when I flew to the plantation to see Doran and check on Cavel's progress. "They've realised the freeze isn't here yet and started flying again. Tomorrow, if the weather is still set fair, I'll put Cavel on one of them and see if my new harness works."

I sniffed the wind, and raised my head to check the skies. "It will be a fine day," I said. "The wind is salt and the clouds are high." I turned my attention back to Miyak. "Have you told anyone else about your plan?"

"Certainly not," he said. "Well, except for Doran, of course, and I told her not to tell anyone."

The next morning, I arrived at the plantation later than I had intended – I had spilled branmeal down my tunic, and had to change it – and by the time I got there it was difficult to see a place to land, because the ground between the plantation and the next cluster was swarming with drax.

Tunics of all shades and colours mingled together on the landing space behind the hill on which the orenvines grew; some had even perched themselves in the tops of the vines, moving their wings gently to ensure they retained their balance.

I alighted where the crowd was thinnest, calling as I glided down to alert those below. As I folded my wings and looked around, Taral came to meet me.

"Miyak has been looking for you," he said. "He has gone back to his dwelling for now, while I fetch more guardflight to help with the crowd."

I dipped an ear in acknowledgement, and he stretched his wings, turned into the wind, and took off at a run. I watched him gain height and turn south-west toward Guardflight Rock, then made my way through the throng towards the plantation.

I caught sight of Swalo the fable-spinner in the middle of a group of younglings, and paused a moment to listen. He was seated on a log at the bottom of the hill, telling them the tale of Tomax the Bold and his battle with the moon-monster, embellishing the story with exaggerated gestures of arms and wings. His young audience sat rapt, and I noticed that there were both winged and wingless among them, all mixed in together. I took it as a hopeful sign, gave a nod of respect to Swalo when he glanced my way, and moved on.

It was like a Festival, I thought, though none had been decreed. Traders shouted over the noise of nineties of murmuring voices to advertise their wares. From the trays strapped round their necks, the aroma of hot groxen pies and the sweet scent of kerzh-fruits dipped in nut-syrup floated across to me on the breeze. As I paused to sniff, wondering what I might trade for a fresh pasty, I caught sight of a bright green tunic over to my right, and turned the other way before Fazak saw me.

Too late.

"Zarda!" That high-pitched call was unmistakable, and though I toyed with the idea of ignoring it, I knew it would be a pointless gesture. Instead, I set my wings and ears to the highest level of respect, and turned to find him hurrying toward me like a raincloud on a feast day. "This is outrageous," he said, not even bothering with the normal formalities of greeting before launching into his tirade. "No-one is doing any work. Look! There are farmers here, fishers, builders, dyers…" He wrinkled his snout as he looked over at the nearest pie-seller. "*Traders* I would expect," he said, his voice dripping disdain, "but nobody else has any excuse for being here."

"Yet here *you* are, Fazak," I said, making my voice as smooth as possible, "along with everyone else."

"I was with Kalis when he sent Taral to find out why such a crowd had gathered without permission," he said, "and came along to satisfy myself that all was being dealt with correctly. Just as well I did, since Taral did not seem interested in sending these drax about their business. I had to remind him of his duty, and sent him to fetch the guardflight."

I wondered when Fazak had been given the authority to order Taral around, but did not voice the thought. Instead, I said, "These drax have had some very difficult moons. I do not think we should grudge them a little enjoyment. Everyone is curious to see if Cavel can ride the vlydh – and if he can, then that is cause for celebration since it means that no youngling need be stranded on the ground."

I looked over at the group surrounding Swalo as I finished speaking, and Fazak followed my gaze. He made a choking noise, as though he was regurgitating a particularly challenging meal, and his mane stood on end. "Murgo!" He bounded across to the little listeners, leaned over the ones at the back of the group, and lifted out a struggling half-grown in a green-striped tunic.

Swalo broke off in mid-sentence and heads turned as Fazak dragged his offspring away from the group. "What have I told you about mingling with those cracked shells?" he barked, and I gasped at his use of such an insult in public. "You are not to go near them again, do you understand? Come along, I am taking you home." And, holding Murgo firmly by the mane, he marched the youngling off through the crowd to find room to take off.

The crowd had fallen silent, every ear turned toward Fazak as he pulled his protesting youngling away. He had dropped his icy cloudburst right over the carnival and left behind a puddle of despondency. As everyone found their voice again and all began to talk at once, I heard several drax mumble agreement with Fazak's stinging assessment of the wingless. Arguments started and younglings in the group around Swalo eyed each other with suspicion; the whole atmosphere had curdled, and even the pies seemed to smell stale.

"Well done, Fazak," I muttered, as I watched him pulling Murgo by the paw into the sky. "You really should have stayed to enjoy your triumph, you miserable—"

Behind me, someone called, "The guardflight are coming!" and I turned to see a 'V' formation of red tunics heading in from the south-west.

"They are not here yet," I said, loudly, determined to salvage what I could from the wreckage of Fazak's prejudice. "Swalo, I'm sure the younglings would like to hear how the tale ends?" I turned to the nearest trader. "Peren, will you take a vial of crushed avalox in exchange for one of your pasties?"

As I moved on toward the plantation, pasty in paw, I heard the traders start calling again, and the conversations I turned an ear towards all seemed to have returned to speculation about the vlydh-ride. I rolled a paw across my tunic, trailing crumbs, and offered a brief prayer of thanks to the Spiral. The gathering was no longer a festival, but at least it had not turned into a riot.

I began to make my way up the hill, through the spiralling ranks of the plantation vines, and met Miyak on his way down. He was leading the elderly vlydh that delivered supplies to the plateau, and behind them, leaping about with excitement, was Cavel. Doran followed them at a distance, her silence and drooping ears telling me that she was contrite about confiding the 'secret' flight to her gossiping friends.

"I'm afraid it has all turned into rather a carnival," said Miyak, his twitching tail betraying his nervousness.

"I don't think you need worry," I said. "The crowd will be leaving soon – Taral and the guardflight are on their way."

I was mistaken. As we emerged from the vines at the foot of the hill, we found that the guardflight had not dispersed the crowd as Fazak had demanded: instead, everyone had been marshalled into a more disciplined order.

Miyak paused, staring. "It looks like a parade."

It did, though not one I had ever seen before, for parades were traditionally conducted in mid-air by drax who swooped and dived as the occasion demanded; the ones in front of us were grounded and still. Nevertheless, it was clear that Taral had used the same principle as the aerial arrangements: spiral formations by trade and seniority.

"They have left a pathway for you," I said, indicating to Miyak that he should go first, with the vlydh.

Extending one wing slightly so that Cavel could hold on to the tip, Miyak led the vlydh onward, and I followed behind with Doran.

The copper-coloured tunics of the artisans were on our right, with Hapak in the central place of honour, his ears betraying his scepticism. There were a half-dozen cluster-criers to our left, their orange tunics bright in the sunlight – though their chief, Fugol, was conspicuous by his absence. Next to them were the farmers, their brown tunics looking drab in comparison, while next to the artisans were the traders in pale blue. The aroma of hot pies wafted from the trays they had placed at their feet, and I realised I was still clutching half a pasty. I gobbled it down in a hurry and hoped that no-one would notice, though a glance at Taral's twitching whiskers told me that he, at least, had seen.

He was standing in the middle of the guardflight in the last of the main groups. Opposite them was a knot of drax in different coloured tunics: a few fishers in deep blue, the turquoise splash of Sifan's distinctive tunic, Swalo in crimson-and-grey, and some in the ochre tunics of the hunters. I spotted Shaya in among them and looked away. I'd not managed to get near her egg before it hatched, and I was sure she blamed me for the wingless youngling that had emerged. At least Ravar was still alive and thriving – I'd seen him earlier with the other younglings listening to Swalo – but I couldn't help but wonder whether he might be 'lost' on his first hunt.

I pulled my thoughts away from morbid speculation, concentrating instead on Miyak, as he halted the vlydh and began to tie an extra strap around its stubby neck. Unlike the usual leading harness, this strap trailed along the animal's back, and was obviously meant for the rider to hold on to.

"Do you need any help?"

"No thank you, Zarda. I've done this many times while I worked it all out."

I saw that Miyak had replaced the panniers the vlydh usually carried with a grox-hide seat, held in place by straps across the creature's belly between its front and middle sets of legs. I strolled around the vlydh, noting the loops that dangled from the seat on each side of the creature, just behind its front wings. I was about to ask Miyak what they were for when he dipped his ears and murmured, "Good thing I already know it works!"

"You do?" I was astonished. "How?"

Miyak grunted, his scent issuing conflicting signals of concern and disappointment. "I tested it myself last night." He tugged at the harness to make sure it would stay in place. "I might not be happy that my nestling's deformed, Zarda, but I'd hardly allow him to be the first to try this. Suppose he fell off – he wouldn't be able to fly to safety. I needed to be sure." He looked over his shoulder at the crowd. "You understand why I told no-one?"

I eyed the vlydh with renewed admiration. The creatures had scales which changed in hue from white to dark green as they aged: the one Miyak had chosen for Cavel's flight was almost black, and I suspected that its final flight to the Great Spiral would not be long delayed. "I'm surprised that it got off the ground with you on its back," I said.

Miyak snorted. "It's used to heavy loads," he reminded me. "I doubt it will even notice Cavel is there." He turned and beckoned to his pup.

The youngling was still small, his head barely reaching the hem of my tunic as he hurried past, but his excitement was clear in his bouncing strides and flicking ears. How strange it must be, I thought, to be over a moon old and to have never left the ground. Stranger still to know that you would never be able to do so without help.

Miyak lifted him onto the vlydh and guided his feet into the loops at the side. "These will help you remain in the seat when the vlydh banks and turns," he said, as the youngling straddled the creature. Passing a strap around both the seat and Cavel's waist, he passed the vlydh's neck-harness to the young rider. "Guide it with this," he said. "Pull gently with your left paw to turn that way, and with your right to go the other."

"But how do I make it take off? Or land?"

Miyak took the leading-harness that looped about the vlydh's head. "I will do that," he said. "All you need do is sit still. If you feel unsafe, or want to land, just call to me, and I will have you back on the ground in a wingbeat. Are you ready?"

"Yes, Miyak-fa, yes! Make it fly!"

Miyak grasped the leading-harness, just as he would have done if it were an ordinary pack-load on the creature's back, and led it along the landing-path, walking at first, then jogging as he extended his own wings, finally breaking into a run with his wings beating. He took off, the vlydh following faithfully, and many of the crowd cheered – though I noticed that Hapak and Sifan remained silent.

Beside me, Doran was hopping up and down with excitement, and I could smell her pride and relief. "It worked!" she called, raising her voice over the noise of the cheers.

I thumped my tail and nodded, glancing up as Cavel's vlydh made another pass overhead and the youngling's excited squeals carried to us on the breeze. "He's enjoying himself." I pressed a paw to Doran's shoulder and she acknowledged the gesture with a flick of an ear, then ran to take off after her offspring. Within moments a whole swathe of the remaining drax had done the same.

"They have already forgotten those ridiculous rumours." I turned to find Swalo at my side. His snout, with its distinctive black stripe, was raised as he looked upward to follow the vlydh's flight-path.

I was surprised. "You don't believe the wingless are cursed, then?"

He shook his head. "I know a fiction when I hear one. In any case, I've seen too many wingless on my travels. If there *is* a curse, they are the result, not the cause."

It occurred to me that Swalo, flying from cluster to cluster to trade his tales for food and board, would have a better idea than I did about how many wingless hatchlings there had actually been – and how many of them still survived. "Would you come to my dwelling tomorrow?" I said. "I would like to hear a *true* story, and I think you can help."

I was sorting through the herb-baskets when Swalo arrived, and I saw his nose twitch as he stepped inside, doubtless trying to identify the different aromas.

"Please excuse the mess," I said, brushing kerzh stems from a section of the table and giving the wood a quick dust with the corner of my tunic. "Pull up a stool, and I'll get you a drink. I have hoxberry juice, avalox tea – or perhaps something a little stronger?"

"Hoxberry will be fine, thank you." Swalo sat down next to the space I'd cleared, and while I located the hoxberry jar, he gave the herbs I'd been sorting another sniff. "Are these all to be turned into medicines?" He reached across to pick up a dried avalox blossom and held it near his nose to give it a brief sniff, before setting it down again on the pile. "I didn't realise that avalox was medicinal. What is it good for?"

"Tea," I said, "and the cooking pot." I set two beakers on the table and poured us each a measure of juice, then pulled up a stool next to Swalo. "I am re-organising the herb stores – I could never make sense of the way Vizan did it, and I'm sure some of the baskets have not been opened for cycles. I can't even identify some of the things I've found – they smell musty and crumble to dust when I touch them. The Spiral only knows what they were, or what they were for. I just hope it wasn't anything important."

"Vizan would surely have mentioned them if they were," said Swalo. He picked up his beaker and took a sip. "This is excellent. Your own recipe?"

"Vizan's." I swallowed a little of my own drink, trying once again to identify the faintly tart taste that accompanied the usual sweetness. "Something else he didn't have time to pass on to me, alas. Once this batch has gone, I will never be able to brew another that tastes quite this good."

"Then I shall savour this while it lasts," said Swalo. His dark mane smelled freshly-washed and his patchwork tunic was cleaner than the one I was wearing. For a drax who travelled from cluster to cluster as he did, it would not have been a simple matter to make so much effort, and I was reminded again that I was no longer Zarda the humble apprentice. I was the Fate-seer, with all the status – and responsibility – that entailed. Swalo took a sip from his beaker and nodded approval. "Delicious. But you didn't ask me here to talk of herbs and recipes."

"No." I took another sip from my beaker and set it down. "It was seeing you with those younglings yesterday. I lost track of what was happening on the Expanse while I was nursing Vizan, but it occurred to me yesterday that with all the travelling you do, you'd have a good idea about how many wingless have hatched. You'd also know…" I hesitated to voice the next thought, but Swalo picked up my meaning anyway.

"…how many still survive?" His ears flattened and he shook his head. "I've heard rumours and stories that would make your fur fall out," he said. It was his turn to hesitate. He picked up the avalox flower again and rolled the stem between his fingers as he spoke, making the petals blur with movement. "I said to you yesterday that I know a fiction when I hear one. That's true, if I can hear it direct, or if I know the source, as I did with that rumour that Fazak started. But if a story comes to me from a drax who has had it from a nest-brother, who heard it from a trader…" A couple of petals drifted from the flower he twirled and settled beside his beaker. "I don't know how much of what I heard is true."

I nodded. There was a dead flisk on the table next to the loose petals, and I dropped the tiny body into an empty bowl as though I'd left the thing there intentionally and intended to make use of it later. "I understand. Go on."

"What I am sure of is that there was many an egg laid that did not produce a hatchling," said Swalo. "But where those nestlings went…" He put down the avalox, picked up his drink, and stared into his beaker as he went on: "Clusters near the sea have no wingless nestlings at all, and half the usual number of winged ones. It's the same story for the clusters near the rivers – and I also heard stories that some drax flew to the Deadlands and left their wingless hatchlings there."

I'd heard some of these rumours before – I'd tried to bring them to Kalis' attention on the night Dru hatched – but Swalo's next words shocked me: "There are even whispers that some took their hatchlings all the way to the Forest."

I gasped and spiralled a paw across my tunic. The Forest was as hostile and alien an environment as the sea – worse, since it produced little food, no offerings, and few glimpses of what might live beneath the ever-moving leaves of its crimson canopy. I had been foolish enough to venture there once, on a juvenile exploit, and the memory of what had happened still chilled me.

"There's worse," said Swalo, "if you can bear to hear it."

I gulped the last of my hoxberry juice, wishing that I'd poured myself something stronger. Still, this was why I had asked Swalo to come; I had wanted the truth and here it was. "Go on."

"This I do know, because I saw some of them myself," said Swalo, and I was alarmed to see his mane standing on end. He leaned close and there was a tremor in his voice as he whispered: "*Smashed eggs.*"

"No!" I spiralled a paw across my tunic.

"As the Spiral is my witness. On the rocks by Far-river."

"Near Paw Lake?"

"Further south. The outcropping beyond the southernmost farms, where the river turns east. And those were just the ones I saw with my own eyes," he said. "As I said, there were rumours and stories in all the clusters. I have been asked for the legend of One-Wing everywhere I fly – though I'm not sure whether it's for comfort or advice." He drained his beaker and I offered another, which he declined with a raised paw.

There was a blob of dried branmeal on the worktop, and I scratched at it as I spoke, "It is astonishing that there are any wingless left at all."

The blob was set hard. It didn't budge.

"The missing pups are mostly from the early hatchings of the harvest batch," said Swalo, "before the connection with the Sickness was established. There have been more survivors in the later hatchings, mainly since Dru came along. The idea that the wingless might be a blessing rather than a curse has helped, too. I wonder where that thought started?"

I said nothing, though my whiskers might have twitched just a little.

"How is Dru anyway?" said Swalo. "Flying about as I do, I seem to have missed the reports."

"There have been none."

He sat bolt upright, slapping his beaker down so hard that the remaining droplets of his drink splashed onto the table. "What? But tradition—"

"Tradition is apparently being rewritten," I said. "Kalis has declined to issue any updates on Dru's progress. Still, if anyone should ask, tell them that he is thriving, and that he will be visiting some of the clusters very soon."

I hoped he would, anyway. I had heard no more than Swalo, though I was sure he expected that I, as Fate-seer, would know more than he did. But I had not been summoned to see Kalis outside a council meeting since the night of Dru's hatching. The single councillor who had was Fazak, and I would let my wings drop off before I asked him for a progress report – or indeed for anything else.

I would have to wait until my appointment with Varna at the end of Dru's second moon, to find out whether my words to Swalo were true.

Eight

W hen I made my way back to the *Spirax*, two moons after Dru hatched, I realised that I had no idea what sort of youngling I might find waiting for me. Though the matter had been raised in Council sessions a number of times, there had still been no official reports issued on Dru's progress, though the 'sitting up' and 'standing' milestones should have been recorded, even if the 'wing-flapping' could not. It disturbed me almost as much as the mutterings about him being cursed, but at least there was something I could do about his isolation – if his parents would allow it.

Morel met me as I entered the *Spirax*, and led me up the curving corridor and along a passage to the nursery. Three levels below the audience chamber, the passageway was so dimly lit that I was tempted to switch to night vision. An odour of damp overlaid with dust and soot gave it an air of neglect and indifference that told me all I needed to know about Kalis' attitude to his pup. If he had been near the nursery even once, the heralds would have made sure the corridor was clean and well lit. It told me too that Varna's standing as the Prime's nest-mate was diminishing by the day. Come the Melt, she would be discarded, likely as not, and a new nest-mate chosen – and what would happen to Dru then, I wondered?

I brushed a paw along the passageway wall, hoping that contact with the *Spirax* might trigger a Vision that would show me the answer, but I got nothing more than greasy soot smears on my fingertips.

Varna was waiting for me, sitting on an upholstered stool on the far side of the nursery. I dipped a bow, and glanced around the circular room, noting the bright dye-work and leaf-patterns on the walls, which depicted scenes from drax legends. Toys were scattered across the floor – a play-nest with smoothed stone eggs, large fabric leaves with word-dots picked out in the same wormspun gold-thread that adorned the ritual tunics, and small drum-logs with nestling-sized sticks to beat them with.

There were also colourful hoops hanging from the ceiling, which a normal nestling would have had fun flying through and around. They had been tied together, gathered into a forlorn set of rings beneath which Dru played. For a moment, seeing him sitting there building coloured pebbles into tiny dwellings, I was afraid he couldn't walk either, but at a word from Varna, he got to his feet and lisped a greeting. I gave him a bow (which, to judge by the snuffling, he seemed to find amusing) and turned my attention to Varna.

"Reaching the Dream-cave will not be easy for him," I said, "but I have given the matter some thought." Though Dru could have ridden a vlydh, as Cavel had done, I was reluctant to take one of the creatures with us, as there were no orenvines near the cave. I had spoken with Miyak about the problem, and between us we had fashioned a new harness, one which strapped around my own shoulders and chest. I had taken the liberty of putting on the harness in readiness, so that I might show Varna how it worked. "Dru will be strapped in front of me with his back against my chest so that he can see where we're going," I said. "We've tried this out with Cavel already, it's completely safe."

Varna wrinkled her snout and flattened her ears. The smell of contempt was palpable as she got to her feet. "You propose to turn the Prime's heir into some sort of live carry-pouch?"

"I propose to take the Prime's heir for his first flight." I dipped another bow in Dru's direction. "If he will allow me?"

Varna bristled, but Dru responded eagerly, snuffling, jumping up and down, and shouting, "Yes! Yes Varna-muz. Let me fly!"

I admired his eagerness, noting the jumping about and the two-legged leaps which took Dru almost to the level of those unused flight-rings. It was something I had seen Cavel do, but was not something normal younglings indulged in. They had no need, being more interested in testing their wings, trying to get further off the ground each day. It seemed that the wingless younglings were adapting to their disabilities by developing other skills. I suspected that before long they would be able to easily outpace many a grown drax on the ground.

"Very well. If there's no other way." Varna still wasn't happy, but like most dams, was unable to resist her pup's pleading. She waved a paw to indicate that I should go ahead, and I knelt to lift Dru into the harness and tie the straps around his shoulders, leaving his legs dangling. It wasn't easy straightening up – Dru was already heavier than a laden carry-pouch – but once on my feet, I gave my wings a careful stretch and turned to Varna.

"It will work very well," I said. "Do you think I might be permitted to take off from the balcony outside the Audience Chamber? It will save me having to carry him through the *Spirax* and across the plateau."

As I suspected, the idea of having Dru carried past the council's cluster was all the incentive Varna needed to grant permission to use the balcony as a launch point, and she summoned Morel to escort me back along the passageway.

The empty audience chamber seemed vast and I heard Dru gasp, smelled his wonder, and realised he had not been allowed into the room before.

"What's that?" He pointed at the see-shell, and I began to explain about the floaters: "They live in the clouds and drift with the wind. Their stingers dangle below them, spans long but very thin, and they catch anything that flies into them – flisks, glittermoths, vlydhs, and even drax if any are careless about how high they fly in bad weather. The floaters' bodies have these shells and—"

"You need to go," said Morel. He shuffled from foot to foot in agitation, his tail shifting from side to side as he looked around to check the doorways. "If Kalis finds you in here – if he finds Dru in here—"

"We have Varna's permission to fly from the balcony."

"And you think Kalis will wait for us to explain that?" Morel scurried across the chamber to the dais at the far end, the scent of alarm trailing behind him. "Even if we did…" He glanced at Dru and his voice faltered, but I had an inkling of what he had been about to say: that Kalis was no longer interested in anything Varna said.

I held up a paw to indicate that I understood, and opened the shutters with the other. "We're going. Come on, Dru – you'll help me look out for floaters, won't you?"

As I took off, and the wind caught and lifted us, Dru's paws clutched at my arms, which I'd wrapped around him, and he gave a strange, high shriek. I thought he was frightened, unused as he was to the sensation of flying, but when he gave a happy snuffle and made the noise again, I realised it was the sound of exhilaration. Dru was enjoying himself! I made a couple of slow turns, spiralled up on a rising air current, then pulled my wings back a little and stooped, the plunging dive eliciting another shriek and much snuffling from my passenger.

"Again!" he shouted.

I repeated the exercise, rather enjoying the whole thing myself, undaunted that it was juvenile behaviour for a grown drax, let alone a Fate-seer. I flew around the *Spirax*, waving to the circling guardflight, before flying straight across the plateau toward the eastern cliffs. A warm breeze smacked into the rocks below us, and like the waves beneath it, burst upward. Dru whooped again as we were carried higher, then began to look around and take an interest in the mesa below us. I pointed out the council dwellings, with my own in the centre of the small spiral formation; the mossy path; the take-off and landing places; the entrance to the *Spirax*.

The sky overhead was dotted with small white clouds, but they were moving fast and were too high to be of any concern. I soared higher, moving farther away from the tor as I did so, then circled to give Dru a wider perspective.

"What's that?" he called, pointing to the monolith that rose from the waters of the southern bay. Smaller than the *Spirax* plateau, it was cone-shaped, like Guardflight Rock, and the lichens on its slopes gave it a mottled grey-green patina. On the north-west side, a few spans below the summit, a cave-mouth yawned black against the hillside.

"That's the Hollow Crag," I said, trying to keep my voice neutral, "Where Fazak looks after the ancient scroll-leaves."

"Varna-muz doesn't like him," said Dru. "She said she had to go and meet him the other day, and I could *smell*."

I gave what I hoped was a non-committal grunt. It wasn't my place to plant prejudice – there was enough of that riding the air-currents as it was. "Perhaps she just wasn't looking forward to the meeting," I said, then changed the subject as I turned and dipped a wing to fly over the black rock stack that sat beneath the *Spirax* balcony. "It's named the Tusk," I said, pointing, "because it looks like the tusk – the big tooth – of a grox." I wasn't sure he would know what those were, so I added, "Those are the big four-legged animals that provide our meat, and the skins for our cold-season tunics. They're kept in the pastures near the rivers."

"Limar told me about them," he said, "my nest-nurse. But I've never seen one."

"Well, we won't have time today," I said, "but if your parents will allow, I'll take you out again each day so that you can see the entire Expanse – and perhaps even some of the land beyond. It's important that you learn more about it."

It was important too that Dru was seen by other drax, though I didn't say so.

Raising my voice a little to make sure he could hear me over the rush of air and the beat of my wings, I pointed out to Dru some of the features of the land he would one day be responsible for. "Over there, in the west, are most of the farms, though they're too far away to see from here. Beyond them are the Copper Hills, and you can see the Skybrush mountains on the horizon."

A wing-flap, a slight turn, and we were looking across the Expanse toward the mountains in the south-west. "Cloudsend is where the Koth live. It's too high for us to fly up there after them." I pointed south along the coast. "Follow the coast far enough that way and you'll come to the Great Ice, where ice and snow stay even in the warm season. My grandsire told me that *his* grandsire remembered a time when the ice thawed into the sea when the melt came, but perhaps it was just a story to amuse a small pup." Though it was true that drax had once lived farther south than they did now: Vizan had once told me of a foolish adventure of his own, when he had packed food for three days and flew as far south as he could. "*I near froze to death, even in the middle of the warmth,*" he had said, "*and I had to turn back after a day and a half. But I saw, beneath the ice, whole clusters of stone-built dwellings*". Perhaps he had simply been spinning me a tale, but if he had spoken true and drax once had lived there, then perhaps the story of the melting ice was true too.

I was beginning to feel chilly just thinking about it, and turned east again toward the sea. I had once tried flying across that, but with no more success than Vizan had had when he flew south – there was just the water, stretching to the horizon, however far I went. It seemed the legends of a "lost land" were just that: legends. I told them to Dru all the same, to keep him amused as I turned north to complete our circuit of the *Spirax* massif.

Dru was heavier than any pouch I'd ever carried and I had to flap hard as I set course toward the Manybend estuary, moving farther away from the peninsula and the *Spirax* plateau with every wingbeat. Beneath us, the sea washed against rocky promontories on which the Fishers perched, their deep blue tunics contrasting with the purple weeds that draped the shoreline.

"Do they eat all those?" Dru pointed to a group of fishers as they hauled a net full of fish out of the surf and flew over the beach to drop their catch into one of the stone-lined hollows near the shore.

I angled my wings to dip a little lower. "They will eat some, I expect, but most of the fish are caught to trade for other things the Fishers need. Any drax might scoop a fish from the ocean – that is surely why the Spiral gave us clawed toes – but imagine how much time it would take to fly all the way from one of the far clusters or from the farms just to catch one."

Dru considered the thought, while I circled over the fish-filled bowl, then said, "Do they always smell so... so..."

"Pungent?" Hints of the stench stuck to the back of my throat, though we were still many spans above the catch. I sometimes wondered whether the Fishers had a blunted sense of smell. Certainly the young drax who were taken as nest-mates or apprentices from other clusters always had problems adjusting. "Only in such large numbers, Dru, when they've just come out of the sea. They smell much better once they've been basted with herbs and cooked – and they taste wonderful. I'm sure Varna will have regurgitated some for you, she loves fish."

A gust of wind from the south buffeted me and I angled my wings to compensate, managing to hover for long enough to give Dru a good look at what was happening below us. "Look, those are Traders in the pale blue tunics with the baskets of goods. They'll exchange those for fish, load up their vlydh, and take the fish to the clusters where the goods came from."

"Where are the vlydhs? I've never seen one except in the pictures Limar drew."

I was appalled that any nestling, let alone the Prime's heir, should have lived two whole moons without seeing a vlydh, but bit back my exclamation. It was hardly Dru's fault, and I didn't want him sensing any negative reactions that he might misinterpret. So I coughed to cover my initial gasp and said, "They'll be in the orenvines over there." I pointed in the direction of the bushes that lay a few wingbeats inland from the catch. "If your dam will allow you to travel with me, as I've asked, I'll take you to the orenvine plantation where my friend Doran lives. There are lots of vlydhs there, and perhaps Miyak will let you ride one."

"Oh yes!" Dru wriggled with excitement and I had to hold him steady to prevent him unbalancing my flight.

Setting course along the coast again, I beat my wings to regain the height I'd lost while we looked at the Fishers. I pointed out the mud-flats at the mouth of the Manybend, where the clouded water mingled with the clean wash of the sea, and showed Dru the rocks that marked the tip of the far shore. Beyond them, the shoreline stretched away, almost flight-path straight as we followed it north. The flat sands washed by the surf rose beyond the high-tide mark to form huge sand-dunes, broken here and there by groves of seavine and scattered boulders. They marked the eastern boundary of the marsh that formed the Deadlands.

I pointed them out to Dru. "Off to our left – there, do you see the clumps of brambletrap? The Deadland marshes stretch for a half-day's flight and more, all the way to those hills in the distance." After a cautious glance upward, I flew higher still, flapping steadily till we began to encounter wisps of vapour that trailed from the patchy clouds. Levelling out, I took a moment to catch my breath, then pointed to the red smudge that lined the horizon far to the north. "That's the Crimson Forest," I said. "The southern edge of it, anyway. No-one knows how far north it stretches, no drax has ever flown far enough to find out. It's a strange place, a frightening place, with poisonous plants and dangerous animals which slither down the vines and creep across the ground."

I felt Dru shiver and placed a paw on his head to reassure him as I started to descend, gliding for a while to give my wings some respite. "Don't worry, we're not going there." Beneath us, the land rose to form steep cliffs which crinkled along the shoreline in a series of shallow bays, and I pointed ahead to a promontory that was as distinctive in its way as the *Spirax* plateau. "Do you see those rocks up ahead? The ones that jut into the sea?"

"I see them! All stripey with the different colours. They look like a giant cut them in two from top to bottom. Look how the sea goes 'swoosh' in the air when the waves come in!"

"They are called the Cleft Rocks," I called, raising my voice a little over the noise of the breaking waves, "and you must not tell anyone that the Dream-cave is there. Not even Varna-muz."

"Or Limar?"

I remembered how fast the news of Dru's hatching had travelled around the plateau. "Especially not Limar," I said.

I flew over the headland, a mere wingspan above the rocks, and swooped down the other side, skimming over the beach to show Dru the patterns made just below the high tide mark by the tiny, burrowing sandweavers. With the tide on the way out, it would not be long before we could reach the cave. Its narrow entrance was hidden under an overhang between the twin outcrops, and was drowned beneath the sea with each high tide. It was why I had wanted to wait until the moon was full before I breathed the Smoke. Varna doubtless thought there was some deeper mystery involved, but the simple reason was that the bigger tide would mean I could spend longer at my scrying, without having to worry about becoming trapped by the incoming waters. It might not matter if I was not seen for several days, but even Kalis might begin to worry if his pup did not return from his first outing by sunset.

Landing on wet sand between towering rocks a couple of spans apart, I folded my wings and unstrapped Dru from his harness. "Can you manage a kerzh-fruit on your own," I asked, as I produced a rather squashed specimen from my tunic pocket, "or shall I regurgitate something I chewed earlier?"

"I can eat it," he said, reaching for the fruit. "I like these."

I left him chewing and stepped into the surf to slake my thirst. I filled the flask I had brought with me, then scooped up water in my paws to wash my snout and ears. By the time I shook the droplets from my fur and walked back up the beach, Dru had finished his fruit and was exploring the narrow finger of sand. He scratched at the striations in the rocks, peered into the shallow pools the tide had left behind, and picked up strands of crimson weed to rub and sniff. It was easy to scent his excitement and curiosity – everything was new to him, from the smells and sounds of the outdoors to the feel of sand, rock and tide. I tried to remember how it felt to be so young, so fascinated by the possibilities of ordinary objects, but although I could recall the actions of reaching for spoons and stones and beakers, I couldn't conjure the feeling of innocent wonder that went with them. I had experienced too much in the cycles since then.

"Don't lick anything," I called, as I saw Dru stick out his tongue in the direction of a colourful seastrand. "Do you want an upset stomach? Leave it alone."

A gleam in the shingle caught my eye as I moved up the beach and I halted where I stood to take a closer look. A spirelle? Could it be? I'd only ever seen one, and that briefly when Vizan had scooped it from the depths of a basket to show me. Tiny and iridescent, its spiral form made it a prize; its rarity made it a treasure. If the tide had washed one up almost at Dru's feet...

No. Of course it hadn't.

I sighed as I leaned down to pick up the pebble. It was the right size, and there were colours in the wet stone, but this was no shell and it bore no spirals.

"What's that?" Dru headed towards me, nose busy, eager to see what I had picked up.

I threw it back whence it had come. "Nothing. Just a trick of the sun." The water had receded from the base of the southern crag and I made my way toward it, beckoning Dru. "Come on – we can get into the cave now."

The highest waves still beat themselves to spray against the broken rocks that were scattered down the shore, but underneath an overhang immediately above me, the cave entrance had been uncovered, far enough over my head that I needed to scramble over several large boulders to reach it. I lifted Dru first, stretching up to make sure he was safely inside, then clambered after him.

"It's dark." He peered into the gloom as he spoke, then jumped with surprise as he heard his words repeat. "It speaks!"

"No, you speak – and I speak. The cavern repeats what we say." I could see that he was still puzzled. "The sound bounces off the cave walls and comes back to us. It's nothing to be alarmed about." I called his name, directing the sound into the cave, and as the echo returned it, he snuffled with glee and proceeded to follow my example. While he amused himself with different sounds and noises, I switched to night vision and looked for the torch that was always kept in a sconce near the entrance.

"What's that?" Dru stopped making the nonsense sounds and turned his attention to what I was doing, pointing to the small stick I had pulled from my tunic pocket.

"It's a firestick," I said. "I am going to use it to light a torch so that we can see where we are going. We have to go through a tunnel to get to the Dream-cave. This is just the entrance."

"Can't you see in the dark?"

"Of course I can, but it's easier with torchlight, and we'll need the fire anyway when we get to the other end."

The cave floor was covered in a deep layer of sand and I pushed the torch handle into it so that I kept both paws free.

"What's that?" Dru poked a finger at the top of the torch, and I realised that he had never seen a torch being ignited before – in the *Spirax*, they would be lit by heralds in advance of his entering a room.

"It's kerzh grass, which has been soaked in zaxel oil," I said, as I stuffed the strands into the top of the torch. "It will burn well, and it will burn slowly, but first we need to light it. Pass me the box of firedust – that's it. Now watch." I sprinkled the yellow power over the oil-soaked stems.

Dru wrinkled his snout. "It smells nasty."

"And the kerzh stems taste bad too, though I use them in my medicines sometimes," I said, as I tucked the empty box back into my pocket. With a brisk downward stroke of my paw, I rubbed the firestick along the torch. In a heartbeat, the torch was ablaze.

"There, you see? The trick is to hold the firestick in such a way that your paw does not get singed when the flame takes hold – that is something one learns very quickly by trial and error."

I picked up the torch and stood, bending my head to avoid bumping it on the roof of the cave. "Come along, we must get this done so that I can take you home before the tide comes in."

He wrapped a warm paw around the tip of my left wing and I gave him an encouraging glance. He did not seem to need it, looking around with a youngling's natural inquisitiveness as we moved toward the back of the cavern. Water dripped from the rocks above us and dampened the sand beneath our feet, while the flickering torchlight dimly illuminated walls worn smooth by the water and dusted white by the salt within it. Dru gave a yell, startling me, but then I realised he was simply amusing himself by starting the echo again.

"The echo will disappear once we are further inside," I said, and he gave another whoop while he still could. At the back of the cave, the passage narrowed to a tiny crevice, a fold in the rock that concealed what lay beyond, and I squeezed ahead of Dru to light the way. In a few steps we were through the passage, and I felt Dru's paw tighten on my wing as he gazed for the first time on the wonder of the cave that held the Dream-smoke. Around us, seams of silver, brighter even than the lights of the Great Spiral, gleamed in the torchlight, and reflected it back a thousand-fold, while the roof of the cavern soared so high that it was lost to darkness. Dru made a small snuffling noise that I realised from the set of his ears was awe, and he let go of my wing to take a few steps into the chamber, turning around as he did so. "Its...pretty," he said.

It was not the word I would have chosen to describe the cavern, but it was apt enough within Dru's as yet limited vocabulary, and I nodded solemnly. "Very pretty, Dru – and very special."

"Why?"

I took a moment to slide the torch into the ancient sconce on the cave wall. "There is a special plant that grows here – the Dream-plant. It likes the darkness, the sea-salt, and the mud on the cave floor, and it will not grow anywhere else." Though Fate-seers had tried for many cycles to coax the stuff into growing somewhere a little more convenient.

"Where?" He shuffled his feet and looked about, sniffing the air for the plant's scent.

"They are all around us," I said, "and beneath our feet." I bent low and plucked one from the mud to show him. "You see? From above, they look like shiny brown pebbles, but they have fat stems beneath, and they grow in the mud. Will you help me pick a few? I would like them put on that flat-topped boulder on the floor underneath the torch."

It did not take long to gather what I needed and heap them onto the boulder. I sprinkled a little firedust over them and reached for the torch. The Dream-plants flared and hissed as the flames sparked on the firedust. I set the torch back in its sconce, unstoppered the flask of water and placed it on the floor, then knelt beside the boulder.

"Come and kneel beside me, Dru." The Dream-plants were smouldering well, and already giving off a thick cloud of purple smoke which smelled of firedust, burnt seaweed, and...whatever it was that made this plant special. As Dru gave the smoke a suspicious sniff, I endeavoured to explain to him what I was going to do, and how I believed it was important that he be there. "When I am ready to inhale the Smoke," I said, "I will take your paw in mine. I believe that it will help focus the vision in the Smoke on you, and tell me what I need to know."

"Won't hurt, will it?"

I shook my head. "Only those with the Sight are able to see anything in the Smoke. It will not be very exciting for you, I'm afraid, and the smoke may make you cough. If it does, take a drink from the flask. I will go very still and very quiet, perhaps for some time, but you must not speak to me while I am Seeing. That is very important – you understand? It will not hurt either of us, but if I'm disturbed the Vision will be lost, and may not come again. So you must be silent. Can you do that?"

"Yes."

"Then let's get started."

I paused for a beat to collect my thoughts, watching the smoke swirl and focussing on the colours and patterns within it, sniffing at the edges of its unique aroma. Spreading my wings, I said the First Incantation, and as the Dream-smoke thickened, I took Dru's paw in mine and began the second chant.

I stared into the smoke, drawing it in with each breath, seeing it change colours and feeling its texture alter and shift. I was used to the sensation by now and ignored it, concentrating instead on the whirling black-and-white vortex at the centre of the smoke. It spun faster, the contrasting shades blending to grey and pulling me inward with them until...

I thought at first that my efforts had failed, for I could still feel Dru's paw in mine. Then the Vision became clearer and I realised that this was an older Dru, adult, and that he was the one leading me. There was swirling snow, an icy wind ruffled my fur. This was what I had Seen before, with Vizan. This time, though, I could also See that Dru had no wings. Above the wail of the wind I could hear howls of triumph, and Dru took a spear from a dead Koth and raised it over his head. The shouting grew louder, nearer...became real, as the vision vanished and I returned abruptly to the present and normality.

The shouting came from Dru, who had pulled his paw from mine and was covering his ears, eyes tight shut as he wailed. I recognised the signs at once, though I was so astonished it took me a moment to react. By the Spiral! He had the Sight! Usually, the few drax who still had the gift would not manifest their abilities until they were half-growns. It is a kindness from the Spiral that they are able to enjoy a normal life until then, without the blessings and the curses of their gift. Alas for Dru, my taking him with me to the cave, and physical contact with the Dream-smoke, appeared to have awakened his ability early.

I crouched in front of him and gently took his paws from his ears. "Dru, listen to me. I want you to visualise the pebbles you were playing with earlier, back at the *Spirax*. See each one in your head: the texture, the colour, the exact shape. Think of nothing else, just concentrate on those pebbles. Think hard, now – you can do it." His wailing stopped at least, and I saw his whiskers quiver as he began to concentrate on the task I had given him. "Now, build those pebbles up in your head. Make a little cairn to keep the Vision in. Put it away until you want to take it out and look at it. Calmly now." I stroked his paws. "You are doing very well. Take deep breaths. That's it."

His eyes were still closed, but his breathing had steadied and I pulled another kerzh-fruit from my pocket.

"I must apologise, Dru," I said, handing him the fruit as he opened first one eye then the other. "If I had known you were gifted with the Sight I would never have brought you here. But you'll discover for yourself that having this talent does not bring with it the ability to predict who else may carry it."

He nibbled at the fruit, and I moved to sit beside him. "You are much too young to have this awakened in you," I said, "but now that it has been stirred, it can't be ignored. I can't control when my own Visions come, so I can't help you do that, but when you're a little older, I'll try to teach you some of the Fate-seers' secrets, if you would like that?"

He put the entire kerzh into his mouth and chewed, closing his eyes as he concentrated on the taste and the texture of the pulp in order to draw his mind back from the Vision. That was a good sign. "Yes," he said. "Thank you." He licked his whiskers and it was obvious he was pondering something. "Was that me?" he said, after a moment. "In the snow?"

I nodded. "My teacher and I foresaw that future for you before you had hatched out of your egg," I said. "I had hoped that by bringing you with me I might See a little more, but alas…" That was not the whole truth, of course, but it seemed to satisfy Dru. "Now, I think you have had enough excitement for one day – and if we don't leave soon, the tide will keep us here all night."

Nine

When I reported the news of Dru's Sight, Kalis reluctantly agreed to call the Council together to debate what to do – then refused to attend the session, leaving all the usual duties to Varna. "You are the one who insisted we keep him alive," he'd growled. "You can take responsibility for what happens to him now."

"A nest-mate in charge of a Council meeting? What next?" Fazak's low mutter was probably not meant to be overheard, but as I pulled up my stool to the end of the table in the Audience Chamber I couldn't resist a response.

"I believe there are plenty of precedents," I said. "Gevar's nest-mate, for instance – Kalis' dam. Did she not chair the Council here while Gevar flew into battle against the Koth?" I poured myself a beaker of hoxberry juice from the jug on the table. "All a matter of record, I'm sure. Perhaps you should look it up, Fazak?"

Fazak looked as though he had bitten into a sour kerzh-fruit, and he made a show of moving his stool another paw-width from mine. "Kalis is in the next chamber," he said, "not skirmishing in the mountains – and for that, there is no precedent."

I wondered if the chill I felt was a result of the draught from the open balcony doorway, which made the torches flicker and the empty hearths seem colder. "I fail to see the difference," I said. "The Prime has designated his nest-mate to take charge of the meeting, as is his prerogative. His own whereabouts are surely irrelevant." I wondered what Fazak's reaction would be if I passed on the hint that Morel had given me – that Kalis was no longer interested in anything Varna said. Yet he had allowed her to preside over this meeting, which suggested that either Morel was mistaken, or that Varna still had some influence the herald was unaware of. I remembered her words to Kalis in the nesting-chamber – "*none of us are perfect*" – and wished once again that I had been able to ask Vizan about what she might have meant.

Varna entered the chamber just then, and there was a scraping of stools as we all stood and bowed.

It didn't take long for her to make her feelings on the subject clear: "Dru is already regarded as different. It would be cruel to set him further apart just now."

"But do you not realise? It isn't possible for him to be set any further apart than he is already." I looked around the table for support. I knew I would find none from Fazak and did not even bother to glance at him. Sifan and Hapak were muttering together further along the table. Broga had her ears turned their way, and though her greying muzzle was pointed in my direction, she appeared to be making a careful study of the wall behind my head. Perhaps she had found some flaw in the slimecrawler shell that hung there.

I looked at Shaya, and to Peren and Miyak who flanked her. All of them had wingless younglings, but though they nodded and set their ears to indicate their agreement with me, none of them said anything. I wondered if they had taken Fazak's words about Kalis being in the next chamber literally, and were concerned that he might be listening to the debate from behind a door. For several breaths, all I could hear was the tiny 'tick-tick' of Fazak's claws scratching notes on his record leaf, and I had given up hope of support when Taral spoke up. "Zarda is right, Varna. The guardflight patrols are asked about the heir wherever they land. I have told them to report that he is progressing well, but—"

"You have no right to tell the drax *anything* about the heir without the express authority of the council." Fazak's bleat had barely dropped from his mouth before Taral was on his feet, stool upended behind him.

"Then tell me what we *should* say!" His teeth were bared, and even with his wings still folded, he looked imposing enough to make Fazak shrink away from him as he glared across the table. The smell of Fazak's fear was a pleasure to the nostrils, but after a moment, Taral collected himself and switched his gaze to each of the other council members in turn, the twitching of his ears and tail betraying his frustration. "You all know well enough that in the absence of news, drax will draw their own conclusions, make up their own reports. My guards have to deal with that every day, on top of their normal duties. In the name of the Spiral, issue a report – say *something* about the pup's progress!"

With a sigh and a shake of his head, he righted his stool and sat down, setting the zaxel stems rustling about on the floor; they were dry and dusty, and gave off a faint smell of feet. Usually, they would have been changed for fresh stems days ago, but despite Sifan's assurances that the raids would not affect our food supplies, we had been left with a shortage of both cobs and stems. Kalis had given orders that all floor-coverings be changed every half-moon, instead of every nine days. Necessary, alas, but not easy on the nose.

Miyak ventured into the silence: "I have to agree with Taral," he said, his ears signalling apology. "I am regularly asked for news of Dru, from those who hire vlydh from the plantation. I...tell them I do not know."

With a little shrug of his wings he subsided, and concentrated his attention on pouring himself a drink. His paws were shaking.

As I glanced away, I noticed that Fazak – recovered from his scare – had opened his mouth again, and I rushed to speak first.

"I've give— been giving the matter some thought," I said, stumbling over the words in my haste. "I believe it is important that Dru be seen – and that he also gets to know the drax he will one day preside over." I held up a paw to forestall any protest. "I know that under normal circumstances he would be taken on the ceremonial cluster-flight by Kalis when the Melt comes. That is too long to wait, especially given the absence of any official reports. So long as Dru is unseen and unknown, it is easy for troublemakers to foment rumours and provoke unrest."

"Such as blaming him for the cold spell we had during the last moon?" said Varna. "Yes – I heard the talk." She gave Hapak and Sifan a hard stare. They had the grace to look away, their ears twitching with embarrassment. "Perhaps we should have just thrown him off the balcony, as Kalis wished to."

"No, Varna." I got to my feet and angled my ears to emphasise my sincerity. "He will defeat the Koth. The Vision in the Dream-smoke has not changed. Vizan Saw it, I Saw it – and now Dru has Seen it too. He knows his destiny."

Fazak muttered something that might have been 'freak' under his breath, but I couldn't be sure as I was re-seating myself as he spoke and the scrape of the stool masked his words. Raising his voice, he said: "May I make a suggestion?" Without waiting for an answer, he got to his feet and said, "It will be easier to convince the drax – to convince all of us – of Dru's true worth if there was some tangible proof that he could carry out all the duties expected of a Prime's heir." He spread his paws, and inclined his head in Varna's direction. "One of those duties is to assist with the blood sacrifice on the Night of the Two Moons." He turned to me. "Do you believe he would be able to do that? To fly around a spiral of hovering drax, and descend to kill the sacrificial kervhel?"

His wings were not set to indicate it, but he had just offered me a challenge.

I accepted.

Getting to my feet again, I extended my own wings just enough to look determined, and signalled my agreement.

"Are you sure?" said Varna. "Dru will not be even six moons old – surely we should wait for another cycle before we can expect him to take part in such a ritual?"

Hapak, the Artisan chief, climbed to his feet. "We cannot wait till he's a half-grown, Varna," he said. "The rumours of a curse…well, they are already taking root. Another cycle and they will be too well established to kill."

Yes, I thought, *especially with drax like you helping them to flourish.*

"Are you all agreed?" said Varna.

"I think it is too soon," said Shaya, with a glare in my direction.

So did I, now that I'd had a moment to think, but I couldn't back down – not if I wanted to retain any credibility, and not if our Vision for Dru was ever to be fulfilled.

Peren and Taral agreed with Shaya, but Miyak, who I might have expected to protest, voted with Fazak. "I'd like some solid evidence that our pups have a purpose," he muttered, though his ears twitched wildly with uncertainty. Varna had the authority to overrule us and set her own terms if she had wished, but – perhaps knowing Kalis' reaction – accepted the consensus.

"There is one other thing," said Fazak, and I felt the fur on my neck stir. Even without a Vision, I knew he was about to utter something fateful. "If the ritual does not go well – if Dru cannot carry out his part correctly, or something goes wrong that can be laid at the feet of the wingless – it will prove that the Spiral does not look favourably on the deformed. They must be sent to the Forest."

"No! That would be certain death." Varna jumped to her feet, sending her beaker spinning to the floor, where the juice splashed stickily over my feet. I backed away a step or two, instinctively moving away from both the liquid and from Varna's horrified anger.

Too late, I realised that this was what Fazak had been working towards all along. If the correct completion of the ritual brought a reward – the acknowledgement of Dru and the wingless as true drax and rightful heir – then conversely there must be punishment if the ritual failed in some way.

"You fly too high, Fazak!" Taral was on his feet too, and I noticed that both Shaya and Peren had set their ears and wings to signal alarm and indignation.

But the other four members of the council – including Miyak – signalled their agreement with Fazak's outrageous proposal, and I knew that even if Varna overruled them, Kalis would not. I was not sure I would still be able to carry Dru in the harness by the time the ritual was due; even if I could, it would mean finding a way to teach a wingless nestling a complex ritual in which he would have to be word perfect.

Still, if that was what it took…

I straightened my wings and bowed my head to Varna, spiralling a paw across my tunic. "I will call for Dru each day, Varna, and take him out among the drax. If the weather is too bad to fly we will stay in the nursery, and I will teach him counting and symbols, history and rituals, in order to prepare him for his future role."

I meant as Prime, though I deliberately left the meaning ambiguous. Let Fazak and his cronies believe that I was referring to the Two Moons ceremony, it didn't matter. There would be time later to discuss semantics.

At least, that was what I hoped.

So, while the weather held, I began to take Dru out and about, making good use of the harness that Miyak and I had made.

I took him first to the Traders' cluster, near the centre of the Expanse, where I had hatched. I had not been back since Vizan claimed me as his apprentice – and I hoped that, with Peren having a wingless youngling, there would be a degree of tolerance for Dru which might not be expected from the Fishers or the estuary clusters.

I was wrong.

Though I had circled over the cluster before landing, and called both my name and Dru's, it took much longer than it should have done for the cluster's Welcomer to reach us. I had had time to land, free Dru from the harness, and remove the straps from my shoulders before Aldan appeared on the pathway. Grey-muzzled, older even than Vizan had been, Aldan had fewer teeth left in his head than any drax I knew. He'd been kind to me a cycle ago, when my dam had been among the first to succumb to the Sickness. Now he reeked of hostility and distaste, even as he set his ears and wings to give the official greeting.

"Fate-seer. I greet you on behalf of all at the Traders' cluster. Will you rest and take tea?" There was a suck in his voice where his teeth used to be as he added, "It is good to see you again, Zarda."

I waited, pointedly not giving the expected response until he had choked out a welcome for Dru too, then bade him lead the way to Peren's dwelling.

"He's not in." Aldan's tiny ear-flick prevented the remark becoming an insult. "You know how busy we get in the moons before the freeze, making sure everyone has what they need before the snows come."

I did know. I also knew that drax who had hatched late eggs would not leave their nestlings unattended. I put a paw on Dru's shoulder as he edged closer to me, and waited.

Aldan gave a sniff and scratched his snout, looked from me to Dru and back again, and dipped a grudging ear. "Jonel will be home," he said. "She doesn't get out much these days." He managed to convey the words 'not with a wingless nestling to look after' without actually speaking them aloud. With another sniff, he turned and led the way along the path.

I had been to many clusters with Vizan, and had seen how the Sickness had left empty dwellings and neglected pathways behind, but still it came as a shock to see what had become of the cluster I had once known so well. For every dwelling with a smoking chimney and a clean-swept entrance-stone there was one that had hacklebrush growing up the wall stones. Weathered doors stood opposite dyed ones; the odour of dust and decay vied with the aroma of vinesmoke. As we wound our way around the spiralling path, I pointed out a weed-assaulted dwelling on our right. "That's where I hatched," I said to Dru. "Of course, it looked much tidier then. When it had drax to look after it."

Aldan grunted agreement and I smelled genuine sorrow as he spiralled a paw over his tunic and said, "May the Spiral take their lights." He glanced over his shoulder as he added, "The empty dwellings will be filled again in a cycle or two, Spiral willing. We have twenty half-growns who will be ready to build their own nests in the next melt. If some of the females are allowed a third hatching…" His voice tailed off. It was obvious to me at least that by 'some' he was referring to the few remaining females who had hatched winged younglings before the Sickness, and I hoped that Dru didn't understand what he meant.

I glanced down to see how the youngling was faring, and saw that his nose was busy, sniffing this way and that as he tried to identify the myriad odours that carried from the dwellings. Herbs, vineleaves, avalox, scroll-leaves, raw meat, cooked meat, smoked meat, zaxel, and kerzh, anything and everything that had passed through the traders' paws in recent days could be detected. "Remember what I told you when we flew over the fishers' catch? That the traders take the goods from cluster to cluster so that every drax has what they need?"

Dru nodded, twisting his ears right and left as a couple of doors opened and half-grown apprentices in striped tunics looked out. "I can't smell any fish, though." Another sniff. "Except for what's cooking."

I heard a snort of derision from one of the half-growns and spun about to confront him. "And what exactly did you know of business when you were two moons old? I doubt you'd got farther than flapping to the ground from your dwelling's cap-stone," I snapped.

"At least I had wings to flap."

"Ordek!" Aldan snarled, thumping his tail in the absence of having enough teeth to bare. "You do *not* insult the Fate-seer. Never, do you hear me? The Spiral speaks and hears through the wearer of the black tunic. Show the proper respect, as you've been taught."

The half-grown's ears were different colours, and he dipped the black one in apology, though his scent told me he wasn't altogether happy about it.

I ushered Dru forward to face him. "Explain to the Prime's heir why he can't smell any raw fish."

Ordek glanced across the pathway, to where the second apprentice stood watching. No doubt the whole scene would be retold to others later, to Ordek's discomfort. Perhaps it would teach him not to be so impertinent. "The fish are taken direct to whichever cluster wants them." His voice was sullen, though he'd angled his ears to display politeness. "They have to be cooked fresh, so the ones brought here are for our own meals. All the other goods can be stored."

Leaving him to sulk with his friend, we continued on till we reached Peren's dwelling, marked out from the rest by having its stones as well as its door dyed blue.

"Why isn't that one the Chief's dwelling?" Dru pointed to the Place of Welcome, next to Peren's residence at the heart of the cluster. "It's bigger."

"The Place of Welcome is not dwelt in by any drax," I explained. "Every cluster has one, and they are all twice as big as the dwellings around it because they are set aside for guests. There are enough nests in there for nine drax, though it's not often that that many will all need to stay anywhere overnight. But, if drax are a long way from home and there are very high winds or a bad storm, they'll make for the nearest cluster to ask for shelter."

As I finished speaking, Jonel opened the dwelling door, and gave us the first genuinely friendly greeting we'd had. "Zarda!" Jonel's ears and whiskers quivered with delight, and continued to do so as she looked down at Dru. "And our Lordling too. Come in and be welcome. Thank you, Aldan, for guiding them to us."

Aldan looked relieved that his part was done. Lisping an acknowledgment, he moved back along the pathway to his dwelling near the landing path with an alacrity that belied his cycles. Inside the dwelling, Jonel moved baskets of goods from stools to the floor, dashed a cloth across the seats, and bade us sit while she brewed tea. Only then did she coax her youngling out from behind the nest-screen. "There's nothing to be afraid of," she said, her voice soft and reassuring. "Look, this young drax has no wings either, he's not here to make fun of you."

A small snout appeared around the edge of the screen, nostrils flaring as they sniffed. Dru and I must have smelled friendly for a moment later the rest of the youngling appeared, ears alert for danger, a toy egg cradled in her arms.

"This is Manda," said Jonel. She brushed a paw over the youngling's head and introduced us to her.

"I've brought Dru to have a look at your cluster," I said, addressing Manda, though Jonel would have been the one wondering why we were there, "and to show him something of what traders do." I looked up at Jonel. "We'll be visiting others too, but I wanted to start here. I'd hoped we would be assured of a welcome."

Jonel grunted. "Manda, why don't you show Dru the basket you've been sorting? I'll bring you both some berryjuice, I'm sure you'll prefer that to a beaker of tea." Only when the younglings had disappeared behind the screen did she settle herself on the stool next to me and whisper, "Aldan doesn't approve. He thinks we should have…well, you know."

I dipped an ear in sympathy, and looked around at the crowded shelves and overflowing baskets that surrounded us, catching the scents of fresh kestox, chalkmoss, needlevine, and nut-syrup. It had been brave of Peren and Jonel to keep their wingless hatchling in the days before Dru hatched. Aldan, and the other traders with winged younglings, would doubtless have pointed out the impossibility of Manda ever flying anywhere to trade.

"Thank the Spiral for Dru," said Jonel, echoing my thoughts, "and for Miyak and his inventiveness. We'll get a vlydh and a riding-harness for Manda, come the melt, and she'll be able to fly about like any other trader."

Her voice had grown firmer and louder as she spoke, and as she got to her feet to stir the pot and pour the tea, a small voice piped up in reply from behind the screen: "Won't need a vlydh. My wings will have grown by then, and they'll be ever so big."

Jonel slumped back onto the stool, liquid sloshing in the beakers she held as her paws shook. "I can't tell her," she whispered. "I haven't got the heart."

For two moons, I alternated days of indoor teaching and rehearsals for the Night of the Two Moons with excursions across the Expanse, to introduce Dru to different clusters and trades. Everywhere, the reactions of the drax we visited were similar to those at the Traders' cluster – contempt, disgust, delight, suspicion – depending on who welcomed us and how many wingless pups survived in the cluster.

As the daylight shrank and our thicker fur grew in, we began to take advantage of the Places of Welcome to stay overnight at some of the more distant clusters – though the welcome we received often fell well short of the usual reception I might have expected for a Fate-seer and a Prime's heir. The metal-shapers gave us water and cold meat; the north-western traders' cluster supplied avalox leaves and leftover stew, which I had to steep and warm up myself. It was a pleasant surprise to be greeted at the gatherers' cluster with hot tea and fresh-baked groxen pie, but Galyn the Healer had always been generous with her cooking, and she was not the only female in the cluster with a wingless youngling.

"We spend more time on the ground than most drax," she said, as she offered sweet loxcakes to follow the pie. "Gather the reeds, gather the crops, gather the fruit. We can't do any of it on the wing." With a sigh and a glance at Dru, she lowered her voice and added, "I don't mean to imply that we're any happier about having wingless hatchlings than anyone else, but at least ours will still be able to learn our trade without too many problems."

We slept well that night in moss-lined nests, and the next morning I took Dru to the low hills beyond Hamor's farm. I pointed out the damaged fields as we flew over them, though they were no longer black with ash and smoke – they had been dug over, and strands of purple showed above ground where fresh roots had been planted. "The other farmers will all have given some of their own roots," I explained, "just as in the last cycle Hamor and Difel gave some of theirs to farms that had been raided."

"Because the Koth come and take what they want?"

"Yes. I'm afraid so."

He growled, a juvenile copy of Kalis. "I want to be grown," he barked, "so I can make them stop."

He smelled angry, impatient, and I placed a paw on his mane, feeling the tension in his body. "All in good time, Dru. For now, you have to keep learning – which is why I brought you all the way out here."

I landed on a hillside that Vizan had brought me to when I began my training. Chalkmoss grew on its steep slopes, thicker where the sun fell, strewn with clumps of yellow camyl in the shade. A few hardy needlevines clung to the summit's thin soil, providing shelter from sun and wind, and a fallen trunk where we could sit and look down on Paw Lake. It was as far to the south-west as I dared go – any further and we would be in the foothills of the mountains, and ready prey for any Koth who hadn't yet retreated to their eyries in readiness for the freeze.

Below us, four wide streams drained into the lake bowl, giving it the appearance from above of an open paw – hence its name. The water was clear enough to see a couple of huge razorfish hunting for the rudhs that they fed on, and I guessed that the smaller fish had hidden themselves in the weeds at the lake edge. As we'd flown in, I'd pointed out the river that flowed from the lake's northern shore, forming a wrist and arm for the 'paw' – the beginning of the Manybend. From the lake it flowed north past the Copper Hills, till its course was deflected eastward by Deadlands Ridge and it began its meandering course around the northern section of the Expanse. "We flew over the other end of that river, Dru, when I took you to the Dream-cave, remember?"

He pointed in the opposite direction, south to where the Far-river sparkled in the distance. "Why doesn't it go that way?"

"Because these hills are in the way."

A couple of glittermoths fluttered up from the chalkmoss as Dru bounded about, and he chased them across the slope, squealing with the joy of a new discovery. A moment later, he was back at my side, ears pricked, as something clattered in the trees. "What's that?"

"Hammer beetles. Burrowing into the vines to feed on the sap."

While I had his attention, I raised my paw to point across the lake in the direction of the *Spirax* mesa.

"Look over there, Dru. Do you see what a great landmark the *Spirax* plateau is?"

From this distance, it was little more than a dark smudge on the horizon, but I could still make out its distinctive shape – like the head of a vast beast with a horn on the end of its nose.

"Can the Koth see it?" Dru looked up at the towering hills behind us as he spoke, and tilted his head to gaze at the mountains beyond.

"I expect so. After all, we can see Cloudsend well enough from the *Spirax*, can't we?" I spread my arms wide, to indicate the vast amount of land between us and the plateau. "There is

112

nowhere in flying range of the *Spirax* that it can't be seen." I meant from the air, but decided it would be tactful not to say so. The mesa was hidden from sight from many places on the ground – the Cleft Rocks were one such spot – but as soon as any height was gained over them, the edifice could be seen. Instead, I turned Dru's attention to the Expanse. "We flew over some of the clusters on our way here," I said, pointing into the distance. I moved my paw about to match my words as I went on: "Now, there are some dwellings in the fields down there, and the hills we flew over, which are not part of the main spiral pattern our clusters make. Why is that, do you think?"

Dru's head turned slowly from left to right as he looked around at the dwellings I had indicated. "They are farms," he said. "The farmers have to be near the grazers – like those over there with the shaggy grey fur – and the crops."

"Very good," I said, "And which particular crop is that one to our left, with the blue leaves?"

He flicked away a flisk that seemed intent on landing on his snout, and rubbed his whiskers as he gave the question some thought. "Kerzh, I think? The zaxel must all have been harvested by now."

"Correct," I said, "on both counts. What will happen to the kerzh when the gatherers have cut it?"

"The leaves are used by the dyers and the fruit is traded for other food and supplies. The stems are crushed, and the juice..." His ears twitched as he thought, but after a brief pause he remembered and went on: "...oh yes! The juice is boiled till it thickens, and the paste can be mixed with other things, like fish-oil or water or," he said, snout wrinkling in disgust, "or waste. Depending on what it's to be used for."

"Very good," I said. "Don't forget the crushed stems. What do we do with those?"

"Use them for the torches," he said, "and you said you sometimes put bits of it in medicine, but not till the juice has been removed."

I nodded. He had learned well. "So. What other crops do you see?" I prompted.

"Marsh-reeds," he said, pointing toward the shore of the lake. "Those are used for grazer-fodder, and weaving. The weavers make harnesses for the vlydh, carry-pouches, and baskets. Oh, and tunics from groxen fur."

I grunted approval. At least Kalis had no cause for complaint about Dru's intelligence. I had just decided to test him further with some questions about the Great Spiral when he startled me by leaping to his feet and pointing toward the lake shore. "Zarda, look! We have to help him."

With that, he leapt off down the hill, leaving me to wonder what he was playing at. Then I saw. Bounding across the moss-bound mud at the bottom of the hill was a small, wingless male in a yellow-striped tunic. He ducked and cowered as a group of juveniles circled above his head, taking it in turns to swoop low and tap his head or shoulder with their feet.

"Cavel," I murmured, recognising the short russet mane and the distinctive tunic of the vlydh-keeper's pup. He was a long way from home for any unaccompanied youngling, let alone one without wings.

Dru was hurtling down the hill at a speed I had thought impossible for one on foot, and when I saw him stumble and roll, I covered my eyes, wondering how I would tell Varna that her son had broken his neck. When I dared look again, Dru had regained his feet and was running toward the wingless nestling and his tormentors. He was waving his arms and snarling words I hadn't realised he knew. I tensed, seeing the winged group leave Cavel and head toward their new target instead. With a sigh, I stretched my wings, ran into the wind, and took to the air.

I made sure I stayed to the west of the circling group, so that the pre-zenith sun would not cast my shadow near them and warn them of my presence. I recognised Murgo's green-striped tunic, and saw that the other two were clad in the pale blue stripes of apprentice traders. Clearly the poisonous talk from Fazak and his allies on the council was having its effect.

I was almost level with them as I started my descent, but it was obvious that they had still not seen me: their attention was all on the wingless pair on the ground. They had reached Dru and began their cruel game over again with him, swooping and striking, their mocking cries carrying on the breeze. Dru, though, was a match for them – he didn't cower as Cavel had. He stood firm, waited his chance, and as Murgo reached him, he grabbed the flyer's leg and pulled hard, dragging him down. Murgo howled as he crashed to the ground, and I heard him yowl again as Dru threw himself on top of him and began to pummel and bite, heedless of his smaller size and oblivious to the other younglings, who were landing to help their friend.

"My wing – he's broken my wing!" Murgo whined, as he tried to fend off Dru's blows and snapping jaws.

"Then *you* will have to walk for a while, won't you?" I said, as I landed just a span or so behind Dru.

The younglings spun around and I scrutinised their faces. As well as Murgo, I recognised Ordek, from the Traders' cluster. The third I did not know, but the white stripe through his amber mane would make him easy to identify.

I helped Dru to his feet and moved behind Murgo to examine his wings. "Do you think it is clever to pick on those who cannot fight back?" I said, addressing all three winged younglings as I checked Murgo's wing membrane and felt for broken struts. "I will ensure that your parents know by day's end that their pups are cowardly bullies who have nothing better to do than terrorise small groundlings."

"We were just having a bit of fun," muttered Ordek, his two-tone ears laid flat against his head with what I hoped was shame.

"I do not see your victim laughing," I replied. I located a small tear in Murgo's wing; nothing serious, though he would indeed need to walk for a few days. I tugged the torn membrane back into place, enjoying his wince of pain rather more than I should have. "Nothing's broken, Murgo, but you'll need to rest this wing for two ninedays," I said, deliberately trebling the amount of time he needed, "so you will have to walk home."

Murgo snorted, though I was not sure whether it was from rage, shame, humiliation, or a mixture of all three. "It will take a moon to walk all that way!" He lowered his voice and added, sulkily, "I'm supposed to be home for supper."

His bravado had evaporated and I smelled a faint trace of fear on him, for which I had no sympathy. "You had better make a start then," I said. "I will send someone to let your sire know where you are after I've taken Cavel home. Perhaps he will ask the guardflight to send a net for you."

I heard a faint snuffle from Ordek, who obviously found the idea of his friend being taken home in a net highly amusing. "Remind me, Ordek, why you and your friend are still here? I would have thought you would have been halfway back to your cluster by now, eager to get back to your dwellings and tell your side of the story before I get there."

"Come on, Bolby, for the Spiral's sake!" muttered Ordek. Without waiting to see if the other youngling followed, he turned, spread his wings and ran up the slope into the breeze. As he circled upward, Bolby said something I didn't catch and followed him, circling on an updraft to gain height, before setting course toward home.

I turned my attention to Murgo, who still lingered as though hoping I might cast some spell to heal his wing. "There is a healer in the cluster to the north-east. Her name is Galyn. Tell her I sent you and she will give you some salve for your wing. It will not make it heal any faster, but it will ease the pain."

Murgo gave a last glare at Dru and Cavel, and I smelled his fear curdle to hatred, but after a heartbeat or two he turned about without another word and set off toward the distant cluster.

At last, I was able to turn my attention to Doran's adventurous youngling. "Did they hurt you?"

He rubbed a dirty paw over the mud on his tunic, smearing it, and lowered his head. His half-flattened ears indicated that he felt he was in the wrong, and I wondered how he had managed to wander so far from home.

"I fell over," he said, "but the ground was soft. I'm alright. Doran-muz will be cross, though. She doesn't like me to leave the plantation."

I nodded. "Now you understand why. But how did you get all the way out here on your own?" On foot, it would have taken the youngling the best part of a moon to make the journey to Paw Lake. Even on a vlydh it would have taken half a day. Had he spent the night in the open?

He shrugged. "Miyak-fa doesn't mind where I go. He harnessed a vlydh for me and said I should go and explore."

"Did he?" I remembered Miyak's disappointment when Cavel had hatched and his lack of support for the wingless in the last Council meeting. Perhaps he had been trying a little too hard to pretend that his pup was normal. "Well, you're a long way from home. Are you hungry?"

Cavel nodded. "I had some of Doran-muz's pie with me, but I ate that yesterday. I was excited, being out on the vlydh. I didn't realise what a long way I'd come till it started getting dark."

"And the vlydhs won't fly after sunset," I put in. The creatures seemed to have no ability to see in the dark and refused to fly even when the moon was full and the Spiral clear of cloud.

I glanced up, half-expecting to see Doran flying toward us. I knew she'd be frantic with worry, but Cavel was more concerned with his stomachs. "I slept under the orenvines by the river, so there was plenty to drink, but I didn't have any more food with me. I thought I might catch a fish this morning, but the water was cold and the fish hid when I waded in to the water. My vlydh wouldn't come out of the orenvine." He was shaking and his voice had risen to a high-pitched wail. "I thought I'd starve! My stomachs rumbled and rumbled…and then the flyers came."

I looked around. Cavel had run all the way across the river-moss on the embankment and we had finished up at the edge of a vast field of zenox stubble. A herd of groxen were gathered at the far end, all looking in our direction. Their young – spawned live in a bag of liquid each Melt – had been nudged into the middle of the group and were pushing against the protective flanks of the adults, honking. If we stayed where we were, it would not be long before their curiosity got the better of their apprehension and the whole lot would meander over to see if we might be edible. While we had no need to fear a nibbling from their tiny teeth, we would be in trouble if any of the full-grown specimens gave us a nudge with the tusks that protruded from their lower jaws. They were built for seeing off predators, and could do us serious damage. "Let's go and sit by the lake," I said. "I have some cold meat in my carry-pouch, and there is enough for all of us. Then, young Cavel, we had better get you home."

"Will Cavel be alright?" Dru's words were muffled, and accompanied by a shower of crumbs from the cold groxen pie Doran had pressed into his hand. It was not, I thought, a dignified performance from a Prime heir, but it had taken us till late after-zenith to get to the plantation; I could hardly grudge him a bite to eat. Fortunately, we were still making our way through the avalox fields that lay between the orenvine plantation and the nearest cluster and there was no-one around to see.

Doran had spent the best part of two days flying around trying to find Cavel, and had given him a fearful nip on the snout as soon as we landed. He'd run whimpering up the spiral path through the vines toward their dwelling, and Doran had turned her wrath on Miyak for letting Cavel borrow the vlydh without supervision. I thought it best we left them to it, but we'd walked only a few spans before she'd flown after us, pies in paws. "Thank you! Thank you for rescuing him." She'd given Dru an affectionate lick on the brow and pressed her snout under my chin in a gesture of friendship and gratitude. Then she'd grasped my wrist and I realised by the set of her ears and wings that there was more worrying her than Cavel's adventure. "I need to speak with you," she said, glancing about as though to make sure no-one would overhear. "But not here. I'll come and see you. Soon."

I was still chewing that over, along with the remains of the pie she'd given me, when Dru asked his question.

"Of course he'll be alright," I said. "His dam punished him for worrying her – but she'll go in to him now and give him a lick and a large slice of pie with a beaker of berryjuice. Now – before we get to the next cluster, tell me how many dwellings it has."

"Same as the other clusters. Ninety-nine." He licked crumbs from his fingers and wiped them down the front of his cream tunic, adding more mess to the stains and mud that already clung to the fabric. I handed him a cloth, though it was too late to be of any use, and he waved it about like a small banner as he began to recite the ancient chant:

> *"Symmetry the Spiral has*
> *Symmetry the Plain below,*
> *Nine the arms we cannot reach*
> *Nine the arms below.*
> *Ninety-nine the dwellings here,*
> *Nine the clusters on each arm;*
> *Ninety-nine the dwellings there,*

Nine fable-spinners, and nine Farms.
Ninety-nine the Guardflight are,
When one falls another's hatched;
Nine the Council, plus the Prime,
Numbers always must be matched."

"Very good." Nothing wrong with his brain anyway. I'd been a least a moon older than Dru before I was able to repeat the entire rhyme from memory. "And the orenvine plantation…?"

"Counts as a farm."

"Which means …?"

This time it took him longer to reply and I could smell uncertainty as he answered: "Miyak and Doran and Cavel are counted in the nearest cluster's numbers?"

"That's right. Just as Hamor and Difel are counted with their nearest cluster."

Dru's head tilted a little to one side, ears twitching and alert – a gesture I'd come to recognise as his thinking posture. "And there are the same number of drax in every cluster?"

"Normally, yes." The ground underfoot was stony and uneven, difficult to see beneath the swaying fronds of avalox, and I took a moment to pick my way over a particularly rough stretch. A corvil fluttered up from the bushes ahead of us, squawking the 'corv-corv' call that gave it its name, and a half-dozen others joined in from points all about us. "They're just warning each other that we're here," I said, as Dru stepped closer to me and put out a paw to take a wing-tip. "They're quite harmless – though those hard plates on its back make them look fierce, don't they?"

"The things that look like unsheathed claws?"

"Yes. They're there so the corvils can graze in the Deadlands without getting eaten themselves. I expect they're more scared of us than we need be of them. Where was I? Oh yes, the cluster numbers."

We had reached the kestox bushes, which marked the boundary between the plantation and the cluster, and I put Dru in the harness I still wore and flew over them; it was easier than trying to find a way through those dense orange leaves. Once on the other side, I flew on until we were halfway between the bushes and the nearest dwelling, then landed and set him down.

Perhaps it would make for a better welcome if the Prime's heir approached unaided on foot rather than be helped to fly in.

As I unstrapped the harness and rolled it up to put in my tunic pocket, I thought about the best way of answering Dru's question, and decided to take an honest approach. I didn't have to. As he straightened his tunic and set off ahead of me toward the cluster, he pre-empted me: "Are there fewer drax because of the Sickness?"

"I'm afraid so. You know that a lot of drax died?"

He nodded, and I smelled impatience, as though the Sickness was ancient history and not something that had directly affected him. "And the females that recovered laid the eggs that hatched the wingless."

"Just so. The drax that died must be replaced. Remember the weeds that grew in the Traders' cluster? How many empty dwellings we've seen in the other clusters we've visited? That's why every cluster was given permission to hatch secondaries in the late season. In the next melt, numbers will be counted again and some of the nesting pairs will be allowed a third egg, a tertiary."

"Ah!" Clearly these were terms he had heard without completely understanding. "So the secondaries will probably stay with their hatching clusters when they're grown, but the tertiaries might be needed somewhere else?"

"You're nearly right." There were a couple of drax chopping vinewood on the outskirts of the cluster we were approaching, and I half-extended my wings in greeting as they looked in our direction. Immediately, one of them hurried off along the spiral path that would lead to the Welcomer's dwelling, while the other put down the axe she was holding and stood with her paws clasped, waiting. Chalkmoss lay under our feet now, its low-growing leaves soft under our feet. As we closed the final few spans toward the cluster, I finished my explanation to Dru: "The tertiaries go to the other clusters when they are half-growns," I said. "That way, they have time to learn the main trade of their new cluster before they are old enough to nest."

He nodded again and I knew that the lesson had gone home. I had not yet needed to tell him anything twice.

"What's that smell?"

He didn't have to explain which one he meant. Even at a distance, the scent of the Dyers' cluster was strong enough to taste, its distinctive, sour odour masking everything else. "It's what dye smells like before it is soaked through our tunics or painted on doors. It's what this cluster specialises in."

"It's horrible."

"It's necessary. And you won't notice the smell when you've been here for a short while, your nose will get used to it."

"Ew. Do we have to go closer?" His steps faltered, dragged to a stop.

"We must go on, Dru. Come along, you'll find it interesting once we get there. The dyers might even let you stir a cauldron."

His left ear pricked up a little, though the right was still flat with scepticism; nor did he move. "What's in it? In the cauldron, I mean."

"Oh, all sorts of things." I thought it prudent not to mention to him just yet that the primary means of making the dyes keep their colour was to add vlydh droppings to the mix. In the plantation we had just left, the odour was kept in check by regular cleaning and the fresh scent of the orenvines the creatures lived in, but in the cluster ahead, the application of heat and water amplified the smell. "The exact mixture depends on what colour they are making."

The tilt of his head told me that Dru still had doubts, but his ears betrayed his curiosity. He raised his snout to sniff the breeze again. "I can stir it?"

"We can ask. In any case, we can't just turn around and go. It would be very rude – especially as the Welcomer has just come to the cluster's landing path to greet us. There – see? Talking to the one with the axe?"

Up ahead, I saw the artisan bend to retrieve her axe before retreating along the path into the cluster, and I searched my memory for the name of the welcomer. I should have asked Doran to remind me!

As we drew nearer, she called the greeting: "Fate-seer. Lordling. I welcome you on behalf of all at the Dyers' cluster. Will you rest and take tea?" At least she'd included Dru in the greeting – but her bow, I noted, was so slight it might have been mistaken for a nervous tic, and we were close enough that I could smell distaste on the breeze.

Perhaps, I thought, it was the grubby state of Dru's tunic that provoked her reaction.

But, in all probability, it was his lack of wings.

Still, the welcome had been given and a response was required. "I thank you...Telin." The name popped into my head just in time. "We are grateful for your welcome, and request shelter for the night."

We followed Telin along the path between the dwellings, Dru's snout still twitching. His head moved constantly as he looked around, and his ears flicked back and forth as he caught sounds that had been lacking in the near-empty Traders' cluster: younglings' voices squabbling in a dwelling to our left; the thud of chopped vinewood being stacked outside a dwelling door further up the path; a clatter of pots; a bark of laughter; and, beneath it all, a constant bubbling roil that I knew was the sound of the cauldrons boiling. "Each dwelling here has a cauldron," I said to Dru, as we spiralled through the cluster, "where other clusters usually have a workbench. Each dwelling produces one colour – though several dwellings may make the *same* colour..."

"Why?"

"I would have thought that was obvious!" Telin didn't bother to look around as she snapped her retort, but her ears and wings still had a rigid set to them that signalled her inner conflict. She had to bid us welcome but it was clear that, like Aldan, she was not happy about having to do so. "Blue, yellow, and red are what we call source colours. We need a lot of them because they are mixed together to make other colours. The nine dwellings nearest the centre of the cluster make these keys. The rest of the dwellings produce the mixes."

Dru, who had been bounding ahead of me, stopped in his tracks at her condescending tone, then scuttled behind me to clutch the wing-tip I proferred. As for me, I was so disappointed by her overt hostility that it took me a few beats to think of a response. "What about colours that are worn by only one drax at a time?" I said, eventually. "Cream, for example, which the Prime's heir always wears?"

As I had hoped, the reminder that Dru was an important drax who would someday be Prime made Telin pause and turn. Her ears flicked back and forth in agitated indecision before she settled on an angle of politeness that was just a hair or two from distaste. "There are special cauldrons." Her tone had been moderated too, and she made the effort to turn and address me, her glance skimming briefly over Dru as well. "We keep them stored in the Place of Welcome. I'll show you, if you would like that?"

It was obvious that there was little she would have liked less, so I accepted her kind offer with gleeful malice. It didn't take long for that feeling to dissipate beneath a familiar wash of discomfort. On either side, as we proceeded to wind our way inward toward the Place of Welcome, I noticed that too many doors were closed; too few drax came out to pay their respects, and those that did were mainly those with wingless younglings of their own.

I had thought the welcome at previous clusters had been lacking, but this was the worst yet. There was a lot of work to do if Dru and the other wingless were to be accepted. The wind was against us, and it was getting stronger.

Ten

The freeze swept in a few days later, bringing with it the snow and ice that made flying unpleasant and landing dangerous. As I stood on the edge of the plateau looking south across the white, frozen land below, I realised that it would be difficult to take Dru anywhere for some time. The snow had stopped for the moment, but irregular purple flashes broke the monotony of the cloud cover, indicating that not all the floaters had yet disappeared for the cold season. A couple of dead ones hung in the sky to the west, and I watched the distant silhouettes of a nine of hunters flying toward them, nets dangling. I didn't envy them their job – the stings of the floaters were lethal long after death, so the netting party would have to take great care as they pulled the things groundward.

I hadn't seen Shaya since the council meeting almost two moons ago, and was sure she would not have anything to say to me if we did meet. Watching the way the hunters angled in toward their targets, spreading their nets between them, I realised it would be impossible for young Ravar to pull down a floater. Even on a vlydh he wouldn't be able to approach one, as the creatures wouldn't go near the things. Still, it was a small part of a hunter's role. Some of their foraging and chasing was already done on foot; Ravar would be extremely useful there, so long as Shaya had the patience to teach him.

Across the Expanse, the wind had whipped the snow into hillocks and valleys, piling it against walls and vine-trunks and softening the outlines of the rocks near the shore. From my vantage point, individual clusters and dwellings had disappeared under undulating white mounds, their existence marked only by the grey smudges of smoke emerging through chimneys. Still, now that the snow had ceased, the artisans would be out clearing landing-paths. It would not be long before inter-cluster flights started again.

There was a clatter of wings and a muffled curse behind me, and I turned to find Doran skidding across the ground on her front, wings askew. She bumped into a pile of soft snow, dislodging some of it onto her snout, and I couldn't suppress a bark of laughter.

"That's the sort of thing I usually do."

"Lights take it," she muttered, digging her claws into the icy path as she got to her feet. "I'll have bruises the size of stew-bowls." With a shake of her fur that sent snow crystals flying, she brushed at her tunic and straightened up, attempting dignity in the face of calamity. "What are you doing out in the cold, anyway?"

"Contemplating the possibility of flying in this weather," I said. "I might ask you the same thing."

Doran grunted. "Flying isn't a problem now the snow's stopped, so long as you wrap up warm and keep low enough to dodge the floaters. Landing, though…" She rubbed at her arms, brushing droplets onto the ice. I remembered her words to me as Dru and I had left the plantation a few days before, and it was clear from the set of her ears that she was anxious to impart her news, but instead of launching into it immediately, she looked around and said, "Let's get inside." As we set off around the spiralling pathway that led back to my dwelling, Doran raised her snout and sniffed the air. "At least this should stop the raids," she said. "The wind has that strange odour that the freeze brings. This is no cold snap such as we had a few moons ago."

It was an obvious point and a trivial one, but since she seemed intent on making idle conversation I went along with it. "No indeed. Are the vlydh settled?" The creatures spun themselves into cocoons when the freeze descended, and slept through the entire season. It made transportation all but impossible for any but the smallest goods, but that didn't matter so long as everyone was well prepared.

Doran grunted. "All except the creature that Cavel rode on. It spun no cocoon."

"Ah. They always know when their time is near."

Inside my dwelling, we smoothed our fur flat in the warmer air, sending drips of melted ice over the floor. I put another log on the fire, put tea in the pot, and pushed two stools nearer the hearth. "Now," I said, as we settled, "what in the name of the Spiral brought you all this way on such a morning?"

We were several spans from the nearest dwelling, and the walls were thick, but Doran leaned close and spoke low. "There are rumours. About the Night of the Two Moons."

I was puzzled. Miyak would surely have told Doran ninedays ago about the council's decision to test Dru at the ceremony. What had changed now, that she was flying through an ice-cold day to talk about it? "Have you been talking to Limar? You know she can't hear a whisper without twisting it into a conspiracy."

"It's not just Limar." Doran's tail quivered with indignance. "When I was flying around looking for Cavel, I spoke to a lot of females with wingless younglings. Nines of them think we'll all be sent to the Forest along with the younglings. They're so worried, they're laying in supplies – trading for extra blankets and bargaining for dried meat—"

"You mean they've *all* been listening to Limar."

"No!" She sat up straighter. I realised she was annoyed at my flippant tone, and I saw her tail was twitching with anxiety. "I've got a carry-pouch in a basket behind Cavel's nest, filled with ointments, salves, nourishing herbs, warm tunics, and firesticks. I'm trying to work out how to carry beakers and a cooking pot."

I shook my head, sighed, and leaned down to stir the pot. "There's no need for that, Doran. I know the ritual is a lot to ask of Dru, but—"

"It's not that." Steam rose from Doran's damp tunic as she leaned a little closer to the fire, turning her arm and pulling at the fur to see how badly she'd bruised herself. "Something else is going on, Zarda." An ear twitched and she flicked her sleeve back into place, raising a paw before I could respond. "Don't ask me what – Miyak's become very secretive lately, and it's worse since Cavel had his little adventure. But I know he's been talking to Hapak and Sifan far more than he needs to – and Fazak's youngling has been flapping about too. Not Murgo. The female. Same cycle, earlier batch."

I realised Doran must be agitated indeed if she couldn't remember a name. "Morla," I supplied.

"That's the one. Came by the day after you rescued Cavel – thank you again for helping him, Zarda, at least he won't be flying anywhere for a while, with the vlydh hibernating. Anyway, Morla came by to hire vlydh, *she said*. Had to fetch more leaves to dry for the archives, before the freeze set in, *she said*."

"And you don't believe that?"

Doran snorted. "Fazak has his faults, but not being organised isn't one of them. He gathers his leaves right through the warm season – *and* keeps enough spare from cycle to cycle to make sure he has enough to last through till the next." She waited while I stood up to get beakers and poured us each a drink from the bubbling pot. Sniffing the brew, she took a tentative sip, then another. Only the twitch of her whiskers told me I'd made it too sweet for her again, as she wrapped her paws around the beaker and resumed her story. "I don't know what she was talking to Miyak about, they went too far into the plantation for me to hear, *but…*" Her ears waggled to signal alarm as she pulled a scroll-leaf from her tunic pocket. "I found this in one of Miyak's fur tunics. He must have forgotten it was there and while I was brushing it for him…well, it fell out of the pocket."

She unrolled the leaf and held it out so that I could look at the markings, but after a brief glance I shook my head, puzzled. "It's a list of names. I don't see—"

"They're all females," she hissed. "Females who have hatched winged nestlings this cycle – and half-growns who will be ready to lay a first egg in the melt."

A tiny ember of understanding flickered. "You're saying that because some of these females have already hatched a winged nestling…"

"They'll be able to hatch more." Doran sighed and her ears drooped, though they still twitched a little at the edges. "Which means I've lost Miyak. Come the melt, all the females with wingless will be discards, you mark my words. The males will be strutting about and showing off their wingspans – competing for the ones who hatched normal younglings, and the ones who weren't grown when the Sickness struck."

I shook my head. "Varna hasn't been discarded, she's still holding court in the *Spirax*. So why would—"

"Take it." Doran put her half-full beaker down on the hearth to keep warm, and held out the leaf for me to take. "These aren't Miyak's marks. I think they're Fazak's, he's the one behind all this." She flapped the leaf as I hesitated. "Take it, Zarda, you can See what will happen."

"You know I can't. Not when I wish it, the way Vizan could. My Visions come at random, when the Spiral wills it, not when I do."

"Try." Her arm was still extended, the leaf wafting gently in the warm air that rose from the fire.

I sighed, put my beaker down and reached for the leaf. "Since it's obvious you're not going to move till I do…"

Fazak. Scroll-leaves spread in front of him on a polished table. The smell of dust and slow decay. The sound of his claws scratching on the leaves, and a single spoken word: "exile".

I gasped and blinked, clutching my stool for support. The drying herbs strung overhead and the warmth from the blazing hearth brought me back to reality, as I stared down at the leaf that had fallen from my numb fingers to the stone floor.

"Your fur's all on end," said Doran, a note of triumph in her voice. She bent to retrieve the leaf and rolled it up. "You Saw something didn't you? What? Was it Miyak?"

I shook my head, picked up my beaker, and drained the tea. "It was too fleeting to be sure, but I think it was the past, not the future. Fazak. He was in the Hollow Crag, I recognised the smell – all those old scroll-leaves in the storage tubes." I shook myself to flatten my fur and made a conscious effort to relax my wings and ears, which had stiffened to signal an alert. I pointed at the scroll-leaf. "He had a pile of those on his table. It may have been that actual leaf I Saw him scratching on. What do you think are the chances that he's had a copy of that list sent to every male with a wingless youngling?"

Doran nodded and tucked the leaf back into her tunic pocket, then fixed me with a stare born of long friendship. "There's something else, isn't there?" She picked up her beaker and passed it to me. "Go on, take it, you need it more than I do right now. I've not seen you look that alarmed since the first time you had a Vision."

I sipped at the tea, pressed the beaker back into Doran's paw, and nodded. "There was a single word spoken: 'exile'." I held up a paw as she gasped. "There was no context. I'm not even sure it was Fazak who spoke—"

"It doesn't matter who spoke!" Doran jumped to her feet and turned away to slam the beaker down onto the table behind us. "It's Fazak who's tilting all the wings, we both know that. He wants us gone, all of us – the wingless, and those who laid the eggs they hatched from." She bowed her head and her wings drooped. "Do you think Kalis will listen to him?"

I stood up and moved to stand beside her, pressing a paw against her shoulder. "There will be no exile," I said, as much to reassure myself as Doran. "Fazak is counting on Dru not being able to complete the ritual on the Night of the Two Moons. My role is to make sure that he can."

Doran nodded. "He's so young. Do you really think he'll be able to do everything just as he should?"

"Yes." I turned away, and stirred the pot for more tea. "Of course he will."

"I will never get it right!"

Dru threw down the shell bowl he had been holding, and slapped his tail on the floor. If he had had wings they would have doubtless been drooping with disappointment, but I was learning to read his moods by other signs – the angle of his ears and tail, and the way he used his feet and paws all provided help in deciphering his meaning. Not that I needed much in the way of assistance just now – he was clearly on the brink of a tantrum.

At just over four moons old, he really was far too young to be learning the rituals and incantations I was trying to teach him. I pushed away the thought that, if Dru had hatched with wings, he'd have had eighteen moons – a whole cycle – till he was asked to learn such things. Unfortunately, with the council's threat always in my mind, I *had* to push Dru beyond what would normally be expected of him. With our lessons moved into the *Spirax's* nursery with the coming of the freeze, conditions were not ideal for preparing a youngling for the Night of the Two Moons. Limar had insisted she had the right, as Dru's nest-nurse and half-sibling, to remain in the room, and had taken offence when I pointed out that the limited space made that impossible. She had huffed off to find Varna, but when she didn't return I assumed that she had been told to stay away while I was there. It didn't prevent her greeting me each day with a barely-civil ear-flick before taking her leave.

Even without Limar in the room, there was not enough space for me to fly, so practicing the practical aspects of the ritual was impossible. The colourful rings that had hung from the ceiling when I first met Dru had been cut down but the frieze around the wall still showed One-Wing, Tomax the Bold, and other figures from legend all flying around the Expanse together.

Each time I visited, I stowed Dru's toys – a small bow, reed arrows, a play-nest, drums and sticks, a toy egg – under the table in the centre of the room; every time I left, Dru pulled them all out again. Leaves had been glued to the wall as targets, their edges cut and torn where the reed arrows had struck, making it clear that Dru spent more time practicing his shooting skills than the ritual. It was hard to blame him, but as my discussion with Doran had reminded me, it was imperative that I find a way to make him learn. I knew that Limar would not offer any help, and I hadn't the nerve to ask.

The bowl Dru had thrown down had split in two, and as I bent to pick up the remains, I bit back my initial retort. Losing my own temper would do no good at all. "Of course you will get it right," I said, forcing my ears upright to project a confidence I didn't feel. "You simply need more practice. But—" I held up a paw to forestall his protest "—not just now." I put the shell shards onto the table. Its scratched surface was about the same size as the space we would have for the ritual on the Night itself, though there was no way to replicate the wind, the chill, or the distraction of a spiral of flaming torches. "Sit down, Dru." I finished each day's work with a story – sometimes of a heroic historical figure, sometimes legends – and Dru particularly enjoyed the tale of One-Wing, who had been revered because he could only fly in spirals. I hadn't the heart to tell him that, as a foolish youngling, I had tried folding one wing in mid-flight, and discovered the hard way that it was impossible to fly at all without both wings extended. My sire had been with me that day, and had continued to remind me of my idiocy until the day the Sickness took him.

As I rolled up the scroll of incantations I had been reading from when Dru's wrong step brought our rehearsal to a halt, I decided that it would be a good idea to tell him something of the Forest. Regardless of whether Kalis carried out the council's threat – and I had to believe that I would have Dru well-enough trained that Fazak's plans would be thwarted – the Forest was a dangerous place, and Dru was old enough now to learn about some of the vile creatures that dwelt there.

"Have I told you of the day Doran and I sneaked off to the Forest, when we were younglings, to try to catch a vinecreeper?" I began.

Truth be known, it was the most terrifying adventure of my life. Doran and I had loved Swalo's stories of serpent-slayers and creeper-catchers. With the foolishness of youth, we had flapped off toward the Forest early one morning with no more than a flask of hoxberry juice and a cutting-knife between us. *"We'll have vinecreeper for lunch!"* Doran had declared, as we banked over the Manybend and flew north over the Deadlands as fast as our wings would carry us. We hadn't realised just how far it was to the Forest. Lunch was long past, I'd rechewed everything in my first stomach, and the sun had almost set by the time we approached the Ambit. If we hadn't spotted a copse of wild

131

orenvines on a low hill south of the river, we would have had to spend the night in the open. As it was, we spent a cold, hungry night blaming each other for the silly idea. We should have turned around and flown home in the morning, but it dawned to such a beautiful day it seemed a shame not to venture just a little further.

On the northern bank of the Ambit, the Forest grew high and dense almost to the water's edge, and as we flew over the vinetops, we had spotted the nests of knotted tendrils in the canopy. The vinecreepers' crimson scales made them hard to see against the leaves and branches, but we spotted a group of them leaping from branch to branch near the top of the biggest vine, crashing through foliage and squeaking.

"We'll have vinecreeper for breakfast!" Doran had called, and as she began to circle, I'd followed her lead. We'd headed for the branch with the biggest nest, and my stomachs grumbled as I caught an animal scent from below, imagining a fat vinecreeper roasting over a makeshift fire.

"How do we catch them?" I'd asked, as we descended. "They're all running across the branches and jumping about. They're so quick!"

"Chase them into the nest, like they do in the stories." Doran had sounded so sure that I didn't think to question whether that would really work. The stories made it sound so simple: chase the biggest, fattest vinecreeper into its nest, cut the tendrils that bound the nest to the vine, and carry the nest away, occupant and all.

But when Doran touched down in the topmost branches of the vine beneath us, it became immediately and horribly apparent that our target was not a nest at all: it was a vine-serpent. They lurk amid the vine-tops and tie themselves into knots which look like nests, in order to lure unsuspecting vinecreepers within reach of their poisonous bite. The one Doran had disturbed sank its fangs into her leg and held on, unravelling itself and then twisting its body around the vine to get a firm hold, while Doran yelled and tried to take off. She had the cutting-knife in her tunic belt, and I shouted to her to use it, but either fear or the poison – or both – made her fumble as she reached for it, and the knife spun from her paw and dropped through the vine-leaves to the forest floor. I angled my wings back and stooped downward, ignoring the leaves and branches that dashed against my wings and bruised my shoulders; my single thought had been to save Doran. The ground was damp and soft beneath my feet as I landed, and I'd struggled to see in the dim light beneath the scarlet canopy. Switching to night-vision, I'd spied the knife atop a pile of leaves, its handle leaning against one of the vine's massive roots. As I bent to retrieve it, the stink of something rotting had assaulted my nostrils, and I'd straightened up to find a mouldworm lurching across the ground, its black maw agape and dripping yellow fluid as it headed straight for me.

I am not ashamed to admit that I squealed with terror. There was no wind beneath the trees, nothing to help me as I flapped my wings in a desperate attempt to take off. The mouldworm had slicked closer, oozing slime from its hairless grey body to smooth the way over leafy mulch, and I'd halted my futile attempts to fly, jumping instead for a low-hanging vine-branch. Fur on end, I swung myself up and began to climb, heedless of the bugs that skittered over the bark, ignoring the swaying leaves that smashed into my face, and the tendrils that seemed to be deliberately obstructing me. A squealing vinecreeper sped down the trunk, probably panicked by the serpent that had bitten Doran; a few heartbeats later, it rushed back up, still squealing, and I'd glimpsed it running along a branch in an attempt to leap to the next vine. It fell, the squeal ending with a dull thud, and I'd wondered whether my wings would save me if I fell too. Gasping for breath, my heart pounding fit to burst, I climbed on, driven by Doran's cries, which sounded weaker by the moment.

Gaining the topmost branch at last, I tore the knife from my tunic-belt and slashed downward, behind the serpent's head. It was a good knife: the writhing body fell away clean, leaving the head embedded in Doran's leg, and she'd collapsed onto the crux of the vine, whimpering with agony and fear. "*My leg's going numb,*" she'd said, as I prised the dead jaws from her ankle. "*I'll die!*"

"It was fortunate for us," I said, as I concluded my censored version of the tale for young Dru, "that we'd been seen heading off over the Deadlands. Vizan and a couple of guardflight flew all night to find us. They had nets with them, I think they expected to find us dead, or too hurt to fly. As it was, Doran would have been too ill for even Vizan to help, if we had not been found quickly." When I had become Vizan's apprentice a cycle later, he took me to the Forest again, to show me some of the healing plants and herbs that grew there, and I made sure that I'd learned as much as I could of the dangers as well. Never again did I want to feel as helpless as I had that day with Doran, when she had lain back on the vine-trunk and I had had no idea how to help her.

Dru rubbed his nose with a paw and his whiskers twitched a little. "Kalis-fa wants me to go to the Forest," he said, certainty in his voice. I wondered if this was something Limar had told him, and how much of the story he actually knew. Before I could form an innocuous enough question, he looked up at me and touched a paw to the top of his mane. "I've *Seen* it. I know."

That was the trouble with Visions, of course. Sometimes they showed you things you didn't want to know.

Eleven

There was no more snow for the rest of that moon, but the temperature dropped like a stooping drax. Snow slid from the sloping walls of the dwellings as the warmth of the fires within warmed them; but it lined the cleared landing-ways to the shoulder-height of a grown male. Only the shoreline was clear, where the tides washed the sands, though the sea was so cold that the fishers had to fly farther out to catch anything. They had raised their trading requirements to reflect the extra effort, so the traders did likewise, and now there were grumbles about the price of fish.

"Paw Lake has iced over, as it always does," Taral reported one evening, "and there's ice in Far-river. But now part of the Manybend has frozen too, from the Lake all the way to Tumblerock Falls. Has that ever happened before, do you know?"

He stood by my table, nursing a beaker of hot berrywine, while I busied myself with a batch of zenox powder that had got damp and turned to mush. I had invited him over because we

135

needed to discuss arrangements for the Night of the Two Moons, but so far we had done nothing but talk of the cold, the wingless, and the shortage of zaxel stems. It didn't help that Taral still exuded that indefinably good smell that I found so distracting, nor that his pale grey fur looked so sleek: my own cold-season coat had a tendency to tangle and made me look permanently uncombed.

I made a point of studying the scroll-leaf that contained Vizan's notes on how to rescue pulpy zenox, in a conscious effort to prevent myself combing my fingers through my fur, and shook my head in response to his question. "Vizan would have known," I said and sighed. There was so much he didn't have time to teach me! "Perhaps the fable-spinners know of stories or legends that mention it?"

Taral flicked an ear and shook his head. "I went to find Swalo as soon as I heard of the icing, but he couldn't recall hearing any such tale – and if Swalo doesn't know..." He nodded as I lifted the berrywine pot, and once his beaker had been refilled, he gave the warm liquid an appreciative sniff before he took another sip. "I'm afraid there are already mutterings among some of the drax that this is another sign of the Spiral's displeasure. That somehow the wingless are to blame."

I grunted, depressed but unsurprised that such nonsense was still being put about. "Fazak and his ilk, I suppose?" I shook my head as Taral flicked an ear and nodded. "I've seen him sign the spiral across his tunic every time one of the wingless goes near him, as though he's warding off evil. Such stupidity! If the Spiral is displeased with us in some way, then the wingless are the *victims* of that displeasure, not the cause." I scratched at my neck, where the layer of longer fur always chafed against my tunic, and added a pinch of ground chalkmoss to the pulp. The texture still wasn't right, so I gave it another stir and added a pinch more. "Taral, how are we going to get the wingless to the ceremony?"

It was tradition that every drax witness the sacrifice, and I knew that neither Fazak nor Kalis would make allowances for the difficulties the wingless would have of travelling to the peninsula from distant clusters.

"Don't worry about that," said Taral. He set his beaker down and bounced a little on his toes, clearly pleased with himself.

"I've already set Miyak to work making more harnesses, like the one you use to take Dru flying."

"That's a good idea," I said, as I looked around for the salt, "but will he have the time to make enough? He still has all the fuel to collect for the pyre." With the vlydh in their cocoons, and little for him to do through the freeze, the vlydh-keeper had always been responsible for constructing the ceremonial bonfire on top of the Tusk. It made sense for him to help with newly-required preparations too, but I didn't see how he would be able to make several nineties of harnesses in the time we had available. And after my last conversation with Doran, I wasn't sure he would want to.

"He's assured me he'll do what he can," said Taral. He picked up a small blue jar from behind the berrywine pot. "Is this what you're looking for?" As I took it, gratefully, he went on: "We'll send nets for those who don't have harnesses. The youngest hatchlings are small enough to be slung in carry-pouches, so there shouldn't be a problem getting them to the ceremonial area. After that…" He picked up his beaker again, ears set forward. "It will be up to you and young Dru."

I put down the zenox powder, which appeared now to be beyond rescue, and picked up my own berrywine. Too late, I realised I'd spilled chalkmoss into it, and I spluttered and coughed, spilling wine on the table and over my tunic. "I'll get a cloth," I muttered, wishing my tail would stop twitching. Once I'd mopped up as best I could, I pulled a clean beaker from the shelf behind me and poured more berrywine. Taral shook his head as I proferred the pot. "This ceremony, Taral – do you think it will be enough for the wingless to be accepted? These grumblings about the river ice – they're just another excuse. If the snow all melted tomorrow, that would be the fault of the wingless too, no doubt!"

Taral stroked his beard, ears flicking as he considered his response. "If Dru can perform the ceremony as he should – Spiral willing – then that will be enough to satisfy most drax – maybe even Kalis himself, but there are bound to be some who will never be content. It will be for you as Fate-seer to make sure you always have an answer for them."

I drained the berrywine and licked the last drops from my whiskers, feeling more inadequate than ever. "How can I answer when I don't know what the questions will be?" I held up a paw to forestall his response. "I may be Fate-seer, but I can't predict what Fazak will ask. Even if I could summon a Vision, it wouldn't be specific enough."

I'd tried. Again and again, to no avail. All I'd Seen was that the sky would be clear for the ceremony. For the rest, the looming Night of the Two Moons was a mystery and a challenge, and would remain so until it was upon us.

Taral grunted and drained his own beaker, cradling it in his paws as he stared down at the detritus on the table. "Well, he's bound to ask what caused the river to ice over," he said. "Probably at the council meeting at the turn of the moon. The anti-wingless faction will get behind him and ask what we have done to displease the Spiral – and right now I have to say that I'm wondering that too. What have we done, Zarda? When?"

I shook my head, unable to give him an answer. The rituals had been observed, the incantations chanted cycle by cycle, season by season, as they had always been. Unless... "Maybe there's something in the archive." Reluctant though I was to believe that we were performing our rites and duties in a different way than our ancestors, perhaps something, some minor detail – a gesture, a posture, a howl – had been missed somewhere, somewhen. I thought of the clusters Vizan said he had seen under the ice: they were so ancient that they had been lost even from the fable-spinners' tales. Did our mistake – if mistake there be – pre-date even that icy encroachment? I was not sure the archive went back that far; I had never had cause to ask.

There was just one problem with searching for the answer there, and the set of Taral's ears told me that he understood it too.

The Keeper of the Records – the drax in charge of the archive – was Fazak.

Twelve

I had been to the Hollow Crag just once before, when I was first apprenticed to Vizan. The visit had been brief – Vizan had introduced me to Fazak, he'd simpered something appropriate, and we'd left without so much as the offer of a beaker of tea. I'd got no further than the entrance cave's landing-stone, and had seen little beyond Fazak's well-filled tunic and a few burning torches in the entrance-way.

But the day after my conversation with Taral, as I folded my wings and moved cautiously through the Crag's entrance-cave to the next torchlit chamber, the smell of dust and scroll-leaves was instantly recognisable. Ahead of me, a brazier had been placed between the racks of scroll-tubes, weighted down with heavy stones to ensure that it was not knocked over. In the brazier's glow, I could see that each rack had a label, and each tube was marked with a colour. The brazier and torches lit the first few racks, but a quick switch to night-vision showed me that they extended through the cavern for many spans, while arched doorways to right and left indicated that there were yet more records hidden from my immediate view.

"Zarda." Fazak's nasal bleat preceded him out of a carved archway to my left. "What brings you here?"

Before I saw the extent of the cavern, I had hoped that I would be able to give Fazak some vague explanation of a search for teaching materials for Dru. But one look at the nines of racks – each one higher than a grown drax – and numberless tubes that confronted me was enough to make me realise that I would have to be more specific: I had no hope of finding anything of relevance on my own.

As I moved toward Fazak, the chilly breeze at my back eased, and I shook out my fur, carefully setting my ears to indicate greetings and respect. "I was hoping to consult the old records, Fazak. There have been reports that the surface of the Manybend has frozen over near the Copper Hills, and I wondered when that last happened."

Fazak scratched his snout and pulled at the point of his beard. "What makes you think it has *ever* happened?" he said.

I ignored the note of contempt in his voice and tried to keep my own tone civil. "I will rephrase my question: I wondered whether the river has ever frozen before. I'm sure with your intimate knowledge of the ancient scrolls, you will at least be able to point me in the right direction?"

He tilted his head and flicked his ears, his twitching nose doubtless detecting the odour of antipathy that the breeze would be carrying from me. It was obvious that he wanted to refuse my request, but I realised with a sudden rush of triumph that he could not: as Fate-seer, I had the right to be shown any record I asked for – or, at least, have the archives searched for what I required.

I straightened my wings a little and brushed a paw across my tunic, in an unsubtle reminder of the colour I wore. The effect was spoiled a little by the grey smudge of grooming-grease down the front, but Fazak got the message anyway. With a growl so faint I might almost have imagined it, he rubbed his paws together and said, "If there is anything at all in the records, it will be in the lower levels. This way."

Plucking a torch from a sconce, he led the way past the brazier, through the middle of the racks, and all the way to the back of the cavern. There, in the floor, a circular opening gave onto spiral steps which descended into darkness. Fazak handed me the torch. "At the bottom of the steps look for the racks labelled in green. The tubes there contain the oldest scrolls we have."

I looked back in the direction we had come. The cavern entrance was a small bright half-oval I could obscure with a single paw, and I wondered whether the room below us covered the same sort of area. "You are not coming to help?"

Fazak all but wrinkled his snout at the idea. "When you arrived, I was in the middle of cataloguing the Artisan reports for the last half-cycle," he said. "I cannot spare the time to chase puffs of wind."

I nodded and set my ears to a suitably determined angle. "Very well. Thank you for your guidance."

"Not at all." With a last flick of his ears, Fazak moved off back towards the daylight. As I leaned over the stairway and sniffed, smelling scroll-leaves, mould, and the faintest hint of ocean salt, he halted and turned back to face me. "Oh, Zarda?"

"Yes, Fazak?"

"Do try not to set fire to anything while you are down there."

He resumed his march; I made a very rude gesture at his retreating back. Then, holding the torch near my feet to light the way, I started down the stairs.

It took some time just to find the correct racks – the torch's yellow flicker illuminated no more than a wingspan or so at a time and the room was, if anything, even larger than the one I had just left. Dust lay everywhere, the thick layer on the ground broken here and there by trails of footprints, which were already softening as they accumulated more dust. Fazak, I guessed, had not been down here for at least a nineday, and many of the tubes had not been touched since he succeeded his sire as Keeper over a cycle ago. So much for his boasts that he knew all about the records!

At last I found the racks I was looking for, their green labels faded and difficult to pick out in the torchlight. Without the sun

141

as a reference I was not sure how long I had been down there, but a glance at the colour of the torch flame as I placed it in a worn sconce on the wall indicated that it was probably near zenith already.

Now that I knew which racks I needed, I blinked to the monochrome shades of night-vision, and let out a groan at the sight of the thousands of scroll-tubes piled one on another on shelf after shelf. The highest were above my shoulder, the lowest down by my feet, and I wondered how many moons it would take me to check through them all, for each rack was over two wingspans in length.

There were labels on the ends of the tubes, and I began to check those nearest to me. The letters were strange, some of them familiar but others appearing to be odd, twisted versions of the scratches I was familiar with. I could at least discern which were labelled 'accounts' or 'tithes'. I felt I could safely ignore those, and since they seemed to form the majority of the scrolls in my immediate vicinity, I hoped that my search would perhaps not be as arduous as I had first feared.

Pulling out a tube with a label I couldn't decipher, I removed the scroll-leaf from its core – and watched in horror as the entire leaf crumbled to dust in my paw. As I stood there with the empty tube in one paw and the remains of the scroll in the other, I heard a faint scuffling at the other end of the chamber, and looked up to see the bright glow of another torch at the top of the stairway.

"Zarda," called Fazak, his voice amplified as it bounced off the rock walls, "don't forget to spit on the scrolls before you take them out of the tubes. Otherwise they may disintegrate."

"Yes, thank you Fazak," I called back, "I remember." I added 'now' under my breath, and sidled between the nearest stack and the wall, hoping that he had not been able to see me in the darkness. Hearing the distant scratch of claws on stone, I peeked around the side of the stack to check that he was not heading my way, but his torchlight had disappeared and I shook out my fur with relief as I realised my hackles were standing on end.

Reaching up, I pushed the empty tube into a gap on the top shelf, and pressed it as far back as it would go, then rubbed my paws together to remove as much of the dust as I could. I brushed my fingers across the front of my tunic to remove the last of the residue, and took a step back to get a better look at the rack. As I bumped into the wall, I felt something move under my paw...

Daylight. Next to a weed-covered rock, a hunk of meat turned on a spit over a fire. Two younglings flapped, testing their wings; a female drax, draped in an animal skin, squatted beside the fire; and next to her, an elderly male scratched at a sideclaw shell with a shard of black stone.

They vanished along with the daylight, and I found myself back in the cavern, swaying a little with the shock of the unexpected Vision. I took a few breaths to recover, and had to remind myself that I was using night-vision to see in the darkness. Then I looked around to find out what had prompted my glimpse of a time long past.

Beside me, wobbling slightly on the hook that held it against the cavern wall, was a paw-sized piece of sideclaw shell with something scratched on the surface.

Carefully – for I felt that I'd already done enough damage – I lifted it from its hook and carried it across to the sconce where the torch burned. When I blinked back to normal vision, I could see that the scratches were crude letters. They were difficult to read, but I recognised the symbols for 'ground animal' and 'last', or perhaps 'final'. Had the scribe been recording the eating of the last of a winter supply?

Sniffing the shell told me that this was the source of the faint smell of the ocean that I had detected earlier – or part of the source anyway; for, now that I knew what to look for, it was easy to see that there were nineties of shells all around the cavern walls. Some were even stacked together beyond the racks, where they looked like piles of flat stones.

Did Fazak know that they were there? Surely as Keeper of the Records the knowledge had been passed on to him, just as he would pass it on to Murgo in his turn. Had Vizan known about them? Was this one more piece of information he had not had time to tell me before the Spiral took him?

I switched back to night vision again and began to make my way around the cavern's curved walls, my attention on the dusty floor. Yes! Footprints leading straight to one of the piles of shells. Their outline was clear, and lowering my head for a quick sniff confirmed my suspicion that they had indeed been made by

143

Fazak within the last moon. He had deliberately misled me. To judge by my Vision – as well as the ancient lettering – the information on the shells was much older than anything contained on the scroll-leaves, yet Fazak had pointed me at 'the oldest scrolls'. Not 'the oldest records'.

"So," I murmured, as I gazed at the pile of shells his footsteps led to, "either you wished me to waste my time down here – or you already know that these ancient records will tell me something you don't wish me to find out."

My main stomach rumbled, and I cursed myself for not having brought anything to eat – I should have known that Fazak would not make this easy for me. Regurgitating a little of my breakfast, I chewed on the half-digested grains, which helped a little, then made my way back along the wall to fetch the torch. Dropping it into the worn sconce near the pile of shells, I squatted on the dusty floor to begin my search anew.

My first thought, when I answered a knock on my door the next day and found Taral standing outside, was that Fazak had discovered that I'd taken a shell from the archive and complained to the guardflight. But Taral's bow and quiver were slung across his chest, and a quick glance at his ears and wings showed that he was not about to start questioning me.

"Kalis has asked me to produce a report about the Manybend for the council meeting," he said, pre-empting my question. "If you're not too busy, I'd like you to come with me – you may be able to discern something that I can't."

My ears were getting cold even as I stood in the doorway, and the thought of flying almost to Paw Lake and back made me shiver. Still, the sky overhead was clear of cloud, and a sniff of the breeze told me it would likely stay that way, so at least there would be no snow.

Taral was waiting for my answer. "I think you are overestimating my abilities again. Still, I would like to see the river for myself. Wait a moment and I'll get my carry-pouch."

We flew north to the estuary, then followed the river west, cutting across its meandering bends and keeping low to avoid the worst of the cold winds that blew straight from the mountains. Reflections rippled in the river, its churning mix of sky-blues and copper-reds a stark contrast to the ground beneath us, where the snow lay in undulating hillocks of glittering white, still and undisturbed. By contrast, the clusters we overflew were busy with colour – tunics bright on hurrying drax, the blue-greys of smoke from the chimneys, and the cleared landing-ways that had been extended from dwelling to dwelling – curling avenues of frosted red lichen, vivid against the surrounding white.

"I would like to find the easternmost point of the ice," called Taral, "and follow it back along the river to the Lake. Then we can head south toward Far-river and check how much of that has iced up too."

I acknowledged him with a wave, too breathless with cold and exertion to form a proper reply. Because we were flying lower than usual, the air currents were sluggish, and we had to flap our wings harder to gain distance. Taral did not appear to be unduly bothered by the extra effort, but I was unused to it and wondered whether I would be able to get all the way to the lake without calling for a rest.

Moons later, of course, I would look back at that flight and think how easy it was to make that journey. But at the time, all I could think about was the ache in my wings, the chill in my ears, and how long it might be before I might get a nice, warm drink.

Up ahead, on the rise that marked the river's high-water point, I saw one of the bankside clusters, and was just about to call to Taral to suggest a rest when he shouted, "We'll land at the Weavers' cluster over there. The net-maker's nest-mate is always generous with her hoxberry juice."

I followed him down, echoing his call of greeting – "visiting Saran" – as we landed. The Welcomer had come out to meet us, wringing her paws as she chanted the greeting. My first thought was that the sight of the Fate-seer and the Guardflight chief coming to visit had caused her undue alarm, but even when Taral had assured her that we were just passing through and would find our own way to Saran's dwelling, she still looked strained and anxious. To my shame, I couldn't remember her name, and when she had scuttled back indoors, duty done, I had to ask Taral.

"Carma," he said. "She had a wingless youngling. He died."

I opened my mouth to ask how, thought better of it, and said instead, "You know the way?" As I followed him around the curving pathway, I sniffed the air to try to identify which dwelling was producing the delicious smell of groxen stew.

"That will be Rewsa's cooking," said Taral, his own snout twitching, "Yes, that's where we're heading. And no, we do not have time to eat. This way."

Lichen crisped under our feet as we moved farther along the spiral path through the cluster, till we reached a dwelling with bunches of reeds stacked on one side of the entrance and folded nets on the other. Taral raised a paw to knock on the door, but before he could do so it opened and a grey-furred male with a black mane stood on the threshold. "Taral," he said. "What brings you this far in such freezing weather? And…" He eyed my tunic, but several beats passed before he added, "and the Fate-seer too. Come inside and get warm."

"Zarda," I murmured to him as I passed. "My name is Zarda."

Saran, I was surprised to discover, had a wingless youngling, a female. While Saran tended to his workbench, and his nest-mate Rewsa poured us beakers of hoxberry juice, Ellet huddled in her nest, splitting the reeds apart lengthwise to expose the tough, flexible fibres that would be dipped in zaxel juice and woven together. Saran and Rewsa used the strands to make nets; others in the same cluster made carry-pouches, vlydh harnesses, and simple lengths of rope.

"Greet our visitors, Ellet," said Rewsa, as the youngling cringed away from us. "They're not going to hurt you."

Flicking an apologetic ear in our direction when Ellet remained silent, Rewsa went on: "She's wary of strangers. There aren't many wingless younglings in the cluster, so the others make fun of her, I'm afraid." She shook her head and stooped to stir the stew, which was bubbling in a pot over the hearth. Quietly, with a glance at her nest-mate's back, she added, "Saran was for putting her in the river. It was only the Prime's heir being wingless that stayed him. All the same, I sometimes wonder if he wasn't right – poor little grounders, what sort of future do they have?"

"You shouldn't underestimate them," I said. "All the wingless younglings I've met are bright and lively, and I'm sure it's the same with Ellet here."

Rewsa flicked a dismissive ear. "Doesn't help her fly, does it?"

Turning from the stew-pot, she poured juice into a small beaker and stepped past us to hand it to the youngling. Ellet took a moment to set the reeds down carefully on the edge of the nest, sheathed her claws, and licked her fingers.

"You are doing a good job with those, they look very straight," I said to the youngling, giving my ears a friendly tilt.

Ellet gave me a stare and a faint answering twitch of her ears, then grabbed the beaker from her dam and concentrated on taking a drink.

Saran had finished up whatever it was he was doing on the worktable – I smelled wet fibres, zaxel juice, and something organic that I couldn't identify – and turned to face us, holding out a paw for a beaker, which Rewsa dutifully supplied. "I assume you were not just passing?"

He addressed his question to Taral, and I suspected that he had forgotten my name again already.

"The Prime has asked me to report on the river ice," said Taral. "Is it much further?"

"Beyond the next bend," said Saran, "upstream from Leafmark Island." He took a gulp from his beaker and looked at me. "They are saying it is a sign from the Spiral. That the whole river will freeze unless…" He stopped and glanced across at Ellet, who had set down her beaker and picked up another pawful of reeds.

"That is not true," I said. "A sign from the Spiral it may be, but the wingless have nothing to do with the message." I licked the hoxberry juice from my whiskers and set my ears straight to emphasise my words. "If you hear anyone else repeat such a rumour, Saran, you may tell them that the Fate-seer knows better."

He grunted, and rather grudgingly set an ear in acknowledgement, but his tail twitched and his wings quivered, so I knew that he did not truly believe me. The sooner I could tell the council what I had found in the archive, I thought, the better.

The council meeting was the last one before the Night of the Two Moons, and the smell of anticipation overwhelmed me the moment I entered the Audience Chamber.

I had not seen Fazak since my visit to the archive. As I had left that day, I had said no more than a polite thank you for his assistance. *"Will you be returning?"* he had asked, his posture and tone betraying that what he actually meant was '*Have you found anything?*' "Oh, I will definitely return, Fazak. There is much to see, and even more to learn," I had replied, as I'd headed for the entrance ledge and extended my wings to test the breeze.

Now, as I picked up the jug and poured myself a beaker of mulled berrywine, Fazak broke off from his murmured conversation with Hapak to dip his ears at me in greeting. I noticed that he had made sure of the best stool – right next to the blazing logs in the vast hearth. I ungraciously sent a prayer to the Spiral that he would singe his wings, and settled myself on the stool opposite him.

Once Kalis had entered and taken his place on the Throne-stool – with a warm brazier set either side of him – Fazak wasted no time in raising the issue of the frozen river.

"Yes," said Kalis, "I asked Taral to investigate and report."

All heads swivelled to look at the guardflight chief, who had risen from his stool next to me as Kalis spoke his name.

"Is it true, Taral? Has the Manybend turned to ice?"

Taral dipped his ears respectfully in response to Kalis' questions, and pulled a scroll-leaf from his tunic. "No, Lord. Only the surface has frozen, the water still runs beneath. Also, the ice is patchy. There is a lot near Paw Lake, as might be expected, and some near the Copper Hills where the river turns and widens, but once past Leafmark Island it flows normally through the rapids and on past the bankside clusters."

He placed the scroll-leaf on the table and sat down. Fazak was on his feet in a moment. "I have heard that younglings are landing on the river ice and..." He sniffed, disdain in every quivering whisker – "...and *sliding about* on it."

I stood to reply. "That's true. I flew upriver with Taral – I thought it was important to see exactly what was happening before I spoke about it – and there were winged and wingless alike having a great deal of fun together."

There had not been many wingless – and the few there were had been younger than Dru – but at least there had been a nine or so of them joining in the fun. From what I had witnessed, they had played *alongside* the winged younglings, not *with* them, but at least they hadn't been physically attacked. I'd thought perhaps the presence of the Guardflight Chief and the Fate-seer might have had something to do with that, but a few questions to the younglings had established that the wingless were tolerated, so long as they kept to themselves. It may have helped that they appeared to be much better than the winged younglings at keeping their balance on the ice. Or maybe it was simply a case of being safer in a flock.

"Perhaps Fazak does not approve of younglings enjoying themselves," said Shaya, from her stool at the coldest end of the table, beneath the see-shell. The outside of the carapace was rimed with frost today, obscuring the view beyond and plunging the chamber into a gloom that was unrelieved by the glow of the torches.

Fazak gave another sniff. "I do not approve of winged younglings mixing with wingless," he said. "You know that already, Shaya."

"They are not contagious," I said.

"As for enjoying themselves," said Fazak, pressing on as though I had not spoken, "I do not approve of anyone making sport of a crisis. And the Manybend icing over is exactly that."

From his stool next to Fazak, Hapak gave a nod of agreement. "Such a thing has never happened before, even in legend," he said. "That it has happened now must surely indicate the Spiral's wrath."

"*If* it indicates the Spiral's wrath," I said, getting to my feet as Hapak inadvertently gave me the cue I needed, "it has nothing to do with the wingless." With a flourish, I produced from my tunic pocket the shell I had found in the archive a few days before. "This ancient record proves that the river has frozen over before – but there's no indication that wingless younglings appeared at the same time. If the Spiral is displeased, then something else is to blame."

Fazak was on his feet, his wings and ears betraying outrage. "You removed a record from the archive without permission?" he roared. "How dare you! Kalis, I demand that—"

"Demand?" Kalis did no more than turn an ear, and his voice was quiet, but there was a menace in his low growl that stilled even Fazak.

"Your pardon, Lord," he said, sketching a hasty bow and resetting his ears to indicate apology. "I humbly *request* that Zarda be reprimanded for removing the record without authority, and that she be barred from the council for three moons."

I was still on my feet, and mirrored Fazak's bow as I said, "I will accept the reprimand, Lord, since I do appear to be at fault, but I must point out that I was unaware that a Fate-seer was not allowed to borrow records from the archive. Vizan, may the Spiral rest him, did not tell me."

Kalis grunted and turned to Fazak. "Where is it written that the Fate-seer may not borrow what she needs?"

For the first time I could remember, Fazak appeared lost for words, and I heard faint snuffles to my right as Taral and Peren stifled laughter.

"I...would need to...look it up, Lord," stammered Fazak, eventually. There was enough venom in his glare to supply a dozen vine-serpents, but I ignored it and concentrated instead on not appearing too triumphant. This was a skirmish merely; Fazak was still intent on winning the battle. "The fact remains—" he said, pointing at the shell.

Kalis interrupted him. "The fact remains that Zarda has found evidence that the Manybend has frozen before, long ago," he said. "That is the matter we are discussing, Fazak. Sit down unless you have something useful to contribute."

Fazak sat, but I could smell his anger from across the table, and my feeling of triumph was tempered with the knowledge that he would doubtless re-double his efforts to prove that the wingless should be sent to the Forest.

Kalis sat forward on his throne-stool, resting his paws on his knees, his ears upright to show his interest. "Now, Zarda. The river – how did the ancestors restore it?"

I turned over the shell. "The letters are not easy to decipher, Lord," I said, "but if I have read this correctly, they offered a sacrifice on the Night of the Two Moons." I reached out a paw and fingered the rough edges of the shell. "It may be that their ritual was the first – that it was the foundation of the Two Moons ceremony."

"Then it is more important than ever to get it right," said Kalis.

"Yes, Lord," I said, forcing confidence into my voice, "I am aware of that. As is your heir."

But my momentary feeling of triumph had vanished, and I realised not only that the pressure for performing the ceremony accurately had just increased; but also that Fazak would do all in his power to thwart it.

Thirteen

"Cavel! Dru! Get down from there at once!"

I was hovering over the Tusk – the pillar of rock that jutted like a broken tooth from the ground beside the *Spirax* plateau – checking that the pile of dry vinelogs and kindling on its summit was being constructed correctly, but at the sound of Doran's voice, I looked groundward just in time to see her start a take-off run, her feet slipping a little on the icy ground. Her gaze was directed at the northern side of the pillar, just below me, and I angled my wings to glide lower on the chill south-westerly breeze.

To my horror, I saw that Cavel and Dru were clinging to the rock's vertical face, about five-ninths of the way up. As I watched, they moved higher, reaching for paw- and foot-holds that seemed to me to be no more than a whisker or two wide.

My first instinct was to shout, as Doran had, but I feared that I might startle them. If they fell...

How had they got so high so fast? Only a few beats ago I had seen them at the base of the rock, putting dry kindling into carry-pouches ready for Miyak to take to the top of the pillar.

"I thought you were watching them?" My question sounded more like an accusation, and I waggled my ears in apology as Doran flew closer.

"I was checking the vinelogs," she called, indicating the pile of logs and sticks near the foot of the pillar, waiting to be lifted into place. "Some of the larger ones were hidden underneath the pile of smaller branches." She waved a paw at the two climbing younglings. "They must have waited till I was busy disentangling…" She was breathless with the effort of her rapid take-off and steep climb. "What shall we do?"

I eyed the Tusk, and flew a few wingbeats closer to it to test the air currents swirling around it. "Perhaps we can get underneath them," I called, "then lift them away from the rock face as we ascend?"

I felt the skip of disturbed air as Miyak flapped down to hover beside me. "Spinning Spirals! How did they get up there?"

In the few beats we had spent debating what to do, Dru and Cavel had ascended several more spans up the pillar, and were approaching the top. "Perhaps we should just wait till they reach the summit?" I suggested, wary of being caught in a downdraught or thrown against the rock face by a sudden change of wind direction.

Doran wasn't listening. Anxious for her hatchling, she angled her wings and swooped in towards the pillar in a dipping glide that would bring her in just below and behind the two younglings. She had almost reached them when she was blown aside by a gust of contrary wind.

"Doran!" I set my wings back and dived, though I'd not given any thought to what I might do if she couldn't recover her equilibrium. I saw her wings flap as she tumbled in the breeze, and for a moment I thought she was going to be smashed against the Tusk. Then her wings flapped again and steadied as she righted herself and glided away from the rock.

"Well, that won't work," she called, as I wheeled in beside her right wingtip. She tried to keep her voice light, but her fur was sticking up all over and the smell of her fright was palpable. We circled on a gentle updraft while she collected herself, turning our heads to keep track of the younglings' progress. I also noticed that Miyak hadn't moved from the spot where I had left him hovering, but if his apparent indifference bothered Doran she made a great show of covering it. "The wind is too unpredictable close to the pillar," she told him, as we flew within calling distance. "One of us should go to the guardflight for a rescue net."

"There won't be time," I said. "Look, they're almost at the summit."

The two small figures pulled themselves higher. Arms reached, paws and fingers found a hold, claws gripped as their legs straightened and stretched. If I hadn't been so worried, I'd have admired the fluid way they moved up the sheer rock, making the climb look easier than gliding on a warm breeze.

While Miyak and I hovered, Doran's frantic wingbeats made her flight erratic, and her paws – no doubt desperate to clutch her youngling – flapped almost as much as her wings. Whimpers and squeals, interspersed with gasps and cries of "I can't look!", floated on the breeze, till Miyak suggested it would be best if we waited on top of the Tusk till the younglings finished their climb.

We landed one at a time on the southern edge of the pillar's flat top. The whole thing was a scant two or three spans across, and most of the surface was now occupied by the growing pile of vinelogs that would be set alight for the ceremony in two nights' time. We had done well to all land safely on the cramped space, and as we edged our way around to the northern side I banged a foot on a protruding branch at the bottom of the pile.

"Be careful, Zarda." Doran's voice was a quiet murmur, and I realised she did not want to call out for fear of startling the younglings below on the rock face.

With a muffled curse and a rub at my bruised toe, I moved on, frost-fringed lichen settling underfoot with a faint crackle.

As we reached the northern corner of the pinnacle, I heard Dru's voice, a moment before a small paw appeared over the edge to grip the rock. "I won!" A second paw appeared, then Dru's head as he pulled himself up. With a deal of grunting and gasping, he hauled himself onto the summit and, to my relief, rolled away from the edge.

When Cavel's paw appeared, Doran could wait no longer. Reaching down, she grasped the youngling's arm and pulled him up, planting him square on his feet next to the kindling. "What were you thinking? You could have fallen to your death!" Doran gave her pup's snout a sound nip, and then, while he was still howling, wrapped her arms about him and gave him a lick. "Don't ever do that again."

"We'll take you home, Cavel," said Miyak, "and you will stay there and attend to your lessons. No more helping with the ceremony preparations for you this cycle."

Cavel's ears drooped and his shoulders slumped. "But—"

"You mustn't blame Cavel." Dru had regained his breath, and stood to face us. "It was my idea." He looked up at me. "I had a Vision last night. We were climbing – up and up, in the cold and the wind – so when I looked at the pillar I thought I would try. Just to see if the Vision was right. To see if I could. When I told Cavel, he thought it would be fun to climb too."

"Fun?" My stomachs churned at the thought of what might have happened if either of them had lost their grip.

Dru turned his head, his gaze taking in the ceremonial area spread out beneath us along the peninsula and the curve of the bays to either side. "We know what we *can't* do," he said. "We wanted to find something we *can* do. Something that the normals can't."

"Normals?"

"It's what the winged younglings call themselves," said Cavel, emboldened by his friend's outspokenness.

"Then you should not encourage them by repeating it," said Doran, though I saw from her glance at Miyak that they knew it was a lost cause. "Come on, Cavel, we must get you home. I'll need to brew some camyl tea to calm my nerves. Zarda, we'll see you after the ceremony."

I dipped my ears in acknowledgement as she gripped one of Cavel's arms and Miyak took the other. Turning into the wind, and beating their wings steadily, they took off together and I watched them glide away towards the Manybend and home.

"So," I said, returning my attention to Dru, "you had a Vision. Why did you not mention it to me before?"

He rubbed at his snout, ears flicking while he thought that one over. "You were busy," he said, "and I didn't think it was important."

"Visions are always important," I said, "though we may not know why when we See them. Next time you See something – anything – you must let me know as soon as you can. Do you understand?"

Dru tilted his head and his whiskers twitched as he looked up at me. "Do *you* understand?" he said.

"Don't be smart with me, young drax," I growled. "You are in enough trouble as it is."

He was right, though, I didn't understand. I had no idea why he should have Seen himself climbing, any more than I understood why the river had frozen.

Or why the Spiral had sent the Sickness and its devastating legacy.

The day leading up to the ceremony began auspiciously. The wind had eased, although as I made my way around the plateau to the usual take-off spot, there was still enough of a breeze to tug at the hem of my tunic. A flisk, no doubt fooled by the sun and a sheltered spot of waste to feed on, behaved as though the warm season was come again and buzzed up to examine my snout, but fled when I swatted at it.

As I flew down to the Tusk, to check once more that we had constructed the bonfire properly and securely, I caught sight of a red tunic beside the spiralling pile of logs. "Taral," I said as I landed, "greetings. Have you been checking the placement of the shelters?"

He dipped an ear to acknowledge me and gave a nod. "Some of the markers got knocked over on the night Dru hatched," he said. "We put them back, of course, but I wanted to make sure we put them in exactly the right place."

I joined him at the edge of the precipice, moving my wings gently to make sure I didn't fall, and looked out across the peninsula below. Red tunics mingled with copper ones as Guardflight and Artisans worked together to drape enormous seatach skins over the huge upright vinetrunks that now spiralled out from the base of the pillar. With the vinetrunk holding up the middle, each skin was then pulled out and down, and the edges anchored to smaller posts. Each one was big enough to hold an entire cluster, with the result that the ceremonial area was transformed into a miniature Expanse. With only a few spans between each shelter, and entire clusters huddled together under one hide roof, they were not comfortable places to stay for long. Still, they kept off the worst of the wind and weather, and would only be occupied for a single night. The members of the council would, of course, wait in the *Spirax* audience chamber until it was time for the ceremony, then move out onto the balcony with Kalis.

With so many shelters stretching over the peninsula it was difficult to see the entire layout from my vantage point, but if markers had been knocked over by the cluster-criers on the night Dru hatched, I couldn't tell which ones they might have been. "Everything looks fine to me," I said, gauging the spaces between the stretched skins, to work out whether there was enough room for every cluster to form a circle around the outside of every shelter.

Taral agreed. "I've flown over it six times now. I'm positive it looks the same as it did in the last cycle." He turned his head and raised a paw to point toward the south-west. In the distance, tiny black specks moved on the wind, an entire cluster on the wing together, moving as one. From where we stood, they looked no bigger than flisks, but Taral identified them with confidence. "The cluster from the Far-river Bend," he said. "They have the farthest to come, but they always get here first."

A hoarse cry from the ground drew my attention, and I winced with sympathy as I saw Jisco doubled over, clutching a paw. A discarded mallet at his feet told me the cause, and with a nod to Taral, I spread my wings and circled down towards him. "Come to my dwelling," I called from the air, "and I will make you a poultice."

He acknowledged me with a twist of his tail, and I turned to fly back up to the plateau. As I gained height, I could see in the distance that more clusters were already making their way toward the ceremonial area, and offered a prayer to the Spiral.

If anything went wrong with the ritual, every drax from every cluster would know: there would be no hiding place, no room for excuses.

No tolerance for the wingless.

Fourteen

As the sun sank towards the mountains and the shadows lengthened, I took Dru out onto the *Spirax*'s parapet to give us both a last look at the pinnacle's ritual space before we made ready for the ceremony. The Tusk had seemed high on the day Dru climbed it, when I waited for him to gain the summit, but from the balcony we looked down on it.

"Do you see how Miyak has arranged the vinelogs?" I said, holding on to the ruff of fur at the back of Dru's neck as he leaned over the balcony edge. "The largest ones form the base, and although you cannot see because of the smaller branches on top, they were arranged in a spiral, with a single log upright in the centre."

"Do they all spiral? All the layers?"

"Yes – as best as can be managed with such straight branches."

"In the middle – is that the end of the upright log?"

"Yes, and it's firmly held in place now by all the logs and branches around it. Watch now – the Artisans are about to fix the platform on top."

At the base of the Tusk, Hapak was pacing about and waving his arms, and I guessed that he was issuing last-moment instructions to the two apprentices with him. They stood on either side of a huge piece of vinetrunk, which had been cut clean across, and polished to show up the pattern of tiny circles within. As Hapak raised his arms, the two drax in copper-striped tunics lifted the slice, flapped their wings, and ran into the wind, lifting off together with Hapak close behind.

"They will fix it to the end of the log in the centre of the bonfire," I explained to Dru, "and the kervhel will be tethered to it just before the ceremony begins."

"Can we watch?"

I pointed to the shelters beyond the Tusk and the ground around them. "Look down there," I said. "What do you see?"

"Drax. Lots of them."

"And what are they all doing?"

The snow that had blanketed the area for the past moon had disappeared beneath a mass of differently coloured tunics. Even at the height we were at, the constant hum of conversations from nines of nineties carried to our ears, while the faint aroma of boiling vegetables and cookfire smoke reminded me that it was past time I ate.

Dru's ears twitched as he listened and he sniffed the wind. "They're talking and eating."

"They are preparing themselves for a long night," I said, "and we must do the same. Come on, we must have our supper, and then we must both get ready."

As I ushered Dru into the warmth of the Audience Chamber, a gust of wind ruffled the fur at my back and I shivered at the sudden chill. I turned and stared again at the unlit bonfire, where the artisans were already lowering the platform into place.

I could see nothing wrong. Nothing.

So why did I feel the need to spiral my paw across my tunic and offer a prayer to the skies?

When I returned from changing into the ceremonial tunic I had last worn when we took Vizan to the Deadlands, the council and the Cluster-chiefs had already gathered in the audience chamber. Fazak was standing near the fire, warming his paws, and murmuring to Hapak and Broga. By the set of their ears and wings, it was obvious that his two listeners were intrigued by what he was saying, but as soon as I moved nearer, Fazak stopped talking and turned to greet me.

"Zarda. How splendid you look in that tunic. Though it is a pity that the harness pulls it out of shape."

I ignored the jibe. The harness was necessary for me to carry Dru. That it creased my tunic and rubbed at my shoulders was irrelevant.

Fazak pressed on. "Everything is set for the ceremony?"

"Everything is ready, Fazak. Hapak here did a splendid job of supervising the platform construction, and Shaya has reported that the kervhel is in place." I gave Hapak a slight bow of acknowledgement as I spoke, and tried not to worry about why his whiskers were twitching.

Fazak's attention had already drifted to look over my shoulder, and he pushed past me without another word to go and speak with Sifan. After a beat of awkward silence, Hapak muttered something about checking the shutters and hurried after him, Broga trailing in his wake.

"What do you make of that?" Taral appeared at my elbow, a beaker of what smelled like berrywine in his paw. "Fazak has been mumbling in shadows with the anti-wingless council members since he got here. I don't like it."

"Nor do I," I said, "but unless you have managed to overhear what they have been talking about, there is nothing we can do."

"You have Seen nothing?"

I shook my head. "I have not had a Vision since my visit to the archive. Have you spoken with Miyak? He may have heard something."

"Zarda, I know he's nest-mate to your friend, but you know you can't trust him. He voted with Fazak and the others to send the wingless to the Forest."

I nodded. I knew Taral was right, but for Doran's sake I still wanted to give Miyak the benefit of the doubt. "He wanted Dru to carry out the ceremony," I said. "The exile motion caught him by surprise, I don't think he really wants it."

"Didn't vote against it, though, did he?"

I conceded the point reluctantly. "But I'm sure he's hoping that Dru will do everything correctly."

Fazak and Sifan had moved to stand near the hearth, and had gathered Hapak and Broga along with them. I set my ears to try to pick up what they were saying, but it was hopeless. Too many others were talking, claws scraping on the floor and beakers rattling on trays as the heralds scuttled back and forth with refreshments.

With a sigh born of frustration and anxiety, I turned to look through the see-shell. It was clear of frost and snow, and in the last of the daylight it provided a good view of the distant mountain peaks. Cloudsend was lost in towering purple clouds that behove storms and more snow on the way. Floaters, too, perhaps, if the clouds were warm enough. I wondered whether the Koth would have rituals to perform this night, and whether they thought it a bad omen that they would not be able to see the sky through the clouds.

"Zarda?"

I shook myself from my reverie as Kalis addressed me, and adjusted my tunic to make sure my Badge of Office was not obscured by the harness. Across the chamber, Dru was wriggling impatiently while Varna fussed over his best cream tunic. She ran a paw through his white mane, which had been combed into submission by his nest-nurse, and gave a snuffle which Dru took for approval. He squirmed away from his dam's ministrations and trotted across to stand next to me, one of his ears betraying his anxiety, the other twitching with excitement.

I gave Kalis a bow of acknowledgement. "We are ready, Lord," I said.

Kalis grunted, his nostrils flaring briefly as he sniffed at Dru. Then he stepped past me onto the balcony and I heard the *spirorns* sound. The council followed him outside, and a moment later the noise of wingbeats filled the air as the Cluster-criers on the ground took their cue to get airborne. Dru picked up the shell bowl from the table where it had been set ready, while I collected a lit torch from the sconce on the wall behind it, and re-checked that my knife was secure on my belt. I gave Dru what I hoped was a reassuring look. "Just as we practiced, Dru," I said.

He flicked his ears and his tail waggled with excitement. "I remember."

And we stepped outside.

I gasped at the bite of the wind, wishing I had put on an extra lining beneath my tunic. At least my paws were warm: one held the torch, the other held Dru's shoulder as I guided him ahead of me to the centre of the balcony. The clatter of drax wingbeats filled the air, along with the smells of anticipation, doubt, anxiety – and a faint but definite scent of mistrust and dislike, though I couldn't be sure whether that was in response to Dru, myself, or perhaps even Kalis.

The moon sat full and bright over the western mountains, while above us the Spiral shone its lights on our offering. But tonight they had a companion in the sky. Tonight, as I turned to face south and guided Dru to do likewise, there was another moon on the horizon. It was small and faint – if I had held up a finger, the claw-tip would have obscured it from my view – but it still had to be acknowledged. Vizan had told me that if it was not, it would remain in the sky instead of the sun, and we would live in darkness forever. I shivered again, though this time it was nothing to do with the wind. If we did not do this correctly…

The *spirorns* sounded again, and I shook away my doubts and raised my voice to deliver the initial incantation, then held the torch aloft to the west, the south, and straight up.

"Deliver us, moons. Deliver us, Great Spiral from the darkness and the cold," I called, and I heard my words echoed by the Cluster-criers, and by the crowds below them, passing from cluster to hovering cluster till at last it descended to the wingless, who had formed a spiral of their own on the trampled ground beneath the Tusk.

Taral swooped in, right on cue, repeating the prayer as he lit another torch from mine. Jisco, Veret, and the six others in the chosen squadron lit their torches from his and the nine of them glided off in formation to continue the ritual. They lit the Cluster-criers' torches, then the criers lit the torches of their cluster-chiefs, as they took off one by one from the balcony beside us. Each moved to light the torches of the drax from their own clusters. The murmur of incantation grew and spread along with the light, as more and more torches were lit, until it seemed that the night sky was filled with flame and shouts. Once Taral had lit the torches on the ground and returned to hover beside the balcony, all the torches were ablaze, pushing the darkness back to the edges of the peninsula, and I raised my arms to still the chanting. The most important part of the ritual had yet to be accomplished.

The Sky Heralds began to direct the Criers into the helix formation that tradition demanded. Many had done this before, of course, and needed little direction, but there were always a few who were uncertain, or perhaps too overwhelmed by the occasion to get their bearings. From where we stood, it seemed that the flames from the torches moved almost of their own accord, and I heard Dru exclaim with delight as he watched the transition of the Criers' hovering torches from the horizontal to a winding spiral of torchlight that descended from high above the *Spirax* to the pile of unlit vine-logs and votive offerings that would become the Great Fire. Atop the pyre, the lone female kervhel that had been tethered there by the hunters was munching a last meal of zenox grass that had been spread in a spiral around her.

"Now, Dru." I dropped to one knee, and Dru pushed the shell bowl into a special pocket that had been sewn to the front of his tunic, before clambering into the harness. He was growing bigger and heavier by the day, and I was sure that I would never again be able to carry him as far as Paw Lake or the Dream-cave. Fortunately, I did not have to go any further than the spiralling torches and the pillar below us, and I was glad of it as I stood and spread my wings to catch the breeze. I felt Dru's grip tighten on the harness as I launched us into the night air, and took a moment to stabilise my flight before circling back around to Taral's raised torch. Slowly, carefully, I flew up to the highest torchbearer, then glided down through the centre of the spiralling passageway the torches made, holding my own torch aloft as I chanted the next stanza of the incantation.

We landed on the platform next to the kervhel, which pulled on its tether and gave a *baa* of surprise. I knelt to help Dru out of the harness, then stood and turned in a circle, the torch above my head. "Dru," I prompted, softly, "the sacrificial rites."

I could smell the expectation in the crowd that hovered around us. Everyone knew that this was the crux of the whole ritual and, if Dru faltered…

I heard him take a breath, then another, and I was just beginning to think I might have to begin the chant myself and risk the Spiral's displeasure when Dru began to speak. His voice, high and clear, edged with a slight tremor that betrayed his nerves, carried on the night wind to the nearest Crier. I uttered a small prayer of my own as I heard the incantation begin to circulate in the air above us, repeated from Crier to Crier. When the chant reached the balcony, the *spirorns* blew, and I pulled the knife from my belt and handed it to Dru.

It was unfair of Fazak and the council to demand that the youngling make the sacrifice, worse that Kalis had not overruled them, and it was an effort for me to keep my tail and ears from betraying my anger as Dru moved to the kervhel. Straddling the creature, as I had taught him, he hesitated. I counted one beat – two – three…then Dru was leaning down, the bowl in one hand to catch the blood, the knife in the other.

It was done.

Dru's snout wrinkled with disgust at the mess and the smell, and I had to bend swiftly to retrieve the knife from where he had dropped it, but he had done his part and done it well. As he walked around me, dripping the contents of the bowl as he went, I spoke the last incantation. Then, lifting Dru once more into the harness, I plunged my torch into the top of the pyre, and took off. As we circled back to the balcony, I looked down and saw other torches joining mine as nineties of drax flew cluster by cluster to drop them on the pile. The councillors flew past me, torches in hand, and I landed on the ledge breathless and exhilarated. Dropping to one knee, I folded my wings. "So, Kalis," I said, as Dru scrambled from the harness and I stood up, "your pup has performed the ritual as you required. All has been done as it should."

Kalis opened his mouth to reply, but before he could utter a sound, there was a shout from the darkness where the torches had been: "No! It has *not* been done as it should, Kalis!"

I didn't need the light from the moons, the Spiral, or the flickering flames from the Great Fire on the Tusk below to know who had spoken. Nor was it the chill of the southern wind that made my fur stand on end as Fazak flew toward us, his ears signalling triumph.

It was the scratched sideclaw shell he held in one extended paw that made me shake.

Fifteen

"This is impossible! It means the ceremony has been incorrect for...for generations."

Kalis was pacing around the Audience Chamber in as bad a temper as I had ever witnessed. He clutched the shell Fazak had found in the archive, brandishing it like a weapon, heedless of the damage he was doing to the delicate record. I suspected he would have liked to simply fling it off the balcony on to the ritual bonfire and forget he had ever seen it, but alas, Fazak's public display made that impossible. Too many people had heard his shouts, too many had seen him waving the ancient shell. The shutters had been closed, the guardflight patrol overhead tripled, but the susseration of wingbeats and the growl of low, angry murmuring indicated that a good portion of the crowd still hovered outside, waiting for answers.

Shaya was among them, as she had not been allowed back into the chamber following Fazak's revelation. Taral and Peren had hurried to join their counsel to mine, but that was of little help when Fazak was preening with joy and his anti-wingless faction reinforced his mood of celebration. Sifan, Hapak, and Broga all had their ears and tails up as they stood together near the hearth, blocking the warmth of the fire. They reeked of triumph, and I'm sure if they'd been allowed to spread their wings and fly around the chamber shouting "Victory!" they'd have done just that. Miyak stood by the table, steam rising from the beaker he held, his ears signalling surprise, but a quick sniff was enough to confirm that he was relieved by Fazak's news, rather than distressed.

"The record is clear, Lord." Fazak stood in the middle of the chamber, bouncing on his toes. His tunic was so strained by his puffed-out fur that it looked a size too small, and he tugged at it and hooked his thumbs into his tunic belt as he went on: "*All* drax must be airborne *and* holding a torch before the pyre is lit." He raised his snout, pulled at the point of his beard, and turned in a circle so that he could make eye contact with each of us in turn, before returning his attention to Kalis. "We all know that nineties of drax were not airborne," he said, contempt dripping from his every word, "nor are they likely to be."

"Drax have always remained on the ground, Fazak," said Taral. His wings were half-extended, his mane bristling, and it was clear from the way his paws clenched that it was an effort for him to keep even that much control. "The old, the infirm, the youngest hatchlings, and their dams..."

"Then it is scarce wonder that the Spiral has visited such appalling tribulations on us," said Fazak. "The Sickness, the wingless, the icing of the Manybend." He flicked a contemptuous ear in Taral's direction before turning back to Kalis with one of his little bows. "As I said all along, Lord, the wingless are a sign of the Spiral's displeasure, and they must be banished from Drax territory."

Taral waved a paw and flattened his ears to express his disgust at Fazak's attitude. "The ritual has been carried out since ages past in the same way it was carried out tonight," he said. "Surely, if the Spiral was displeased, the Sickness, the ice, and the wingless would have appeared long ago."

I felt my neck fur bristle with anger and frustration – mostly aimed at Fazak, though some was reserved for my own foolishness in underestimating him. "Dru completed his part in the ritual perfectly. He did all that was asked of him – and at a younger age than any drax before him."

A vinelog settled in the hearth in a shower of sparks, its sap hissing as it burned, loud in the stillness of the room.

Fazak, though, was implacable. "The fact remains that the ritual has not been completed accurately, and has not been for many cycles. Little wonder we are visited with..." He caught himself as he looked over at Dru, who was still standing next to me. Varna had rushed from the chamber, howling, when Fazak loosed his poison, and no-one had thought to send the youngling out of the room with her. I placed a paw on the youngling's shoulder and felt an unwarranted swell of pride as Dru set his ears upright and returned Fazak's stare. Fazak hesitated only a beat before he continued, "...with the Spiral's wrath."

Kalis, however, understood the unspoken message – and, it seemed, agreed with it. He stepped up onto the platform to stand in front of his throne-stool, wings set at full pinion and ears upright with determination. His whiskers quivered a little, but when he spoke it was with the solemn edge of leadership: "The ice on the Manybend is not the problem here. We have been cold before. The Sickness, terrible though it was, seems to have passed. But the deformed, the wingless..." He looked across the room at Dru, shook his head, and clasped his paws together, turning his head to gaze into the brazier on his right. "We must be rid of them," he said, "and Fazak, you must search the records for a suitable penance – Koth sacrifices, perhaps, who knows?"

Fazak dipped his head and his ears respectfully, though his tail was quivering with triumph. To his right, Hapak, Broga, and Sifan formed a trio of snuffling glee. Peren's reactions mirrored mine – wings flexing with agitation, fur on end, ears twitching with distress, and I glanced at Miyak, hoping that he had reacted in the same way as Peren. But instead, he dipped his ears and inclined his head. His left shoulder rose and fell in an almost imperceptible 'I don't care' gesture, and he stepped toward Fazak. After a moment's hesitation, both Peren and Taral flattened their wings and fur, and set their ears to the correct level of respect. I was close enough that I could smell their anger, but I had to admire their control.

With Shaya outside howling to be let in, no-one else was left to speak for the wingless, so it fell to me to broach the next question. "Kalis, since you are determined to enforce the council's ruling and send the wingless to the Forest, may I ask that they are allowed to stay where they are until the snows melt? Since they cannot fly, it will be difficult for them to move very far while the freeze lasts. Unless of course you are going to issue their dams with carry-nets?"

The logs in the hearth crackled and popped, filling the air with the scent of burned vinepod as sparks flew upward; on the platform, Kalis continued to gaze at his brazier as though seeking inspiration. I counted ten breaths before he turned back to face us, his head lowered and his wings shifting with discomfiture while one paw traced the spiral embroidery on the front of his tunic. "There are no carry-nets to spare," he said, without so much as a glance at Taral. "They may have one moon, Zarda, and one moon only, to prepare. The wingless and their dams are to remain in the shelters at the base of the plateau until then."

"Lord..." I was about to object to a Prime command, and dropped to one knee before I said anything more, to demonstrate that I was not issuing a challenge. "The weather may have worsened by then. Surely—"

"They will leave from the peninsula, Zarda, in one moon's time, and make their way to the Forest. Once their journey has started, no dwelling, no drax, no cluster must send shelter or aid to them." He looked at Dru, folded his wings, and tossed his head, making his mane stand on end. "They are cursed, and the Spiral will not look on us with favour until they are gone from here – and their dams with them. Now, get on your feet, go to the balcony, and announce my decision." He pointed at Dru. "And get that out of my sight."

"I failed."

It was all I could manage to say when I entered the shelter that had originally been assigned to the Dyers' cluster and found Doran, Shaya, and several nines of the other wingless' dams gathered together in there. There were no males with them, no winged younglings – "*Already flying back to the cluster,*" Doran had said, her voice bitter, when I'd asked where the rest of the drax were.

Doran had pressed a beaker of berrywine into my paw, but my nostrils had detected disappointment, fear, and hostility from the other females, and my soot-stained fur stood on end as I'd wondered to what extent they blamed me. At least they'd allowed Dru to get settled – Limar had all but snatched Dru from me when I landed and had wasted no time in swaddling him into a nest of blankets at the back of the shelter, next to a stack of well-filled carry-pouches and surrounded by other wingless. His whimpers of disappointment and unhappiness had been stilled by a few drops of zenox powder in warm hoxberry juice.

The berrywine tasted sour and made me want to regurgitate, but with Dru asleep and no more reason to postpone my excuses, I forced a mouthful down.

"Sit, Zarda." Doran's voice was gentle as she pointed to a bench near the fire at the shelter's entrance. "None of this is your fault." As I sank onto the rough-hewn log, I saw her glare in the direction of the other dams, and guessed that some of them at least were holding me responsible for what had happened.

I don't know what might have been said if there'd been no interruption, but just then, everyone pricked up their ears and turned their heads to listen to what was going on outside. There were distant shouts, a clatter of wingbeats, muffled cries. A moment later, the shelter's flap was twitched aside, and more females scurried inside, their wingless offspring cradled in arms and harnesses, carry-pouches dragging beside them. Taral came in behind them, breathless, his chest heaving. "The Artisans turned all their wingless out of their shelters," he said. "I've had to deploy the guardflight to protect them."

"Hope you do a better job than you did with your own nest-mate, then."

I couldn't see who had spoken, but I didn't have to. I knew by the tone and the words that it was Limar. She'd hatched no youngling of her own, wingless or otherwise, but it seemed that her association with Dru – or, perhaps, her relationship to Varna – had been enough to have her sent to join the other unfortunates. I wasn't surprised that her distress at being punished for something she'd had no part of had made her angry, but for her to turn on Taral...

There was a collective gasp of shock, the smell of indignance. Doran whipped around so fast that she almost tripped on her own tail. I jumped to my feet, spilling berrywine, but it was the healer, Galyn, who spoke first: "We all know of females who flew to the Deadlands, or the rivers, or the ocean, Limar. Taral is trying to help, I see no reason to insult him." She moved forward a pace, her auburn fur bright in the torchlight, and gave Taral a dipping bow of apology.

Taral's mane and ears were erect, and his wings half-extended, but at Galyn's gesture he shook himself and folded his wings – though his eyes stayed on Limar as she grunted her disagreement and moved toward the back of the tent. Muttering and shuffling ensued as she proceeded to help the newcomers find space to nest for the night. Taral watched for a moment, then took a step back and shifted his gaze to Doran and to me. "A lot of the winged drax are already leaving," he said. "There's been too much excitement for anyone to rest. This shelter and the eight surrounding it will be assigned to..." He broke off, doubtless groping for a term that was not too insulting.

"Call us what we are." Rewsa, her copper tunic a glaring contrast to her grey demeanour, stepped from the shadows. She heaved a sigh of utter wretchedness, and I saw everyone's ears droop. "Exiled. Banished. Unwanted. Discarded. Pick one – we've heard them all and worse since Zarda stepped onto that balcony and announced Kalis' decision."

Limar, unable to resist listening to the conversation, had crept back to the edge of our circle and I caught sight of her tail spasming as she whimpered agreement. At the back of the shelter a youngling howled. A cold breeze blew through the entrance flap, carrying with it the burned smell of scorched berrywine.

"Oh lights!" Doran's nose twitched and she rushed past Taral to pull the cauldron away from the fire. She gave it a sniff and a stir, grunted, and tipped it over. "Spoiled," she said, as the liquid pooled on the ground, purple against the leached moss.

"Never mind." Galyn stooped to pick up the spoon and right the pot. "We have more berries, we'll brew another batch." Without another word, she handed the spoon to Doran and scurried away into the shadows of the shelter. A few beats later I heard jars clinking together as she rummaged about.

"I'll leave you to it, then," Taral muttered, grasping the opportunity to leave with dignity and courtesy more or less intact.

Through the open tent-flap, I watched him skirt the sticky puddle as he left, and I hoped that Limar hadn't offended him too much. I was sure that I should have said something – anything – to help smooth his fur, but couldn't think what it might be. The night had been long and upsetting, and my own failure struck me anew as I sank back onto the bench and licked berrywine from my fingers.

I took a sip from the beaker, but I still felt nauseous and it took an effort to swallow it down. "I Saw Fazak planning exile. I Saw it! I thought we'd done enough to thwart him." I shook my head. "I should have Seen there was more to it. Vizan would have known."

"You can't be sure of that." Galyn sidled up to Doran and held up a clean cauldron, smaller than the one that had scorched. "We've plenty of berries," she said, as Doran peered into it, "but there's not much avalox left. We'll have to trade for more before we..." Her ears drooped and she scurried to set the pot on the fire.

"Trade with what?" Rewsa's gloomy outlook was nothing new, but she did have a point this time. "We came here for one night. I doubt any of us brought more than two days' food and drink. I don't even have a fresh tunic with me."

I thought of the fat carry-pouches I'd seen at the back of the tent, where the younglings were, and knew that Doran was not the only dam who had brought her 'emergency pouch' with her. Either Rewsa had not heeded the rumours, or no-one had bothered to repeat them to her. Likely it was the latter, given the awkward silence that followed her statement, but it was a little late to be telling her now.

"We'll think of something." Doran handed the spoon she'd been clutching to Galyn and moved back into the shelter to settle on the log beside me. "Right now, we're all too tired to think. We should get some rest – and you—" she patted my arm "—need to stop blaming yourself for not Seeing Fazak's scheme. Vizan was a great Fate-seer, but even he didn't always have answers."

Galyn looked up from the pot she was stirring and gave a nod. "I remember him howling at the death ceremonies when the Sickness struck. He was as shocked as anyone – more so, perhaps, for not having Seen it coming."

"He had a Vision of empty dwellings," I said, remembering what Vizan had told me, "but he didn't understand what it meant until it was too late." I forced down another mouthful of berrywine; it was nearly cold, but it tasted a little less sour.

Doran nodded. "And just as we were beginning to fill some of those empty dwellings with new hatchlings, they'll be cleared again," she said, her ears twitching with agitation.

Rewsa sat down on a bench on the opposite side of the entrance flap, pulled her tail around into her lap, and began to pluck at the fur on the tip – a gesture of stress and tension I'd heard about from Vizan but never witnessed. "How in the name of the Spiral are we to even get to the Forest with younglings who can't fly?" she said. "There's the Manybend to cross, the Deadlands, the Ambit – and everything's covered with snow! As for the Forest…" Her voice rose almost to a howl as she finished: "We'll die! We'll all die!"

"Oh hush, you'll wake the younglings." Doran rubbed her leg where the serpent had once seized hold of her. Even now, the fur above her right foot bore two patches of white fur where its fangs had sunk in, a contrast to her thick russet coat. "We have a moon to prepare. We just have to be practical about it, and think of what we might need on the journey."

Her words would have been more convincing if I hadn't noticed the way her tail quivered, but I did my best to reinforce her point. "I expect the guardflight will net the wingless over the Manybend," I said, thinking aloud. "After that, they'll have to walk – you can't carry them and a full pouch of supplies. If you take the younglings along the coast instead of through the Deadlands, you'll avoid the worst of the snow and the marshes. After that…" I swallowed more berrywine and scratched my whiskers, making a conscious effort to keep my ears from drooping with fatigue and hopelessness. After that…what? Would the guardflight or the fishers give them nets? It seemed unlikely, especially as the wingless had nothing to trade in return. And even if they could get across the Ambit, with its mudbanks and yawning estuary, the Forest was a terrifying prospect. "I'm sorry, I'm too tired to think straight. Doran's right, we all need to get some sleep. Once we've rested, I'll find the notes I made when Vizan took me to the Forest."

Doran nodded. "And anything you might spare for us of basic medicine and salves. We have healers, but I have a feeling we'll need every remedy we can carry." She looked over at Limar and Rewsa, and sighed. "It's going to be a long journey. And the Spiral knows where it will end."

Sixteen

The Spiral's light was already giving way to the rising sun when I returned to my own dwelling. Ashes lay in a cold hearth, and the see-shell was opaque with claws of frost, even on the inside, but I was too tired to do more than pull an extra blanket from the store box and roll myself into my nest.

My feet were cold when I awoke some time later, but the sun had crept around to almost zenith and meltwater was running down the see-shell. Stiff and still tired, I stretched my wings, took off my creased ritual tunic, and gave my fur a thorough lick and comb. With a fresh tunic buckled on, a cold meat pasty inside me, and a pot of tea brewing on the relit fire, I felt able to make a start on searching for my notes on the Forest, as I'd promised Doran I would do. But hardly had I pulled the first basket from the shelf when there was a firm knock on the door. I knew who it was even before I heard Taral's voice call my name.

"One moment." I smoothed my fur, tugged my tunic straight, and stepped across to the hearth to add more leaves to the pot before I opened the door. "Come in. I was just looking for some notes. I have some scroll-leaves somewhere with scratchings about the Forest." As he ducked inside, sniffing, I pulled the basket across the table and peered into it: rolled up scroll-leaves jostled for space with ointment jars of various sizes, a broken beaker, an unlicked spoon that would have to be boiled clean, a couple of horn knives, and an elderly kerzh-fruit that had shrivelled to half its edible size. I sighed and looked around at the rows of baskets lining the shelves around the walls. "It might take a while." I indicated the stools beside the hearth, and Taral sat down. He looked uncomfortable – even seated, his back was straight, his wings not quite folded flat, his paws resting on his knees. It took me a moment to identify the scent he carried with him: alarm. I felt the fur on the back of my own neck start to bristle, and raised a paw to brush it flat. After the night we had all just endured, I doubtless smelled alarmed too. "Tea's just brewing."

"Thank you." Taral coughed, scratched his beard, and looked around at the dusty, basket-lined shelves and the drying herbs that hung over the workbench, as though he needed to remind himself that this truly was the Fate-seer's dwelling. I followed his gaze, suddenly and horribly conscious of the beakers soaking in a bucket, the dead flisks on the table, the half-made ointment in a pestle on the floor, and the warm-season tunics that I'd washed days ago and had hung over a couple of the stools to dry. The zaxel stems on the floor hadn't been changed for a moon.

"I've not had much chance to tidy up recently," I said, as I hastily pushed the tunic-draped stools under the table out of the way, and plonked the pestle next to the basket on the workbench, "though I do have clean beakers." I pulled the last two unused ones from the shelf and bent to pour the tea. "I can brew it longer if you prefer it sour?"

Taral took the filled beaker, sniffed it, and took a sip. "This is fine. Thank you." He waited while I poured my own tea, moved the pot from the flames to the warm hearth stones, and sat down. "I was summoned to the *Spirax* again this morning."

I shivered, as though a draught had blown down my back, and my ears stiffened and turned toward Taral, alert for every nuance. "I take it that Kalis has not thought better of his declaration?"

Taral shook his head. He stared down at the beaker in his paws for a beat, then lifted his head. He glanced over at me and set his ears in apology. "He's instructed me to have the guardflight break the wings of the females before they're taken across the Manybend." He rubbed his whiskers, looked away, and coughed, as though embarrassed. "It means we'll have to net them all across—"

"It means they'll start their journey in pain – *and* reduces their chances of survival." I was outraged. Bad enough that so many would be sent away to an uncertain fate, but to add to their suffering by deliberately hurting them, ensuring they couldn't fly... "And you're prepared to do this?"

I was being unfair – I could smell his discomfort and disgust at the orders as easily as I could read the determination in the way his wings were set – but chose to react only to what he had said. I saw his ears twitch a little at my harsh tone, and he set his beaker down on the floor before he leaned toward me, paws upturned. "What choice do I have, Zarda? Kalis is Prime, hatched of Primes. If I don't do as I'm bid, he'll name another of the guardflight as Chief and have my wings removed – and no drax will question it."

I knew he was right. All the same, I had to stand up and move away from him, turning to set my beaker down on the table. "This is Fazak's doing. He was there, I suppose, when Kalis gave you this order?"

"Not in the Chamber, no." The stool scuffed against the floor and cloth rustled as he got to his feet. "But I could smell that avalox he coats his fur with. He was on the balcony outside, I'm sure."

My jaw ached with the need to bite something, and I growled low in my throat, grinding my teeth together. The blob of dried branmeal that had stuck to the table moons ago still mocked me with inanimate defiance, and my temper twisted around and focused on the stubborn splodge. I pulled one of the knives from the basket to scrape at it, though I knew the effort was futile. I drove the knife at it, stabbing and prodding with a force that bent the blade and threatened to snap it. I threw it onto the table and snatched up another. "How did this happen, Taral? How did

Fazak become so trusted by Kalis that he won't listen to anyone else?"

"He *has* been listening." Taral paused and I glanced round long enough to see him shift his weight forward to brace his paws on the table. "The problem is that it's not just Kalis that Fazak has spoken to. It wasn't one drax who pushed to have the wingless exiled, remember – the majority of the Council voted the same way, including one who has a wingless pup of his own."

I sighed and renewed my attack on the stubborn stain. "Vizan was sick, I was fresh out of the egg. Fazak saw his chance, I suppose." The blob had gone glassy, tougher than the vinebark it adhered to, and I knew that however hard I stabbed at it, I'd be unable to remove it without damaging the table. It made no difference. Still I jabbed and scraped, the blade-thrusts growing fiercer, till splinters flew from the table and I stuck the knife-point into it with a roar of frustration. I kept hold of the handle, gripping it in tight fingers while I made an effort to regain control of my temper. When I spoke again, my voice was level. "I could cheerfully put this through Fazak's curdled heart."

Taral gave a brief bark of laughter. "No-one would want to eat it."

He had a point, and I managed a faint snuffle. "True. Pure poison, that one." I pulled the blade free of the table and set it down, rubbed at the mark it had made, and moved back toward the hearth. A vinelog rolled, hissing and sparking as it settled, and I took a moment to set another log on top of it. I could still taste the tea I'd sipped earlier, but now it had an unsavoury tang and the thought of drinking more made my stomachs roil. I waved a paw at the stools. "I'm sorry, Taral, it's not you I should be angry with. Sit. Finish your tea."

He sat, straight-backed still, though his wings and ears were a little less stiff. "You know," he said, "they were always close, those two." He reached down to collect his beaker from the floor, sniffed the contents and sipped. "Kalis and Fazak, I mean. You've not enough cycles to remember, but even as younglings they flew together."

I clamped my teeth together as I imagined fastening them around Fazak's nose, though I knew I'd never have the nerve to actually do such a thing. Besides, there would be consequences and I knew they wouldn't be in my favour.

I paced back toward the table again, picked up the half-made ointment and gave it a sniff. Adding more camyl from the worn container on the shelf behind me, I began to mash it, pressing the pestle hard against the glossy yellow leaves. I took the bowl across to my stool and resumed my seat, twisting the pestle rhythmically as I thought back to what Vizan had told me of Kalis' life. "Kalis and Kalon hatched from the same egg," I recalled, "but Kalon emerged first."

Taral nodded. "Kalis was a spare male where there should be none. I suppose if Kalon hadn't died, a place would have been found for Kalis on his council, but as a youngling he spent most of his time flying about with Fazak." He paused, rubbed at his beard, and nodded. "I remember my sire pointing them out to me when I was still a nestling. We'd see them flying over the Manybend – heading for the Deadlands, or coming back from the edge of the Forest – and Ralet-fa would tell me that I'd need to watch them when I was Guardflight Chief. *'They'll be nothing but trouble, those two'*, he said." He sighed, took another sip of tea. "He didn't know how right he was."

"Fazak was with them both on the day Kalon died, wasn't he?" The story was almost a fable by the time I was old enough to hear it: the two shell-brothers flying together on their Proving Flight, each with nine chosen friends, and two guardflight apiece. They'd gone to the Copper Hills in search of Koth, but it was the Koth who had found them as they rested overnight in a grove of orenvines. Only Kalis and three of his friends had returned – wings torn, limbs bitten – and Gevar had spent his remaining days howling with grief. Or so Swalo told it. Vizan had snorted when I told him what I'd heard, and said that Gevar had taken a hunting party to the mountains and spent a moon trying to catch a Koth. *"But of course, he couldn't fly high enough. They just stayed above the clouds and waited him out."*

Taral drained his tea and set the beaker down on the floor again. "Yes, Fazak was with him, and Jisco's sire, who died of the Sickness. Varna too. She was guardflight back then."

Which set my thoughts in another direction: "Where *is* Varna? If Kalis is so set on ridding himself of the wingless and their dams, why isn't she out there in those makeshift shelters with the rest of them? Did you see her this morning?"

Taral's ears twitched with puzzlement. "No, I didn't. Not that that's unusual, but..." He scratched his snout and combed his fingers through his curly mane as he pondered. "It's strange that she's not been sent to wait with the other females. Kalis wasted no time sending Dru from the *Spirax*. Even Limar's out there. Why not Varna as well?"

I remembered again that moment when Dru had hatched, and Varna's words to Kalis, and spoke them aloud: "*None of us are perfect.*"

The camyl had been reduced to a pulp and I set the bowl down on the hearth to warm it. "That's what Varna said to Kalis on the night Dru hatched." I had lowered my voice so that Taral had to lean toward me and turn both his ears in my direction, though there was no-one to overhear. "It wasn't just the words," I added, as he opened his mouth to respond, "it was..." I waved a paw. "Perhaps it was nothing. It was one of those moments when I sensed there was more unsaid than had been spoken aloud – and it was then that Kalis agreed not to throw the hatchling from the balcony."

Taral grunted. "You think Varna knows some secret that allows her more leeway with Kalis than he would otherwise allow?"

"It would explain a good deal."

The initial shock of Taral's news had worn off, and I stood up to pour myself a beaker of tea. The pot had stood too long on the hearth and I grimaced at the taste. "Would you like another?" I offered. "I have nut-syrup to sweeten it if you'd like?" As I spoke, I took the syrup container from the shelf, set it on the table, and spooned a few drops into my beaker.

"Thank you, but I must be on my way." Taral stood and set his beaker down. "About breaking the wings," he said, extending a paw to touch the handle of the knife I'd used earlier. "Say nothing to Doran or the others yet. It may be that between us we can persuade Kalis to change his mind."

I nodded, though I think we both knew it would be as futile as trying to remove the branmeal bead from my table. "I will pray to the Spiral for guidance," I said.

Taral dipped an ear in acknowledgement. "I'll let you get back to your…" He looked about, at the untidy basket, the cooling tea, the tunic-draped stools, the stubborn blob of branmeal, and the discarded knives, looking over his shoulder as he sniffed at the scent of warming salve on the hearth. "Uh…your work," he finished.

My ears drooped with embarrassment. Vizan had always been so organised! "It's more orderly than it looks," I said.

I was talking to the closing door.

"Notes," I muttered. "That's what I was looking for." I removed the encrusted spoon and the rest of the knives from the basket, threw the wrinkled kerzh-fruit onto the fire, and put the broken beaker into an empty basket which I'd set aside for discards. The scroll-leaves were recipes for ointments and salves, and after I'd glanced through them, I put them all back in the basket, scratched a label for it, and put it back on the shelf.

As I put a paw on the handle of the next basket, I paused. Should I be doing this? Now? With so many drax under threat of exile and injury?

I half-turned, intending to collect my fur tunic and make for the shelters. As I did so, the room spun…

Vizan stood in front of me, the black stripe on his snout marking him, though he looked younger and more vigorous than I had known him. He reached up to the highest shelf, pulled down the three baskets that were stored there, then stretched up again, his paw reaching for the empty shelf…

The basket I had grasped dangled from my paw, the dried roots it had contained spilling out over the floor. Shaking, I set it down on the table, which I leaned on while I collected my thoughts. Once I'd recovered, I picked up the scattered roots, put them back in the basket, and took a deep, steadying breath.

The top shelf. The one up near the apex of the roof, where it narrowed and curved inward so that there was only room for three baskets. The high one I couldn't reach without standing on a stool.

"This is just to get me to tidy up, isn't it?" I muttered, imagining Vizan's disapproving stare at the state of the place. I moved the drying tunics from the stools and put them on the hooks behind the door where they were supposed to be, then dragged one of the stools to the middle of the room. "If I fall and break a wing, Vizan…" I kept one paw on a lower shelf to help me balance and stepped up. Bunches of dried canox brushed my ears and the scent of old leaves and dust made me cough. My wings half-extended as I felt the stool wobble beneath me; somehow I stayed upright, though my fur was on end and my fingers were clutching the edges of the shelves on either side.

"This had better be worth it." I reached up, eased one of the baskets toward me, and balanced it on the edge of the shelf while I used my free paw to feel around on the shelf behind it.

Nothing but cold stone and rough mortar.

I replaced the basket, shuffled around on the stool till I faced the second basket, and repeated the process.

Still nothing.

I turned again, hauled the third basket aside, and reached behind it…

My knuckles scraped against stone once again, and I almost let go of the basket in my despair. I reached a little further along the shelf, and a finger's-breadth more. There! Something soft – cloth – a bag? Yes, there was something beneath – inside it?

Straining upward, I stood on my toes as I reached to hook a finger-claw into it. The stool wobbled, the basket tipped, and I made a last frantic grab before I fell.

I landed with a curse and a thud, the stool skittering across the floor on its side, the basket narrowly missing my head as it dropped. My wings had extended in a futile attempt to break my fall, and one wingtip scraped painfully against the nest-screen, while the other was near enough to the hearth to feel the heat from the fire. I pulled them into a half-fold as I clambered to my knees, flinching as I jabbed a knee against one of the spiky cones that had fallen out of the basket.

My wings were unbroken, the rest of me no more than bruised, and having established that, I turned my attention to the bag I clutched in my right paw. It was heavy, the contents making a faint rattling noise, shifting beneath my paw as I patted it. The bag was made of the same black-dyed material as a Fate-seer's tunic, though the nap was worn, the colour patchy with age, and a draw-string secured the neck. I righted the stool I had fallen from, seated myself at the table, and unfastened the string.

The scent of the ocean filled my nostrils, along with the distinctive smell of fish and shell, and I gasped at the message my nose was communicating.

Spirelles.

Trembling with excitement, I clutched the bag in both paws and set it down with the utmost care. It was bigger across than my paw, and twice as deep, its sides bulging.

"So many," I murmured. "It's not possible."

Cautiously, as though the entire bag and its contents would disappear if I moved too fast, I reached inside it and closed a finger and thumb around the first hard sphere they nudged. I closed my eyes. *It's a stone,* I told myself. *Just a stone washed by the sea, like the one I picked up by the Cleft Rocks. That's all it is. Don't be surprised. Don't be disappointed.*

I withdrew my fingers, opened my eyes.

My fingers tightened their grip. I stared, astonished, at the perfect, knuckle-sized shell I held, admiring its tiny, perfect spiral, and the sparkle of blue iridescence that seemed to give it an inner glow. It was the biggest spirelle I'd ever seen.

Placing it reverently onto the table, I reached for the bag, coaxed a few more shells out onto the vinewood surface. Spirelles. More spirelles. Nines of them. Nineties of them...

I upended the bag and drew it gently across the table, allowing the shells to spill into an untidy, glistening pile. It must have taken several lifetimes to accumulate so many, and I wondered how many Fate-seers had been responsible for gathering such riches. Had any of them Seen that one day they would be used to trade for basic necessities?

For there in front of me lay the means to barter for anything the wingless needed. Blankets, tunics, roots, beans, meat patties, containers, harnesses...

I sat back. The empty bag dropped soundlessly from my trembling fingers as I spiralled a paw across the front of my tunic, the mess and my bruises forgotten.

It appeared that I had finally done something right.

Seventeen

"Where do you think you're going?"

I was half-way from my dwelling to the plateau's take-off spot when I heard Fazak's challenge, and for a heartbeat I considered ignoring him. The wind was whipping fresh snow into stinging swirls around my legs and the ocean was heaving itself against the cliffs with a roar; it would be easy to pretend I hadn't heard him.

Unfortunately, that would just antagonise him further, and I saw no point in making more trouble for myself. So I folded my wings, forced my ears to a level of politeness he did not deserve, and turned around.

"I'm going to fly down to the shelters, to see how the wingless are faring." I decided not to mention the additional journey I was planning, to the outer clusters. Fazak would hardly approve of the Fate-seer using precious shells to trade for supplies for the unfortunate groundlings he hated. Or had he heard about the

185

flights I'd already made over the past nineday? Perhaps he wanted a spirelle for himself?

Fazak spiralled a paw across his tunic, as he unfailingly did whenever the wingless were mentioned. The wind carried his scent away from me, but I doubted he was praying for them. "I fail to see how they are any concern of yours," he said.

"Quite apart from the fact that they are drax, Fazak, and that some of their dams are friends of mine, I have Seen that one of them will overcome the Koth. Of course they concern me."

"What concerns *me*," he said, shifting his wings with an air of self-importance, "Is the amount of food they are consuming—"

"They trade for it—"

He continued on as though I had not spoken. "—and the amount of goods they are accumulating. I have heard reports that they have an entire shelter full of blankets and fur-lined tunics, which would be put to better use keeping *real* drax warm."

The wind eddied between the plateau dwellings, throwing little claws of stinging ice against my back, and I wished heartily that Fazak had chosen a cosier spot to have this conversation. "If you have a point to make, Fazak, would you please get to it?" I said, moving my wings gently up and down in a vain attempt to stay warm.

His ears flicked, his snout wrinkled, and his whiskers quivered with ill-disguised contempt. "I thought I just had."

"In that case, I will bid you good day." I shook snow from my fur and turned away from him to resume my take-off run. I slipped twice before I managed to catch the breeze and leave the treacherous surface behind. As I lifted off and circled to find the best air current, I could hear Fazak's roar of laughter below me.

I hoped he was laughing at my clumsiness, but when I glanced back, I saw him moving across the plateau towards the distinctive turquoise tunic that Sifan wore. I shivered again – and this time, it had nothing to do with the wind.

Doran greeted me as I landed, Dru and Cavel on each side of her. "I just met Fazak," I said, once our greetings had been exchanged, "He was whining about the amount of goods you've gathered for the journey."

Doran snorted. "He's got his own way with sending us to the Forest," she said, "You'd think he'd be content." She sent Dru and Cavel into the shelter behind her with instructions to find Limar and study their leaf-scratching, then led the way to the shelter in the middle of the temporary camp. "Some of the pups' sires have brought what they can. Then there are the supplies you have been trading for." We reached the central shelter and she pulled back the flap for me to enter. It was difficult to get inside for all the items stacked around its stretched-skin walls, and in the absence of natural light I switched to night vision as I looked about.

"Surely there is too much here to carry!" It was difficult to even turn around amid the piles of blankets, pots, pans, carry-pouches, and fur-lined tunics. My wings brushed a stack of plates on a makeshift shelf, and I hurriedly put out a paw to steady them as they swayed, then turned back to Doran. She had lit a torch, so I adjusted to normal vision again. In the brighter light, the piles of goods looked even more impressive – and daunting. "Have you made lists of what is here? Of what is still needed?"

She shook her head. "We did try, when the first bundles started arriving, but the traders have been coming every day." She raised her torch to illuminate a half-dozen knives in skin sheaths, hanging from the shelter's central post. "Even the guardflight have been generous."

"It's good to know that some drax at least are trying to help while they can." I turned in a circle, sniffing. "Where is the food?"

"What we don't eat we store in a separate shelter," she said. "There's not much to spare, though, not with almost five nineties to feed each day."

That was worrying. How would they manage to get enough to eat on the journey if they had consumed most of their supplies before they even left the peninsula? I thought of Fazak's laughter as I had left him, and of his remark that the supplies were being 'wasted' on the wingless. What had he meant? If I could but See his intentions!

No Vision came, but even without one I felt that keeping all the supplies in one place was a bad idea. "Make lists," I said. "Give the younglings a leaf each and get them to help, it will find them something to do and something to learn. While you're counting, distribute everything you have here – start with one of each for everyone, but make sure no-one has more than they can actually carry."

Doran must have caught something in my tone, or perhaps the lay of my ears, for her own were signalling alarm as she said, "You think these things are not safe here? Taral has set a guardflight patrol—"

"There are only two of them," I said, "and their attention is on the drax flying in from the Expanse." I squeezed past Doran and exited the shelter, waiting till she had followed before I looked up at the mesa's cliffs towering over us. "Suppose someone flew down from the plateau, as I just did. The guardflight circling the *Spirax* didn't take any notice of me, and the ones guarding you may not even know I'm here."

She gasped. "But surely...?"

"There are drax up there who begrudge the wingless sharing the air they breathe," I reminded her. "I am not saying that they *will* fly down here and take things, but if there is a chance that they *might*, then you need to make it as difficult as possible for them to find your supplies." I gestured at the shelter behind us. "Empty that. List what you have and what you need. I'll go and see if I can get more food from the farms out near Paw Lake."

As I stretched my wings and turned into the wind to ready myself for take-off, another thought occurred to me and I half-turned to call over my shoulder. "Doran? The food – remind everyone that there will be nothing given and little to gather on the way except the fish they catch. Even the hunters won't be able to find much in the snow out there. If all the stores are eaten before you set off, a lot of you will starve long before you even reach the Ambit."

She dipped an ear in acknowledgement. "I'll find Shaya and gather the females together," she called. "We'll be better organised when you get back."

I checked that my carry-pouch was fastened securely, spread my wings, and ran into the wind to take off. Despite the spirelles

I carried, my last three flights to trade for food had ended in failure. I prayed to the Spiral that this time my efforts would be rewarded.

As I neared Paw Lake, I glimpsed Hamor's dwelling off to my left, and angled my wings to change course toward his farm. With everything else that had been going on, it had been some time since I checked on the condition of his fur-clump, and I wondered too how he and Difel were faring in the freeze without a crop to trade.

My flight path took me over the stream where I'd filled the bucket on my first visit. It meandered back and forth across the hill slope, making its way downhill to feed the Far-river. Ice clung to its surface here and there where the current slowed, and snow blanketed the slopes beyond, save for the sheer faces of the dark rocky outcrops. When I saw the drax in a brown tunic crouching at the foot of one of those outcrops, my first thought was that he must have fallen somehow, but as I dipped a wing to circle about, I saw from his pale mane and long snout that it was Hamor, and that he was hunched over something in the snow. A something that moved and writhed and bleated, and which stilled as Hamor's blade flashed in the sun.

He was hunting! Hamor had just killed a kervhel, though the creatures were supposed to be sacrificed only during rituals!

Tilting my wings, I glided down to land in the snow beside him, my approach silent, my landing less so thanks to a gust of wind that whipped around the rocks and almost unbalanced me at the last moment.

I landed with a thump amid a tumble of displaced snow, and I smelled terror as Hamor gave a cry of alarm, his fur on end, ears upright. Quick as a striking serpent, he brought the knife up; then he shook himself, lowered it, and dipped his ears. "Zarda." He looked from me to the dead kervhel at his feet, and I scented shame mingled with defiance. "For a beat there I thought you were a Koth."

"It was a little thoughtless of me to take you by surprise," I conceded, "but I was a little shocked myself when I saw what you were doing."

"It fell from the outcrop. I saved it from a slow and painful death." Hamor's fur – still patchy with the fur-clump he'd suffered from – was fluffed out against the biting wind, but his ears were set in defiance.

My own ears were numb, as was my nose, but I was able to detect enough of Hamor's scent to know that he wasn't being truthful. The outcrop was scarcely higher than a grown drax, and I'd seen kervhels leap happily from twice that height without so much as missing a step. As Fate-seer, I would be well within my rights to report Hamor to the council and request that he be fined.

But what good would that do? I'd seen Hamor's burned crop for myself, I knew he couldn't afford to pay a fine.

Hamor stooped to wipe his blade on the white fur that, in life, had helped to camouflage the creature. Now, snow was softening beneath the blue pool which the animal lay in, and the metallic tang of the blood was so strong I could taste it. "Tell me the real reason why you killed it," I said, as Hamor sheathed his knife, "and I'll help you carry it back to the farm."

"We have nothing to trade." Difel's ears drooped with unwarranted shame as he confirmed Hamor's story. He tucked in readily enough, though, to the stew which Hamor had prepared from the kervhel he had killed, and it was obvious from the skilled butchering of the beast that it was not the first one to go into their pot.

I had to admit it did taste good after a long, cold flight. I endeavoured not to notice that the bowls still bore some of the residue from previous meals. "But having no crop shouldn't mean you don't eat." It was drax tradition that those with surplus should give to those who had suffered misfortune during a cycle. The Spiral would turn, fortunes would change, and in the next cycle the necessity might well be reversed. Especially with the Koth around to raid at random.

Hamor ladled stew into his own bowl and pulled up a stool next to me. "The crops have not been so good this cycle," he said. "Not for anyone. The Sickness took so many—"

"—and crops need encouragement – weed-pulling, waste-spreading." Difel waved a paw. "Never mind the details. The point is that the yields are all down."

I set down my spoon and sat back, puzzled. "But the Council was told…" I thought back to the meeting moons ago when Sifan had insisted that the crops would be unaffected by the Sickness, the wingless, or the Koth, and that the *Spirax* would receive the same tithes as in the previous cycle. "This is why I've not been able to get food for the wingless." The realisation jolted me, and I inwardly cursed my own stupidity.

Difel snorted. "The wingless? If you ask me, they're to blame for this whole—"

"Difel, enough. There's no need to rant." Hamor held up his spoon for a moment, till he was sure Difel wasn't going to say more, then placed it in his bowl and turned to address me: "We heard you're offering spirelles – and we'd love to have one or two, but we can't eat shells, and even if we wanted to give you food for the wingless, we've nothing to trade."

"Nothing." Difel's voice was a snarl. "Thanks to those cursed…" He caught Hamor's warning gaze and gave a grunt before continuing on a different heading: "Which is what I told Sifan when he came to tell us we still have tithes to pay. I asked him 'what with?', but he just said we would have to find a way."

Hamor cut in. "I took Sifan all around the farm. I showed him the pit where the Koth had burned the cobs, opened the doors of the storage shelter to show him it was empty, but he just kept sniffing as though he smelled something bad and made notes on his record-leaves." His mane bristled, and there was anger in his voice as he spoke. "He said that we still had the roots – which is true, but they're no good for anything but animal fodder, and they fetch almost nothing from the Herders."

"We would be living on Orenvine bark and snow, if Hamor hadn't found an injured kervhel one afterzenith," said Difel. "He put it out of its misery, and it seemed a shame to waste it. Since then, well…you have to admit they taste good."

Hamor licked his spoon and his whiskers, and pushed his empty bowl aside to gather another crust of dried residue. "Will you tell Kalis?" He scratched his arm where the fur was still growing back, and I resolved to send more tincture and salve for him the next day.

I pushed my own bowl aside, unlicked. "Do you mean will I tell him about the tithes," I said, "or the kervhel we've just eaten?" They looked embarrassed, and I flicked my ears to indicate that I was not being entirely serious. "I'll request an audience," I said, "though I can't promise he'll see me. I'll try to get word of your hardship to him somehow." I left unspoken the thought that Fazak would do everything he could to thwart me. "Meanwhile, be careful that no-one else sees you with the kervhels. If the guardflight catch you, or you're reported to the council, I'll not be able to help."

It was late when I flew back to the plateau, and dark as I circled to land. Clouds obscured the moon and the Great Spiral, and I had switched to night-vision, expecting that my way would be lit dimly by the torchlight that flickered through the see-shells of the dwellings below.

But as I made my approach, I saw lit torches moving about on top of the mesa, and more of them around the base of the Tusk where the wingless were sheltering.

I felt a chill that had nothing to do with the cool air currents that blew from the south, and as I flew lower, it was clear that several drax were gathered outside my dwelling. I could hear the noise of them hammering on the door even as I circled over their heads. "I'm up here!" I shouted. "What is it you want?"

"Zarda, thank the Spiral!" I recognised Doran's voice, and by the light of the torch she was holding, I picked out her green-and-black checked healer's tunic and russet fur. Three guardflight in their distinctive scarlet tunics surrounded her, and at first sight I thought they were the threat; then I saw a flash of turquoise at the edge of a small knot of males, and realised that the guardflight were protecting her.

"Get back to your groundlings and take your accusations with you," I heard Sifan call. "Steal from you? What would any of you have that we would need? You fight among yourselves and blame us."

It all sounded urgent enough that I decided to ignore the usual landing path and aimed instead for a spot on the narrow path between my dwelling and the next. I went in a little steeply, slid in the snow, and came to a halt in a rather undignified heap at Jisco's feet; at least I managed to hurt nothing but my pride. "What's going on?" I said, getting to my feet and brushing snow from my fur and tunic.

"We were raided," said Doran. Her ears were upright and her wings set back as she glowered at Sifan and the drax surrounding him. "When the sun went. By a group of cowardly drax in undyed furs and hoods. Four of them. They came from the plateau." She turned to look at me. "You were right to tell us to move our supplies, Zarda. They made straight for the central tent where we used to keep everything. Shaya heard them and howled an alarm, but before the guardflight arrived she was bitten and her wings got torn." There was a note of triumph in her voice as she added: "Whoever did it, all they found were a few empty shelves and a couple of spent torches."

I stepped onto my threshold and opened my dwelling door, then paused and looked over Doran's head at the guardflight. "I trust you will take care that this doesn't happen again?"

Jisco nodded and dipped his torn ear. "Taral has already posted more guards around the shelters, and one of us will stay on the plateau, too, till the wingless leave."

I supposed that that would have to do. There were healers with the females – Doran among them – but I felt I needed an excuse to fly down to the shelters, and spoke over my shoulder. "I will fetch liniment and canox, and tend to Shaya in a beat or two."

Doran flicked her ears in acknowledgement, and I moved inside the dwelling, but before I could close the door, a roar from the direction of the *Spirax* halted everyone in their tracks.

"Zarda!" It was Kalis. His mane was awry, and his tunic hung loose from his shoulders where it had not been securely fastened; but it was the position of his wings and ears that held my attention: stiff with rage, they signalled that he had not taken kindly to being awakened in the night with tales of brawling drax. Nor was he likely to be amused that I had not been in my nest when I was looked for. His next words, low and menacing, delivered with a snarl that would have made a Koth retreat, confirmed my fears. "The guardflight have been searching for you," he said, "as have I. Where, by the Lights, have you been?"

I realised that telling him I had been looking for food and supplies for the wingless would just provoke him further. So, with Jisco's torch warming my snout, and the snow freezing my feet, I explained that I had been visiting Difel and Hamor. "They are being asked for tithes they cannot provide," I said, "and the worry is making Hamor's fur-clump recur. I stayed a while to tend him. Of course, had I known that my presence was required here—"

"You are a Fate-seer." Fazak. I should have known he would be creeping around in the shadows behind Kalis. His scent was masked by the Prime's, but I glimpsed him rubbing his paws together as he spoke, and his breath misted the air beyond Kalis's wings. "Surely you should have Seen what would happen here?"

I felt my mane bristle, then realised that Fazak had inadvertently handed me a reason to be flying in after dark. Running a paw over my neck to settle the fur, I addressed my reply to Kalis: "I would hardly have flown straight back here in the middle of the freeze if I had *not* Seen that something was amiss. Alas, the Vision was unclear, but it was enough to make me decline the guest-nest that Hamor offered and come back as soon as I could." I dipped him a bow. "I regret that I cannot be in more than one place at the same time, Lord. If the Spiral wills it, perhaps there will be more Seers for me to apprentice very soon."

Kalis grunted, but the relaxation of his ears and wings told me that the worst of his anger had left him. "It's too cold for anyone to be loitering about out here," he growled. "Get what you need and tend to the wounded."

"Yes, Lord." I shivered with relief, and masked it with another bow, while Kalis spun on his claws and marched back into the *Spirax,* Fazak running at his heels. Sifan muttered something I couldn't quite hear, though the hostile set of his wings was clear enough. He regurgitated something and spat it into the snow before following Kalis' example and stalking off toward his dwelling.

Left with Doran and the guardflight, I looked from Jisco to Veret, whose scar made him look intimidating in the flickering torchlight. For a moment, I wondered if the guardflight had had any part in the raid, but these two at least smelled trustworthy. Besides, they were Taral's wing-flyers, the guardflight who had been given the honour of taking Vizan to his last nest. Surely that distinction and trust had not been misplaced? "Has anyone searched the dwellings up here for undyed furs?"

Veret shook his head. "Taral went to Kalis to ask his permission, but Fazak was already there. Didn't take much for Kalis to be persuaded that the wingless had been fighting among themselves and were lying about who was really to blame."

Jisco had been watching Sifan and the drax who had gathered around him, as they retreated into the shadows. As doors creaked and slammed in the darkness, he raised his snout a little and said, "One of them at least had the smell of fresh hide still on his fur." Then, to me, he added, "Come on, Zarda, before our wings freeze off. You can't do anything about Sifan and the others, but you can help the healers with Shaya."

He was right, though that did not make the fact any easier. "Take Doran down to the shelters," I said. "I will gather what I need and fly after you as soon as I can."

Eighteen

The pounding on my dwelling door woke me, and I had scarcely managed to force my eyes open before the door creaked open and Morel stuck his snout inside. "Kalis has called an emergency council meeting," he said, as I blinked and tried to remember where I was. "Your presence is required immediately, Zarda."

"Immediately," I repeated, confused, half-understanding. Then I registered what he was saying, though it took some moments for my body to catch up with my brain, and I rolled and thrashed about several times before I managed to get out of my nest. I must have looked ridiculous on my knees on the floor, but Morel didn't so much as snuffle.

"Let me help you," he said, extending a paw to assist me to my feet and passing me my grooming-brush.

"What time is it?"

"After dawn. But the sun's still over the ocean."

196

I groaned. No wonder I was still tired! It had taken me half the night to finish tending Shaya's wounds, and listening to the wingless tell me about the attack. I'd crawled into my nest well after moon-zenith and now, with the sun hardly risen, here Morel was, helping me brush down for a sudden council meeting. "Do you know what the meeting is about?" I said, as though I couldn't guess.

"I'm just a Herald, Zarda, I take messages and fetch whatever is needed, nothing more. Kalis would hardly see fit to confide in me."

"I haven't been Fate-seer for long, Morel, but I know better than to believe that." I threw the brush onto the workbench and hunted through my tunics for one that was reasonably presentable.

He started to tidy my brushes into a line – an automatic action, I supposed, born of his heralding duties – and his ears flicked nervously as he considered what I had said. Eventually, he set his ears straight and confided, "I may have overheard something about the departure of the wingless. I believe someone has suggested to Kalis that they are causing too much trouble, and should leave now, instead of at the end of the moon."

"Fazak," I hissed, and he didn't contradict me.

"Your snout," he said, handing me a cloth, and while I rubbed at my matted fur, he plucked my badge from the hook by the door and pinned it to my tunic.

I smoothed fur and fabric. "I smell like an old nest."

"You don't have time for a thorough lick. Come on – Kalis is waiting, and the rest of the council will already be there."

I splashed some avalox juice on my paws and rubbed it over my neck, then followed Morel outside and into the teeth of a gale.

I was so intent on planning what I might say to Fazak and his cronies that I was halfway across the *Spirax's* vast Feasting Hall when I realised it was no longer empty. The massive tables and carved stools that were used for the ceremonial feast had been stacked along one side of the hall.

"Morel, what are these doing here? Morel!" He was several paces ahead of me and seemed not to hear, but I saw him rub his snout as though afraid it might get bitten again, and I could scent his alarm. It was clear that I'd get no answer out of him – at least, none I could believe – so I had to leave it be. I tried to persuade myself it was a routine *Spirax* matter, some sort of cold-season inspection or tidying that happened every cycle; perhaps it was not going well, which would explain Morel's anxiety.

In any case, I had more immediate concerns than a stack of displaced furniture, and as I hurried up the curving passageway, I prayed that the Spiral would send a sign, a portent, a new and clearer Vision that would help persuade the council to listen to me.

All I saw was Morel, opening the door to the Audience Chamber.

The room was warm, bright with lit torches. A fire blazed in the hearth, which even Fazak's bulk could not entirely block. The other members of the council were already gathered around the table by the time I took my seat, with Shaya's stool occupied by Rysel, who clearly had no qualms about seizing his nest-mate's place. I acknowledged his presence with a polite dip of my ears, but was spared from having speak to him when Kalis entered the room – he must have been pacing about in his antechamber, listening for my arrival.

"Fazak, you have a proposal for the council," he said, without preamble. "Let us hear it."

Fazak stroked the point of his beard as he got to his feet, smoothing his tunic as he set his ears and wings to the correct angle. "The wingless are worse than useless," he began. "They take our precious resources and give nothing back—"

"They are younglings," growled Peren from his stool on my left, "what do you expect?"

"Their dams are not," said Sifan, who was seated in his customary place next to Fazak. "They have failed to produce useful offspring, and now they sit around being fed and clothed by the rest of us."

I couldn't resist. "I've not noticed *you* contributing toward their well-being, Sifan. Quite the opposite in fact."

"What they eat, the rest of us cannot."

"—and furthermore," Fazak went on, as though no-one else had spoken, "they are occupying far too much of the guardflight's time."

"I have been using the situation as a training exercise," said Taral, who was next to Miyak and opposite Fazak. "It's what we do at this time of year, when there are no Koth to guard against."

"You also have a duty to guard the plateau," said Fazak, "and to intervene in any disputes that might arise."

"You know very well that guarding the plateau is nothing more than a tradition," said Taral. "Apart from the guardflight, only the hunters carry weapons, and they know better than to approach the mesa while they're carrying them." He held up a paw to forestall Fazak as the Record Keeper opened his mouth. "In any case," Taral went on, "the patrols don't occupy all of our time. That's why we use the freeze to train. The apprentices—"

"—need to learn how to shoot and bite," said Fazak. "Not spend their time herding groundlings."

I saw Taral set his ears upright and his mane bristled. "You know very well that that is not what we are doing."

"I do beg your forgiveness, Taral." Fazak placed a paw on his chest, over the spiral beads on his tunic, but his ears were not set for an apology and the smell of his contempt reached me even from the other end of the table. "Your guardflight are, of course, keeping the peace between the groundlings and those who might wish them harm – though, if those poor wingless drax are to be believed about what happened last night, your troops did not do a very good job of protecting them."

I heard Taral growl low in his throat, and I half-feared that his next response would be to leap across the table and rip out Fazak's throat. Fortunately for both of them, Kalis intervened, raising his voice to call from the platform: "Fazak. Your proposal. Get to it."

"Of course, Lord." This time, his ears were angled to convey deference and respect, and for good measure he dipped a little bow in Kalis' direction. For a moment, I wished I had the courage to rip his throat out myself. "In view of the problems they are causing, and the resources they are consuming, I propose that the wingless and their dams leave for the Forest at first light tomorrow."

"Seconded," said Sifan, almost before Fazak had finished speaking.

I didn't need to look around the table to know which way this would go. Miyak and Rysel both voted with Fazak, any ambivalence over their offspring evidently resolved. Besides myself and Peren, only Taral, in a vain attempt to sway a few votes to the 'nays', spoke against, pointing out that the logistics of moving so many flightless drax at such short notice would be all but impossible. I doubt if he would have said even that much had he known what was coming, but in any case it made no difference.

"The proposal is accepted," said Kalis, without even moving from his throne-stool. "See to it, Taral, and don't forget my instructions regarding their wings."

"It will be done, Lord." Taral's fur was almost standing on end, but his ears and wings were perfectly correct as he bowed; it was clear that he would carry out the Prime's instructions, however much they might repel him.

No-one, least of all Kalis, had listened to my input as Fate-seer. I might as well have been a rock in a black tunic for all the notice anyone had taken of me, and I knew that I couldn't let that pass. Not if I was to retain any semblance of dignity or respect for my office. My paws were shaking. I braced them against the table to mask the tremor, pushed myself to my feet, and took care to set my ears and wings to convey absolute deference. "Kalis." My voice came out as a squeak and I cleared my throat, tried again. This time I managed a scrap more authority as I spoke. "Kalis. Surely it's enough that the females are to be banished along with their offspring. To send them out without enough food in this weather is cruel. I would remind you that Dru has been Seen to be the drax who defeats the Koth." I heard Fazak snort, and turned on him, my anger overcoming my nerves. "I know you have little regard for my own talents," I snapped, "but it was Vizan's vision before it was mine. The Dream-smoke shows true, and it has not changed since Dru hatched. I implore you—"

Kalis stood, spread his wings, and bared his teeth. "I have spoken, Zarda. How dare you question me."

Everyone had gone very still. Even Fazak sat unmoving and silent as the Prime raged, and I felt as though I was growing smaller by the moment. Dropping to one knee, I folded my wings tight, bowed my head, and concentrated my attention on Kalis' feet as they stamped about the platform and kicked at the Throne-stool. "If Vizan were here..." He roared and ranted, but all I could think was that if Vizan were here none of this would be happening. He'd have found a way to undermine Fazak, to reinforce Kalis' belief in the Fate-seer, in the visions, in Dru. I heard Kalis snap his wings shut, caught the mingled scents of his contempt and Fazak's amusement, felt the heat of the fire that blazed in the hearth...

...and Kalis' pacing feet became smaller and paler, a youngling's feet, with others' feet beside him, black and sticky with mud. Doran's voice was calling me, I could smell the black sludge of the Ambit estuary, feel it suck and pull against my feet...

"Zarda?" Taral was crouched beside me, a paw on my arm as though to steady me. "Did you See something?"

"Just the wingless," I said, thinking it best to leave my own part out of it, "crossing the Ambit's estuary mud."

Kalis, who had stopped his tirade and now stood at the edge of the platform glaring down at me, gave a bark of disgust. "Your Visions are utterly useless, Zarda. What good does it do to tell me that the wingless will cross the mud flats? Better if you'd told me you saw them getting sucked into them!"

I dipped an ear apologetically, though in truth I barely registered his words. I felt cold, though the fire still blazed, and my thoughts were reeling. I knew what the Vision meant: that I would cross those mud-flats with the wingless. I would be with them on their journey. It was a terrifying prospect. True, I felt unwanted on the council, and Kalis paid no heed to anything I said, but...to leave? To go with Dru and the others into the Forest? Yes, of course Dru would need help and guidance if he was ever to fulfil the destiny we had Seen, but the thought of leaving everything I knew, of leaving the remaining drax without a Fate-seer, chilled me. Could I really do such a thing? Could I even contemplate it?

After Kalis hurled a last insult and closed his jaws with a snap before leaving the room, I let out a breath and got to my feet. Vinewood scraped on stone as stools were pushed back and everyone stood, voices filling the Chamber as everyone felt the need to speak at once.

Taral gave me a hard stare, his gaze laden with curiosity, and I knew that I hadn't fooled him for a heartbeat with my half-truth of what I'd just Seen. After a moment he looked over at the others, grouped now into twos and threes as they chattered, and instead of questioning me he said, "I have to go and finalise our preparations."

I flicked an ear in acknowledgement – both of what he had said and what had been left unsaid. "And I must go and see the exiles," I said, "and tell them what the council has decided."

As I banished thoughts of returning to the cosy warmth of my nest, and turned to follow Taral out of the Chamber, Fazak stalked past, his bearing triumphant, his manner superior. He sniffed as he passed me and turned to address Sifan, who was trailing behind him as usual. "How very odd. Sifan, do you smell nest-mould?"

Nineteen

"It is the worst time of year to be travelling." I stood on a stool beside the glowing brazier near the middle of Doran's shelter, surrounded by nines of anxious faces. I had asked that the younglings be temporarily taken to a different tent while adult representatives from each shelter gathered in the central one. It meant I would not have to reiterate my message. Word would spread swiftly enough without me repeating myself, and it churned my stomachs even to deliver it once.

Outside, the wind was throwing sleet against the shelter's flapping sides, and an icy draught blew under the edges, between the pegs that secured it to the ground. My ears almost brushed the sloping roof, and I put a paw on the central pole to steady myself as I felt the stool wobble on the uneven ground. The last thing I needed was another undignified tumble. "I'm very sorry. Taral, Peren and I voted against, but the majority of the Council voted that you leave in the morning…"

"*All* the rest? Even Miyak?" Amid the sobs and the angry murmurs, Doran's voice, edged with rancour and disappointment, carried from the shadows at the back of the shelter.

I sighed. "Even Miyak. Rysel too – he was there in your place, Shaya. I'm sorry."

Doran stepped nearer, pushing her way through the crowd till she stood a mere wingspan away. To my surprise, she smelled more of determination than of anger or resignation, and as she turned to address the others, she raised her ears as well as her voice. "They want us gone. Our Prime, our nest-mates, our fellow drax. So be it." Her voice shook, but she turned in a slow circle as she spoke. Her eyes flicked over the faces around her, while her nose hunted for scent and her ears stood alert. The murmurs died away. "Now or at the end of the moon, the weather will not have changed much," she said. "It's the leaving itself that will be hard, the 'when' does not matter. We just have to make sure that we all carry as much as we can. We must leave nothing behind."

Shaya, ever one to take charge, hopped onto a stool next to me and combed her fingers through the thick brown fur around her ears. Anger radiated from her as she barked, "Doran's right. We have no choice about going, but we *do* have a choice about surviving. We've got blankets and spare tunics, we've got beans and pulses, meat patties and pans to cook them in. There won't be much to hunt, but if we stay near the shore we can fish, we adults have got wings—"

"Wait." I held up a paw. A murmur of speculation hissed around the shelter and there was a good deal of shifting about while I wondered whether I should break Taral's confidence and tell them what Kalis had planned for the morning. I'd promised to say nothing, but I couldn't stand by and let them assume they would be able to pull fish from the ocean with a glide and a stoop. "About the wings…"

I got no further. With a collective howl, the crowd surged for the tent-flap. The post trembled, my stool went from under me, and I fell with a squawk of surprise against Shaya. We landed amid hurrying feet, some of which trampled right over us, and I heard high-pitched squeals of pain as someone barged into the brazier.

"Be careful!"

"Watch where you're going."

"Look out! That's hot!"

"Mind who you're stepping on…"

"…shouldn't wait, we must leave now…"

"…go before they take our wings too…"

The sounds and smells of fear and panic assaulted me along with the pounding feet, and I rolled onto my side, folded my wings in as tight as possible, and covered my head with my arms.

Then I heard the roars from outside.

"Those are males." Shaya's voice.

I lowered my arms, raised my head, and cautiously looked around. The rush for the exit had halted. Now drax were pushing their way back in, and I used the fallen stool to help lever myself to my feet. Beside me, Shaya was already brushing down her tunic and licking her paws, though she spared me a glare as she rubbed her snout.

"Guardflight?" I could think of no other reason for the females to be rushing back into the shelter. "Taral left the council to fetch them, but…how have they got here so fast?"

"They haven't." The shelter-flap was flung back, throwing a shaft of weak sunlight into the shelter, and Fazak strode in, Murgo at his wingtips. The younger drax was wearing a tunic colour I'd never seen before – maroon with a blue edging – and carried a half-drawn bow with an arrow already nocked. Fazak took a moment to stroke the point of his beard and smooth his mane, then strutted across to stand beside the brazier and raised his chin as he barked, "No-one will leave until the morning!" He turned toward me as he added, "My Elite Guards are eager to prove their worth to the Prime. I suggest no-one gives them cause to practice their shooting."

He pivoted on his heel and stalked back toward the entrance. I doubt I was the only one who was sorry he didn't singe his wings in the flames from the brazier as he turned – the stench of loathing was overpowering.

Drax drew away from him, a path clearing through the mass of protesting females as though they feared he might contaminate them, and I followed right after him. "Fazak!"

He swept out of the shelter without a backward glance. Murgo held the shelter's flap aside for him and let it go just as I reached the exit, allowing the rough hide to slap my snout and bruise my shoulder. I punched it aside and stormed out, catching my breath as the wind bit into me, sharp after the relative warmth of the shelter. "Fazak!"

This time he turned, his movement one of haughty disdain.

I pointed in Murgo's direction, indicating his new tunic, but my words were addressed to Fazak. "What is all this? I was with you in the audience chamber six moons ago when Kalis dismissed the idea of an Elite Guard."

He struck a haughty pose, chin up, wings set just so, his paws clasped across the front of his tunic – which, I noticed, had had an extra panel let into the front to contain his considerable bulk. Clearly he was eating a good deal better than Hamor and Difel. "Fortunately, I was able to persuade Kalis to reconsider," he said. "He agreed to set up a pilot scheme of eighteen Elite, to test their necessity."

At a nod from Fazak, Murgo pulled back the shelter's flap again and growled that the females should each return to their own shelters for now. "They're guarded," he added, as the dams began to leave. Though they moved in groups of two or three, none of them spoke as they scurried across the frozen ground, Murgo's words filling the air behind them: "Don't try flying anywhere."

Fazak raised a paw to preen his whiskers. "I think it's clear that the females would all have taken their worthless pups and fled across the river by the time Taral returned with more guardflight. Kalis' orders to break their wings could not have been carried out." He paused, while I shivered in the freezing wind that snapped at the shelters and ruffled our fur. "I wonder..." He pulled again at his absurd beard, but this time I couldn't see the humour in it. "I wonder who might have told the females about their punishment? Kalis' orders to Taral about their wings were supposed to be confidential."

"Were they? I wouldn't know." I set my ears to indicate sincerity, and hoped that the wind would carry any sniff of deception away from Fazak's busy nose. "I had a Vision that their wings would be smashed before they left. I felt I had a duty to come and warn them."

"I see. It was not Taral who told you, then." His voice dripped with disbelief.

"It was Taral who triggered the Vision when he brushed past me in the Chamber," I lied, "but he said nothing to me directly, nor I to him. I Saw what had been ordered, and I came straight here."

Fazak's ear dipped – just a whisker – in acknowledgement, and he looked across at Murgo, who still stood in the entrance to Doran's shelter. "In that case, I suggest you return to your nest," he said. "There's nothing more for you to do here."

No doubt he was right, but I wasn't about to flap back to the plateau on Fazak's say-so. "Actually—" I gave him a nod of dismissal, as though I had control of the conversation "—I have friends to visit."

And with that, I turned my back on him, and stalked away to find Doran.

It was dark when I left the shelters. The wind had dropped and a sea-mist had crept across the peninsula, blanketing the hides in damp droplets and making take-off from the ground a wet, laborious effort. The *Spirax* and plateau reared out of the grey swirls, seeming to rest on the mist like some huge beast on a sea of cloud. As I gained height, the Great Spiral shimmered over my head, and as I circled upward, I sent my prayers toward it: *By the lights of our ancestors, show Kalis he's mistaken.*

There was no wind, even at the top of the mesa, and this time – without an audience to witness it – I managed a perfect landing. The odour of stale nest and boiled herbs assailed my nose when I opened my dwelling door, and I sighed with relief that I was home. A moment later, my mood fell like a tumbling boulder as I realised what I would be leaving behind if I was to travel with the wingless. Closing the door against the chill night air, I wasted no time in banking up the fire in my hearth and putting a pot of water on to boil for tea.

In the stillness and warmth, I brushed droplets of icy water from my tunic, and stood for a while, staring into the flames that licked the base of the pot, while I contemplated what it would mean for me to pack up and go. Did I have the courage to fly from the safety and comfort of my dwelling, knowing I might never return? And what about those I left behind? The drax would have no Fate-seer, no-one to perform the sacred rituals or pray over the dead.

"Am I doing the right thing, Vizan," I murmured, "is this what you would do?"

The water in the pot was bubbling and I threw in some avalox leaves to steep. Then I sat on my stool near the fire, closed my eyes, and spiralled my paw across the front of my tunic, seeking guidance. My vision in the Chamber had shown me that I was destined to travel with the wingless, but did they need me right now? Perhaps I might postpone my own departure for a short time, fly after them when the freeze was done?

I opened my eyes. No revelation had arrived from the Spiral, no further Vision had come, but I already knew the answer: I could not delay. Dru's future was set, and I must fly alongside him. The rest of the wingless would need help too, and there was no-one else willing or able or allowed to give it.

I didn't doubt that Kalis – or, rather, Fazak – would happily appoint another Fate-seer in my place. It wouldn't matter that they didn't have the Sight: all they'd need to do was repeat well-known rituals and whatever words Fazak put in their mouths.

The tea was ready. I poured it into a beaker and sipped at it, savouring every drop. Then I stood, shook out my fur, and turned to the workbench to begin to sort out what I would need for the journey.

Twenty

My first attempt to decide what I needed produced enough belongings to fill three carry-pouches, and it took half the night to whittle them down to the absolute minimum. Even then, I had to sacrifice a haunch of dried meat for the bag of spirelles that my predecessors had collected. The shells couldn't be eaten or worn, but instinct said that they would ultimately be more useful than a few mouthfuls of meat, and Vizan had taught me to listen to my instincts.

With a beaker, pans, a bowl, and a ladle tied to the outer straps, plus blankets, two of my old blue tunics (one fur-lined, the other for the warm season) and the shells, medicine jars, bags of herbs, and a small pot of beans stuffed inside it, the carry-pouch was almost as heavy as Dru had been on our last flight together. When at last I was satisfied that I'd packed as many useful items as possible, I pushed the pouch under the table and surrounded it with stools, then I settled into my nest for one last comfortable doze.

It was still dark when I woke, though a glance through the see-shell told me that it was past sunrise. Clouds as grey and threatening as a clenched paw had moved in overnight, and as I put my waste-bucket outside for collection, a feeble drizzle of sleet dampened my snout. At least there was no sign of lightning-storms and it was too cold for floaters. Back inside, I banked up the fire and brewed tea, washed, groomed, and pulled on my warmest black tunic – all the while sending up prayers to the Spiral that Kalis would reverse his decision. All the same, I made sure I had a large jar of salve and a basket of canox tincture ready in a carry-pouch when Morel knocked on the door to tell me it was time.

"It's going to snow," he said, sniffing the air as we made our way to the rim of the plateau to take off. "Those poor groundlings, how ever will they cope?"

He stepped back from the take-off point as I spread my wings and I looked over my shoulder to check what his problem might be. "Aren't you coming?"

"Certainly not! Kalis sent me to make sure you didn't miss anything, but he said nothing to me about watching it myself."

He scurried off and all I could do was call after him, "I hope their howls reach you, and stay with you, Morel."

I landed near the central shelter where all the excitement had taken place the previous evening. Already, several guardflight were unfastening the pegs and beginning the task of dismantling the structure. Most of the other shelters had already been taken down, the hides rolled neatly and stacked in a pile at the base of the Tusk. The wingless were huddled together in the lee of the great rock-stack, getting what shelter they could from the elements. Even without the circle of guardflight around them, I doubt they would have strayed very far, and I wondered why Taral had placed so many of the red-tuniced drax around younglings who posed no threat.

Then I saw that the females, who had been herded into nine protesting groups where their shelters had stood, were guarded by half-grown drax clad in the maroon-and-blue tunics of Fazak's new Elite Guard.

As I folded my wings, Taral appeared at my wingtip, his mane on end and his tail swishing. "It seems Kalis doesn't trust me to carry out his orders," he said, glaring in the direction of Murgo. The half-grown was flying over the groups of females, swooping low over their heads as he banged two heavy stones together in a rhythm of casual menace. Taral turned his back on him, his voice a growl that I strained to hear over the frightened howls of the females. "Don't mistake me," he said. "I'm glad I won't have to ask my guardflight to break all those wings, but for Kalis to set up the Elite and put a half-grown in charge? Then to have them do my job..." His lips peeled back from his teeth as he spoke, and I was glad that his anger was not directed at me. "It's an insult."

I was alarmed at the strength of the scent issuing from him. "You're not going to challenge him, are you?" Taral was a head taller than me, and a good deal stronger, but Kalis was half-a-head taller again, and kept his claws sharp and his teeth sharper. If he was challenged – even by Taral – there would only be one outcome.

Taral shook his head. "That was my first instinct, but now's not the time." His voice was a low growl and he kicked hard at a ridge of snow, dislodging a frozen wedge and sending it skimming across the icy ground. "Kalis is two cycles older than me," he muttered, "and he'll get old and slow before I do. When he does..."

The volume of the howls and cries behind us increased, and the scent of terror and pain made us stop and turn. Murgo had stopped his incessant stone-clashing and had moved in on the group of females nearest to us to start putting the rocks to a more painful use. One by one, the females were pushed away from the group, each with a wing trailing over the uneven ground, each of them yowling with pain.

They headed toward the Tusk and their younglings, and I hefted the jar and basket I'd brought. "I must go and help tend to them," I said. "If you've no objection?"

"Of course not. Best not let Murgo see what you're doing, though."

I tried to lighten the mood. "He's just a half-grown." I waved a paw dismissively. "Even I could knock him over."

"Ah." Taral glanced up at the *Spirax*. "But how would you manage after he'd flapped off to Kalis to bleat about how you'd treated an Elite Guard?"

I acknowledged the truth of that with a dip of an ear and a nod. In the shadow of the Tusk, the younglings joined their howls to their mothers' and the reek of agony was palpable. As I started toward them, Taral kept pace with me, our claws scratching for grip on the rutted ice. The wind had a fresh, untainted smell to it that spoke of the icy southern wastes, and I felt it tug at my cold-season fur as though trying to cut bites from it. Beyond the wingless, three drax in patchwork tunics stood watching: fable-spinners, come to witness events so that the story might be passed on to future generations. I looked for Swalo and flicked an ear to acknowledge him. He'd been sympathetic about the wingless when I'd spoken to him moons ago, but what sort of tale would be told while Kalis and Fazak had ears to listen?

"I see the weather has kept the spectators to a minimum."

Taral dipped an ear and nodded. "I brought so many guardflight because I thought we might have trouble between those who sympathise with the wingless and those who are glad to see them gone." His mane writhed as the wind howled about us, and he rubbed his paws together in what I knew would be a futile attempt to warm them. "But it looks like any drax who does not need to venture outside has stayed at home."

I looked around, noting that even some of the faces I had expected to see were not there. "I can understand why Miyak and Rysel didn't come, but what about Rewsa's nest-mate? And Peren? I thought they at least would have come to say their goodbyes."

"Peren was here earlier," said Taral. "He said he didn't want to wait around to see Jonel have a wing damaged. A few others came in the night. As for Miyak, haven't you heard?"

"Heard what?"

We had reached the circle of guardflight surrounding the wingless, and Taral nodded to the nearest pair that I should be allowed through. He waited till they were behind us before he answered my question: "He has a new nest-mate."

"Already? Could he not have waited until Doran and Cavel have left before moving on to next season's choice? Who is she anyway?"

Taral flicked his ear, his tail swishing with annoyance. "Morla."

I halted where I stood. "*Morla*? Fazak's eldest?" Snatches of my conversation with Doran, moons ago, edged across my memory: "*Morla came by...had to fetch more leaves to dry for the archives before the freeze set in, she said...*"

Ahead of us, Limar made her way across the open space between the younglings and the corralled females, her broken wing trailing. I wondered again why Limar was being punished. She didn't even have a youngling, she was...

Like the sun emerging from cloud, my thoughts coalesced and I finally understood the extent of Fazak's ambition. "Fazak wants Morla to produce a proving-egg," I said, and saw from the lay of Taral's ears that he had just reached the same conclusion.

"He wants her to become Kalis' nest-mate," he said.

We finished the thought together: "He wants to be grandsire to a Prime."

The ground near the Tusk was free of ice, slushy and yielding where it had been trampled. I stamped my feet down hard, partly to warm them, partly with frustration that there was nothing we could do about it. There were few living females with winged offspring for Kalis to choose from, so of course he would likely wait until the younger ones had hatched a winged nestling. And of course Fazak would advance Morla to the top of the list of candidates. A cycle and a half, two cycles at most, and Fazak would have put his family in the *Spirax*...

Taral rubbed his whiskers. "We can't worry about that now," he said, pointing his snout toward one of the howling figures with a trailing wing. "There are more immediate problems to deal with."

"Doran!" I hurried across to her as fast as I could, though the basket and jar I carried almost unbalanced me. "Here – I've brought salves to help with the pain."

"Doran-muz!" Cavel reached her before I did, and sensing that she was in pain, began to lick one of her paws in a gesture of comfort and sympathy. Doran clutched my shoulder as I bent to set down my basket and her fingers gripped tight enough to hurt even through my fur. She was whimpering with pain.

Dru bounded up as I lowered the basket to the ground, and he immediately began to sniff at it. "Medicine?" he asked, as I lifted the lid off the jar of salve.

"Yes," I said. I looked around at the growing crowd of whimpering females. "Dru, you can help. Go and find the Healers – the ones wearing green-and-black checks like Doran – and bring them here. I'll see to them first, then they can help with the others."

Dru flicked an ear and bounded off, his head turning left and right as he looked about. Taral, I saw, had retreated to stand with the circle of guardflight, and I supposed that that was just as well: there was nothing he could do save get in the way.

I set to work, starting with Doran: straighten the broken struts, smear on the salve, add a canox leaf to bind it, pray to the Spiral for a swift healing. By the time I'd helped my friend, Galyn had made her way over to me, and I noticed that two more healers were also moving through the knots of keening drax in my direction. After that, all I was conscious of was the feel of broken wings in my paws, the sticky salve, the scent of the canox, as female after female, broken wing after broken wing, arrived beside me.

"We should have fought back," muttered Shaya, as I smeared salve onto her wing. The wounds that she'd suffered two nights before had been reopened, and a strut newly broken: she would not be in a fit state to fight anyone or anything for some time. "We've got spears, we've got teeth—"

"Murgo and his cronies have teeth too," I reminded her, "and even I know that an arrow from a bow will fly further than a thrown spear."

She winced under my paw and snapped at me to be more careful. "Didn't Vizan teach you anything?"

"Not nearly enough," I said, dipping an ear in apology, "though I did learn that a broken wing will heal more quickly if it isn't flapped. Make sure you keep it folded for now."

As the healers and I moved through the growing crowd of wounded females, Murgo finally realised what was happening, and stormed over in a flurry of angry wingbeats. "I did not give permission for any healing to be done." His ears were up, his wings still half-unfolded.

"I didn't ask permission." I smeared my fingers around the inside of the jar, which was now almost empty, and applied the salve to Limar's wing. "A Fate-seer does not need permission to heal anyone. It is a part of what we do – what we have always done." Around us, the howls of pain were giving way to low grunts and occasional hisses, as the healers did their work. I could smell the relief from Rewsa to my left as Galyn bound her wing, and I felt Limar relax under my paw as I daubed the salve across her broken struts, then pressed a healing leaf into place. I heard Murgo growl and turned to face him, only to find that Taral had already moved from the encircling guardflight to confront him.

"What were *your* orders, Murgo?" Taral stood in front of the younger male, his stance and his ears rigid with anger, though his wings were folded. As he drew himself upright, emphasising the difference in their heights and maturity, the message was clear: Murgo was not worth the effort of a traditional challenge. "Well?"

For a beat, it looked as though Murgo would be stupid enough to extend his wings and snarl. Had he done so, Taral would doubtless have ripped his throat out, but after a long pause, while his wings juddered with indecision, Murgo realised that juvenile bravado would not bring him much glory. He folded them flat, with ill grace, and spoke through his teeth: "I was told to break the wings of the females who had hatched these wingless abominations."

"And you have done so," said Taral. "Now, are you and your Elite Guards going to help the guardflight net them all across the river?"

Murgo wrinkled his snout and waved a dismissive paw. "Certainly not. Our remit is to take care of the *Spirax* mesa and the peninsula as far as the boundary with the Expanse. I would not want you to complain that we were overstepping our bounds."

Taral opened his mouth, possibly to retort that the mere existence of the Elite overstepped a number of bounds – but fortunately, perhaps, he was interrupted by one of Murgo's guards. Beneath the maroon-and-blue tunic that flapped untidily in the breeze, I recognised Ordek, the half-grown who had been with Murgo on the day Dru had spoiled their sport with Cavel. "That's everyone, Murgo. Except for Varna."

Murgo nodded. "She will be here shortly. Kalis asked me to send two Elite to escort her down here. I would have expected them back by now…" He looked up in the direction of the plateau. "Ah! Here they come."

Far above us, two drax in Elite Guard tunics took off from the mesa and turned in unison to catch the wind. There was something between them, and at first, half-blinded by the sleet, I thought it was Varna taking flight. Then I realised that the third figure had not spread any wings. "What is that?" I said, though my stomachs lurched as I realised I already knew the answer.

"A net," said Taral. "It looks as though Varna didn't come willingly."

"She's certainly setting up a howl about it," said Rewsa, flattening her ears as Varna's cries carried to us on the breeze, growing louder as the net and its carriers descended toward us.

Not until the net had been grounded and the occupant released did we understand why Varna had had to be carried, and the reason for her constant howling. Her wings had not been temporarily damaged, as had been the case with the other females around us.

They had been removed.

Twenty-one

"I swear by the lights – I had no idea what Kalis intended to do." The way that Taral's mane stood on end told me that he spoke true: he looked and smelled as shocked as I felt. "If he'd spoken of it, I would have suggested he consulted the Council first. It's an outrage!"

I wasn't sure whether he meant the de-winging itself, or the fact that Kalis had not involved the council or the guardflight, but it didn't matter now. It was done.

Murgo and his Elite Guards, having carried out their brutal task, had wasted no time in returning to the plateau, and I wondered where they were all going to dwell. It was clear they must have gathered in the *Spirax* to put on their new tunics, and without a cluster of their own, they would have to be housed with the heralds and cooks...

The tables. The ceremonial tables in the Feasting Hall that I had noticed when I last went to the *Spirax*. That was why they'd been taken out of storage – to make room for the Elite Guard to live. They must have flown up there in ones and twos, just before the guardflight patrols changed each day. It must have taken days for them to assemble – and their weapons had doubtless been smuggled in by Sifan, Hapak, and Fazak, who the guardflight were used to seeing on the plateau.

No wonder Morel had been so reluctant to answer my questions!

I returned my attention to Varna, who stood howling in the lee of the Tusk. Dru bounded across to her and raised his snout to rub noses in greeting, but she ignored him. He tried licking her paws instead, but still she didn't respond. "Galyn, would you bring some salve?" Picking up the basket of leaves, I flattened my ears against Varna's deafening yips and yowls, and went across to examine the stumps where her wings had been.

The pinions had been sawn cleanly, though the muscles and skin around the bone were raw and bleeding. "Hold still, Varna, this will hurt." While Galyn held the jar, I dabbed on salve and pressed a leaf against each stump. It didn't take much imagination to see that, exposed as they were, the leaves and salve would not withstand the weather for long. "Dru, see if you can find a small square of seatach skin," I said, as Varna's howls subsided to a whimper. "If I can secure it in place, it will protect the poultice from this sleet."

He scampered off in Doran's direction and I moved around to stand in front of Varna, intending to give her a comforting lick. "I'm sorry," I said. "If I had known—"

"You would have challenged Kalis would you?" she snapped, her teeth missing my snout by a claw-width. "Taken the blade from him?"

I took a step back, alarmed that her anger should be directed at me. "I would have reasoned with him, Varna," I said, setting my ears to their most contrite. "Pointed out that—"

"We have tried 'reason'," she spat. "You, Taral, Peren, Shaya – you all sat in the Council meetings, angled your wings so as not to cause offence, and made your arguments. It has not made one whisker of difference, except to delay our exile. We would have done better to leave when the last egg hatched, before the freeze started. See where your 'reason' has brought us!"

She was being unfair, but given that she was badly wounded and in pain, her hurt and anger were understandable. Behind her, Galyn put the lid on the jar of salve and edged away.

Dru returned just then with a corner of seatach hide whose ragged edges spoke of being cut roughly from a bigger piece.

"That is perfect, Dru, thank you."

With twine from my pocket, I secured the hide around the poultice. As I pulled it tight, and offered a prayer to the Spiral that it would hold secure, Taral stepped across and I noticed with a start that he had taken his bow from his shoulder, carrying it in a semi-defensive mode.

"It's time," he said, and pointed his snout up at the plateau.

On the balcony outside the Audience Chamber, Kalis' white tunic was just discernible through the sleet.

"So he came to watch," I said. As I spoke, another figure moved onto the balcony and through the damp haze I caught a glimpse of bright green behind the white. "Fazak." Just saying the name made me choke. "I might have known."

"The guardflight will net you all across the river, and escort you for the first day of your journey." Taral raised his voice over the noise of the wind, while the wingless and lamed gathered up their carry-pouches and back-packs. "They will make sure there is no trouble from the anti-wingless faction."

"They are all warm in their dwellings," said Doran. She had put on a second cold-season tunic over the first, and wore lined foot-covers, but the fur on her snout was so damp it barely stirred in the wind and I saw her shiver as an icy gust almost knocked us off our feet. "Your guardflight will manage to fly in this? Are you sure you wouldn't all rather wait for a warmer day?"

Taral scratched his snout and brushed droplets of melted snow from his whiskers. "If I am not seen to be enforcing Kalis' orders, I will lose *my* wings," he said. "You know that. I sympathise, Doran, but I have no wish to join you in a march to exile."

"A march to death you mean." Like the wind that swept her words away, Doran's voice had a caustic edge. "We are skirting the Deadlands, crossing the Ambit, and going to the Forest. If any of us reach it, what hope will we have in there?"

"There must be hope, Doran." I pointed toward Dru, who was pulling at Varna's paws, still trying to get some sort of response from her. "The Vision was clear, and if Dru is destined to survive and grow, and defeat the Koth, then there must be drax to help and guide him. We all must believe that."

I took her cold paws in my own and pressed my snout against hers. This was supposed to be a farewell forever, and all those looking on had to believe it, but I was close enough now to speak for Doran's ears alone: "I will join you all as soon as I can. Say nothing to the others."

I heard her gasp, felt her paws tighten on my fingers, but she had sense enough not to give any outward sign to those watching.

I gave her paws a final squeeze and loosened my grip, then spiralled a paw in the air. "May the Spiral watch over you," I said.

Doran's grunt was not one of devout conviction, but she dipped her head in acknowledgement, and signalled to Cavel to come over for a blessing. Then, as they moved toward the Guardflight and their waiting nets, she gave a howl. It was not the howl of farewell I expected; it was a death-howl, with the sort of desolate edge I had not heard since Vizan was taken to his last nest. Everyone in the group followed suit, first filing past me for a blessing, then beginning a howl as they moved over the ice toward the nets. The baying rebounded from the cliffs and set up a mournful reverberation that made my fur stand on end.

"Kalis won't like that." Taral still stood close by, Jisco and Veret flanking his wingtips. Each of them held a wad of blank record-leaves, and scratched names on them as the females passed – an accounting for the archive, something else for Fazak to gloat over.

I glanced upward, just in time to see the figure in the white tunic retreat from the balcony. Fazak lingered a moment longer, then he too disappeared inside. I doubted that the Audience Chambers' shutters would keep the noise out, and wondered how far inside the *Spirax* the din would still be audible. I raised my voice to a shout to make sure Taral could hear me: "Are you not going to order your guards to stop it?"

In answer, Taral set his ears and wings to full mourning. Then, raising his head into the wind, he joined his howls to theirs.

Twenty-two

"What is it you want?"

Kalis' begrudging growl was accompanied by flicking ears and stiffened wings as he stood on the Audience Chamber dais and gazed down at me. Only a couple of torches burned in the wall-sconces and the fire was unlit. The Council table stood empty in the middle of the room and the throne-stool that Varna had occupied until recently had been removed – presumably until Kalis selected a new nest-mate from the names that the Council proposed.

At least there was no sign of Fazak, for which I heartily thanked the Spiral. He must have slithered back to his dwelling or his Records, once he had made sure the wingless were on their way. Perhaps even he found Kalis' foul mood hard to bear.

"I seek permission to fly to the Dream-cave, Lord," I said, dipping a bow, and trying to ignore the smell of contempt that Kalis exuded. "The future that was foreseen must be revisited."

"You mean 'revised'," said Kalis. His tail swished, his ears flicked back and forth, and I realised with a shock that he had utterly lost faith in the Visions. I had never heard of such a thing happening before, not even in legend, but here was our Prime, all but sneering at my wish to carry out my allotted task.

It took me several heartbeats to gather sufficient wits to reply. "I cannot say whether the Vision will change, Lord," I said. "The Dream-smoke will provide the answer, I cannot."

"Then let us hope it provides a more believable answer than it did the last time."

"It may take several days," I said. "The future has been…unsettled. Disturbed. It may take time for the Vision to clear."

The claws of his feet drummed on the platform and he waved a paw. It was obvious he didn't care how long I might take. "Go," he said. "Come back when you have something constructive to tell me."

I dipped another bow and scurried out, almost knocking over Morel as I hurried through the door. He was right outside and it was obvious he had been straining to hear what was said, but at my appearance he brushed at his tunic and hoisted the torch he was carrying as though he had merely been waiting to escort me outside.

Neither of us spoke as we followed the spiralling corridor down and around the *Spirax* interior, but as we reached the entrance, Morel paused and looked around to make sure there was no-one within listening distance. "Do you honestly believe that the Dream-smoke will show you a different Vision?" he asked. "Vizan saw it too. How could you both be mistaken?"

I shook my head, lifting one shoulder to indicate my own bafflement. "It will be as the Spiral wills," I said.

For once, though, I already knew the answer: Visions seen in the Dream-smoke had never been wrong. Why should this one be any different?

It felt strange, looking around my dwelling for the last time. There was so much I had to leave behind: the comfortable nest, the big cooking pot that Vizan had inherited from *his* teacher, all the furniture, the spare beakers, most of the bowls. Several tunics hung behind the door, and I ran a paw over the soft cloth of the ceremonial one that I had worn so little – and so disastrously.

The badge of office hung next to the tunic; on a whim, I plucked it from its hook and pinned it to my tunic. There was no other Fate-seer to claim it, and the thought of what Fazak might do if he found it made me determined to bear its extra weight.

My carry-pouch was stuffed to the brim and beyond, so heavy I had to rest it on the table while I tightened the straps around my shoulders. The blob of branmeal still stained the work surface and I rubbed at it with a claw, then stepped back, supporting the weight of the pouch with my paws. It was just as well that I intended to fly low – I would have difficulty gaining any height at all! Turning in a slow circle, I breathed in the scents of the half-burned candles, the dying embers of the fire in the hearth, the herbs that still hung from the hooks beneath the shelves. My nest, stale and untidy, but warm and safe, tempted me one last time to forget my foolish plan and remain where I was. But I thought of Dru and Doran, of Galyn, Shaya, and Rewsa, and their despair as they had stepped into the nets with their younglings. Kalis had no use for me, he'd made that clear: so be it.

When I opened the door, I almost changed my mind. The night sky matched the black of my tunic – no lights shone through the clouds, not even the moon – and a sniff of the wind told me that more snow would be falling before long. There was a faint smell of self-importance in the air too, and I realised it came from the Elite Guard who now circled the *Spirax* instead of the guardflight. I would need to be careful that they didn't catch sight or smell of me as I left. I had Kalis' permission to fly to the Dream-cave, but a pouch full of belongings would take some explaining.

Before I stepped over the threshold, I listened warily, and sniffed the breeze again. The slap of wingbeats cut the air to the north and the south. I listened while both flyers headed toward the *Spirax*, then waited as they circled back. It was cold standing on the step, but by keeping my wings against the door I was at least sheltered from the worst of the wind, while my tunic would make me difficult to see even with night-vision. As the sentries' flight-paths crossed once more, on the seaward side of the plateau, I sniffed the air again: Murgo and Ordek. Two half-growns I would not have entrusted with a bent stick, let alone a bow and arrows, yet there they were, circling the plateau on a current of conceit. What under the Spiral did they think to achieve?

The wingbeats receded, circling back around toward the west. I pressed a paw against the smoothed bark of the dwelling door, and for a heartbeat I fought the temptation to push it open and go back inside. But if I did that...I would have to face Fazak in the morning – and the day after that – and the day after that – all the while knowing that Kalis placed no value on anything I said.

No. I was not needed. Not on the plateau. Not in the *Spirax*. Not anymore. I would miss Taral – the angle of his snout, his curly mane, his wisdom, his scent, his reassuring presence. Would he agree with my decision? Would he want to come too? Perhaps I could...

I squashed the thought of asking him almost before it could form. He was Guardflight. He was sworn to protect the entire Expanse, not just the Prime. And in any case, why would he want to leave everything behind to join me and a gaggle of howling females on a journey to nowhere?

With a sigh, I dropped my paw from the door, turned, and hurried to the seaward edge of the plateau to take off.

I didn't look back.

The entrance to the Dream-cave was colder and damper than it had been on my visit with Dru, but once through the passageway and into the Cave itself, the atmosphere was little changed. The veins of silver in the rock winked and sparked as they caught the light from my torch and threw it back, and for a time I stood and admired its beauty, while I breathed in the comforting smell of the Dream-plants. For the first time in days I felt that I was in the right place, doing the right thing.

I sniffed about for the best Dream-plants and gathered a pawful onto the rock ready to ignite.

"Lights guide me," I murmured, as I sat down on the damp sand beside the rock. "Great Spiral, show me what will be."

I placed my torch on the rock, and as the Dream-plants flared and began to smoke, I closed my eyes, listened to the whisper of the sea against the beach beyond the cave, and breathed in the distinctive fungal smell...

Smoke swirled, or was it cloud? Arrows flew – the knife from the Audience Chamber wall spun past me, its blade bloodied – a huge drax with black fur and a grey mane snarled – water roiled and crashed – a wingless Drax with a white mane lifted a fallen Koth banner...

When my eyes opened, I was lying on my side and the torch was guttering. I sat up, rubbing my snout as I tried to make sense of my Visions, and allowed the torch to go out. The taste of the Dream-smoke lingered in my throat as I sat there in the dark, reflecting on what I had Seen. One thing was clear: the Vision of Dru defeating the Koth had not changed. His exile to the Forest was part of his destiny, not the end of it. I could make little sense of the other scenes I'd glimpsed, though I recognised the blood-covered knife as the one I'd Seen on the first occasion I had acted as Fate-seer. That was little more than six moons ago, though in some ways it felt as though cycles had passed, for so much had happened since then. I was sure now though that the knife was part of the future, not a glimpse of the past as Kalis had insisted. The rushing water, the arrows...they were important, otherwise the Great Spiral would not have shown them to me, but I couldn't imagine how such things might affect the lives of wingless exiles.

But it was the drax with the pale grey mane who lingered in my memory, for try as I might, I couldn't shake the belief that it was Kalon – Kalis' shell-brother. Kalon who had died, several cycles past, in a skirmish with the Koth.

At least, that was what we had always been told.

Yet, if he was dead...why was I Seeing him in a Vision of the future?

The thud and hiss of water on rock drew me back to the present, and I adjusted my eyes to find my way through to the entrance cavern. As I squeezed through the passage, sea water rushed over my feet and retreated – the tide was coming in.

Hurriedly, I gathered up my carry-pouch – damp now at the bottom – and waited until the next wave had drawn back from the cave, then scrambled down to the rocks under the entrance and glided to the sand, above the high-tide mark. Daylight. The second day of exile for the wingless and their dams. How would they be faring as they struggled along the shoreline? At least the wind had dropped and the threatened snow was not yet falling. A chill dampness hung in the air, undaunted by the frail sun which dyed the clouds crimson as it rose from the ocean.

For me, shelter, such as it was, lay between the Cleft Rocks, and after taking a moment to gather some of the scrubby sea-reeds from the dunes to the south, I flew over the outcrop, and landed beside the moss-covered cliff-face which Dru had explored the last time I'd been here. Sea-vines, bare of foliage and grey with salt, clung to the sand, and I snapped a few branches to add to the reeds. I set them down between two massive boulders that had fallen from the bluff in some long-ago storm and coaxed a flame from them before filling my bowl at the water's edge. Sitting between the fallen rocks with the cliffs at my back and a blanket wrapped around me, I set the bowl to heat on the fire, raised my fur against the damp, and settled down to wait.

I dozed, and when I woke, the water had boiled half away. I moved on cramped legs, stamping my feet as I staggered to the tideline to get more. Once it had reheated, I pulled a bundle of kestox leaves from my carry-pouch, dropped them into the bowl, and used the blade of my knife to stir them. While they steeped, I dug through my pouch to find a reflector, a blue tunic, and a meat pattie. The latter I placed in the flames to cook, while I balanced the reflector against a boulder. I poked the kestox again with the blade, which came out sticky. It was ready.

Carefully, I pulled the bowl from the fire and let it cool – which didn't take long in the chill, damp air. I lifted out one of the leaves, crushed it, and rubbed it against the fur on my arm, turning it from its normal nondescript mid-brown to a deep russet. Limb by limb, leaf by leaf, I changed the colour of my coat, finishing the effect by rubbing a couple of leaves over my snout and ears. When I looked in the reflector to check that I'd coated my head evenly, I was a stranger even to my own eyes.

The pattie had burned a little, but I scratched off the worst of the blackened edges and wolfed it down. When had I last eaten? More importantly, when might I next eat? Only the thought of having to eke out supplies for the next moon – and perhaps beyond – prevented me from cooking a second pattie. There would be no fish on the menu if the storms were bad – the waves would be too high, the fish too far from land, too far below the surface. Besides, until all those damaged wings healed, I would be the one female in the group who was capable of flying and I mustn't draw attention to myself by fishing. Even if the guardflight didn't watch us, the Elite Guard surely would. It would be many days – ninedays perhaps – before we had travelled too far for them to pick out individuals or see what we were doing.

The tide had reached its height. Waves lapped at the base of the boulder to my right, and I sluiced out the dye from the bowl and rubbed it with the fine dry sand that lay beyond the reach of the waves. The first few meals I ate from it would doubtless taste a little odd, but every item I now had with me was too precious to use only once.

Lastly, there was my tunic. There was no point dyeing my fur to disguise myself if I then continued to wear the distinctive black of the Fate-seer, but still it was a wrench to take off the colour I had worn for the past six moons, the colour I alone was entitled to put on.

It was cold, too, despite my thick fur and the shelter the cliffs provided. Hastily, I scrambled into the fur-lined blue tunic I would have worn if I had not developed the Sight. What would my life have been like, I wondered, if the Visions hadn't come and I had been left to fly and trade like my sire and dam before me? I was old enough to have hatched an egg of my own. Would I have been thanking the Spiral for a normal youngling, or been one of the wretched females netted over the river?

As I rolled up the discarded tunic, the badge of office pressed hard against my paw. I unpinned it from the cloth, held it against my chest where the fur was thinner, and ran my fingers across the spiral relief that decorated it. This, even more than the colour of my tunic, denoted who I was and reminded me of my purpose. I couldn't bring myself to put it in the carry-pouch with the black tunic. Instead, I pinned it inside the high neck of the pale blue tunic and offered a brief prayer to the Spiral to seek forgiveness for the deceit.

There was nothing left to do then but wait until dark.

The cooking pots strapped to the outside of the carry-pouch clanked together as I ran along the wet sand, flapping my wings to catch the breeze. The storm that had been threatening for two days had finally broken over the mountains and lightning flickered on the southern horizon. There would be gales, avalanches, and falling rocks where the tempest raged, but for the moment, the clouds above me held nothing but sleet, which beat against my snout and chilled my ears as I flew higher. Even without the lights of the moon or the Spiral, it was easy to see my way. All I had to do was follow the coast beneath me, its white coating of ice and snow providing a stark contrast with the deep black of the sea.

"Am I doing the right thing, Vizan?" I murmured. "Is this what you would do?"

I didn't expect an answer. I was still trying to process what I had Seen in the Dreamsmoke – and, I suppose, still trying to reassure myself that I'd made the right decision. But as I spoke, the clouds overhead thinned and parted, and I glimpsed the centre of the Great Spiral watching over me, its lights making the snow and ice beneath me brighten and glisten. As the clouds moved, so the bright patch on the snow moved with them, and I checked my course and circled about, watching the track of that single luminous spot as it raced northward – from the Cleft Rocks, across the Deadlands, over the Ambit, and onward toward the Forest itself.

The clouds drifted together again and the brightness vanished. Hovering, I spiralled a paw across my tunic and breathed a prayer of thanks. I was following the right course. The Great Spiral itself had shown me the way.

229

To the south, the Manybend estuary cut through the snow; beyond it, the *Spirax* and the mesa it stood on formed a single black silhouette against the night sky. On a triangle of flat land to the north of the river, nines of flames showed me where the exiles had made camp.

I checked my course, increased my wingbeats, and flew into the wind to join them.

END OF VOLUME ONE

Acknowledgements

Sincere thanks to everyone at Mirror World for pulling 'Unreachable Skies' from their submissions box and taking it on so enthusiastically. I'm especially grateful to Robert Dowsett for the thorough line edits, and to Justine Alley Dowsett for not only designing the striking cover but also for answering my "first time novelist" questions so patiently.

To my family and friends: thank you one and all for your patience and support over the years while I scribbled my stories – your encouragement and feedback enabled me to persist with my writing and, eventually, to dare to submit it to competitions, anthologies and publishers. Special thanks go to Annie Smith for the initial read-through of my manuscript; Patrick Masters for the writerly talks in the University post-room; and of course to James Swallow for providing the fantastic cover quote.

About the Author

Brought up in Staffordshire, England, **Karen McCreedy** now lives in West Sussex and recently retired from the University of Chichester.

She has written articles on films and British history for a number of British magazines including 'Yours', 'Classic Television', and 'Best of British'. In 2009, her essay on *'British Propaganda Films of the Second World War'* was published in *'Under Fire: A Century of War Movies'* (Ian Allen Publishing).

She has also written a number of online articles and reviews for The Geek Girl Project (www.geekgirlproject.com), as their British correspondent.

Karen has had short stories published in anthologies by Fiction Brigade (2012, e-book), Zharmae Publishing *('RealLies'*, 2013), Audio Arcadia (*'On Another Plane'*, 2015), Luna Station Publishing (*'Luna Station Quarterly'* December 2015), Horrified Press *('Killer*

Tracks' and *'Waiting'*, both 2015; and *'Crossroads'*, 2016), and Reflex Fiction (*'Voicemail'*, published online 2017). She also won second prize in Writers' News magazine's 'Comeuppance' competition in 2014 with her short story *'Hero'*.

'Unreachable Skies' is her first novel.

You can follow Karen on Twitter @McKaren_Writer, or check out her website at www.karenmccreedy.com

To learn more about our authors and their current projects visit: www.mirrorworldpublishing.com or follow @MirrorWorldPub or like us at www.facebook.com/mirrorworldpublishing

Why 'Mirror World'?

We publish escapism fiction for all ages. Our novels are imaginative and character-driven and our goal is to give our readers a glimpse into other worlds, times, and versions of reality that parallel our own, giving them an experience they can't get anywhere else!

We offer free delivery within Windsor-Essex,Ontario, an all-you-can-read membership program, blind-dates with books, and you can find our novels in our online store, or from your favorite major book retailer.

To learn more about our authors and our current projects visit: www.mirrorworldpublishing.com, follow @MirrorWorldPub or like us at www.facebook.com/mirrorworldpublishing

Or keep reading for a sneak peek of:

Shelf Life

By

Rob Gregson

1. Death and Taxis

Knock, knock.

A gloved knuckle struck the café window. It was the merest tap, but coming so unexpectedly and so close to her ear, it might as well have been an air horn. Finn's wrist responded with a jolt that sent a hot slop of cappuccino leaping for the sanctuary of her lap.

"Dah!" Snatching up a napkin, she pressed it to her jeans, glancing aside as it began its transformation from a pristine white to a sad and soggy beige.

Outside, a tall figure in a smart winter coat waved a greeting. It was directed at Chrissie, her sister. The attentions of sane, attractive, eligible men always were.

"Is that Tony?" Across the table, her mum gave Chrissie a nudge.

"Yup. That's him." A grin lit her face, though whether it was prompted by the new arrival or the spectacle of Finn's quietly steaming trousers, it was impossible to say. Perhaps a little of both. She turned her smile upon her friend. "You coming in?" Her question was partly spoken, partly mimed; her lips made comically exaggerated movements.

Tony shook his head, pointed along the street and mouthed something that was lost to the noise of the café. The place wasn't busy but the baristas were showing off their determinedly buoyant personalities to two punters at the till. By way of accompaniment, a Miles Davis album contended with the mechanical snarl of an ice blender.

"He's nice, Tony, don't you think?" Her mum watched the young man leave, seeing him off with a coquettish wave of her own.

Chrissie shrugged. "He's alright." She'd always had her pick of admirers. That they went out of their way to grin at her through coffee shop windows was something she took entirely for granted - like oxygen or perfect cheekbones.

Her mum adopted an expression of casual innocence. "He's from your office, isn't he?" She took a keen and constant interest in their respective romances, despite Finn's continuing failure to deliver anything worthy of discussion. Keeping her bookshop afloat was demanding all her focus right now and it left scant time for men. A brief smooch at a midsummer barbecue was about the sum of her contributions to that particular topic, and now it was approaching Christmas.

"He worked at the last place." Chrissie took a sip of her coolly unspilled espresso.

"Oh, I see." Her mum gave a rueful nod.

"Mm. He got a bit funny after I got the promotion."

Finn leaned back and dabbed at the damp, chocolate-stained patch on her leg. Here sat the two dearest people in the world, but the discussion was taking a predictable turn. They'd do their best to include her, but this was very much Chrissie's story.

Since leaving university, Finn had grown used to performing this minor supporting role. Her sister was only a year older but she led by far the more interesting life - all centred on a bright and breathless fast-track career in financial journalism. While Finn could only regale her family with tales of imaginative window displays and rising damp along the back wall, Chrissie's anecdotes were of foreign capitals, famous moguls and hastily-arranged interviews in airport departure lounges. Different lives for different temperaments.

Once, long enough ago for its title to have faded from memory, Finn had read a book about a man who seemed forever fated to live an unremarkable life. Some unspecified, epoch-making change was evidently unfolding right across his city but, at every turn, the most trivial events would always conspire to lead him the other way. She saw a lot of herself in that: an ill-fitting extra; a bit-part player in someone else's tale.

"So what about your new place, Chrissie?" Her mum's eyes twinkled. "Anyone interesting there?" They both knew what she was really asking; the desire for grandchildren was never far from her mind.

Chrissie smiled over her cup. "They're *all* interesting, Mum. I work with all sorts of amazing people."

Her mum pursed her lips and turned to Finn in mock annoyance. "Does she tell *you* anything, Cathy? She doesn't tell me a thing."

Finn shook her head. "Not a peep. I think she's secretly working for MI5."

"Nothing she does would surprise me." Her mum returned to her interrogation. "Come on, Chris. You fly off to all these places, you meet all these celebrities..."

"They're not celebrities. They're just business people."

"Oh, you know what I mean. You're hardly in the country these days. Your old mum just wants to know what's going on in your life."

Finn flashed her sister a conspiratorial smile and looked away. To her final breath, their mother would always proclaim an equal pride in both her daughters, but there was no hiding the fact that one of them prompted much more interesting conversation. Chrissie played things down, never pretended to be anything more than she was, but her burgeoning career and her growing absences from home inevitably put her centre stage whenever the three of them got together. By contrast, Finn was the dependable stay-at-home sister who saw her mum at least twice a week - and that was fine with her. She wouldn't swap places.

Now, as the talk turned to chance meetings in the snowy streets of Manhattan, Finn let her gaze drift through the window into the Great British drizzle beyond.

There was nothing wrong with staying here and being who she was. Her old university tutors might have frowned to see a promising student immersing herself in the vulgar world of retail, but literature was still a big part of her life. In an odd and unforeseen sort of way, she was still doing what she loved.

And who needed ice skating in Central Park when they could have all this? Finn stretched out her legs and did her best to luxuriate in the early Yuletide ambience. Who could say no to the warmth of good conversation? To the cheery parp of a passing black cab? To the Lowryesque figures who passed by the window, hunched and bent beneath their umbrellas?

Well, okay, maybe that was stretching things. Ideally, she'd be doing much better business in a smarter part of town - some place where legitimate customers outnumbered the drunks; where kebab-disposal wasn't regarded as the chief purpose of her shop doorway. For just a while at least, it might be nice to be somewhere interesting; somewhere a bit more encouraging of a passion for art and literature.

As though to illustrate her point, a white van mounted the kerb outside and juddered to a stop. A thin, dangerous-looking yob flung open the door and advanced with aggressive gestures towards someone just beyond her view.

"Cathy."

Finn looked back. Mother and sister were looking at her expectantly.

"Mm?"

"Take a photo, would you, sweetie?" Waggling her phone, her mum leaned towards Chrissie wearing the sort of smile one might instinctively associate with an abuse of medication. "She'll be off again at the end of the week; we've got to capture her while we still can."

"Oh, right. Yeah." Finn took the phone and fiddled with the zoom. "You ready? Say... *titular*."

The two of them grinned. "Titu..."

Bang.

The sound was abrupt and momentarily stunning; loud enough to rattle the window in its frame.

Outside, the young thug was pointing a pistol. It fired again.

"Shit!" Chrissie spun in her seat.

Finn tensed, barely processing what she was witnessing. As she did, her camera-phone produced a brilliant white flash.

The shooter was striding back to the van's open door when the bright burst drew his attention. He looked across at the café window and, for a moment, he met Finn's gaze. Two unreadable eyes narrowed; then the driver's arm was tugging at his sleeve and drawing him inside.

Wordless and white, Finn watched the vehicle speed away. From behind her came agitated shouts and the sounds of chair legs scraping tiles. She could only stare. The flash had been an unlucky accident - she'd been pointing the phone in a different direction altogether - but that wasn't really the point. The gunman might easily have formed a very different impression.

Outside on the pavement, someone screamed.

* * *

The longer Finn drove, the more she felt a strangeness settling. The city had a sullen cast. The moments passed, close and weighted, like the quiet, bated minutes before a storm.

Movements in doorways, the cars that drew up alongside her - everything appeared differently now, though it wasn't a transformation any camera would detect. It was she who was altered. Her world was impressing itself upon her in the age-old language of the hunt and, within her, some ancient survival instinct was responding.

Brake lights flared, snaking back through the dark and drizzle of the early evening. Checking her mirrors, she clasped the wheel tight - angry at being forced to leave like this; angrier still at how the experience was shaping her.

Outside, the world of the everyday rolled to a halt, all fancy falling away. Streets looked hard; the parks and the riverbanks unwelcoming. They offered no comfort now. The sentiments she'd attached to them were hers, not theirs; no more lasting or reciprocated than tattered poems pinned to the bark of a tree. The gingham-striped lawns wouldn't miss her. Shops would still trade, rocks would still grow smooth in the river. Her little exodus would go unnoticed.

Ahead, the stabbing reds dulled, distancing themselves as the line of vehicles moved on.

She glanced at her fuel gauge and saw the needle drooping to the quarter mark. What remained would take her well clear of the city. That would do. There would be plenty of opportunities to fill up somewhere on her long drive north.

Normality: that was all she wanted. Living like this felt surreal; somehow ridiculous. Gangland killings and criminal investigations were the province of dark-browed action heroes, not a woman like her. She ran a bookshop. She listened to *You and Yours* on Radio 4. She had a goldfish. Everything she owned and enjoyed declared her rightful place amongst the ordinary. Even now, in the midst of her flight, a pair of old running shoes sat in the footwell behind her, muddy and loosely wrapped in an Asda bag-for-life.

But normality had become elusive. Fear and unreality had suddenly intruded into her life, and all just because she'd chosen the wrong seat by a café window. Those few short seconds had been enough to overturn everything.

Yesterday had seemed endless but, in the early evening, an earnest-looking detective inspector had recommended she take herself *far away* for a while. His presence, his very title had seemed absurd - like something that belonged on the other side of a television screen - but still she'd taken it for sound advice.

So here she was, just twenty four hours later, fleeing organised criminals in a green Fiat Panda; abandoning her flat, her friends and her business in exchange for a period of safe anonymity somewhere in the Pentland Hills.

First though, she had to make things safe. Her mum and Chrissie had seen nothing of the killer, but who could say what he'd seen? His eyes had met hers - that she knew - but would he recognise her again? Had he seen enough to track her down? Had he noticed she'd had company?

Probably not. Real life was messy and hurried. All-knowing super-villains were the stuff of cheap fiction. But then the formidable D.I. Holland had considered the risk serious enough to express his concern, and if there was indeed a credible threat to her, then it might also extend to those closest to her. She wouldn't rest easy in her Scottish bolthole knowing there was still an address book on her shop counter listing the whereabouts of all her family and friends.

Turning at the next junction, she saw the unlit frontage of her little bookshop, its darkness conspicuous amongst the bright facades of the newsagents and the betting shops around it.

Stopping the car, she slipped out and remote-locked the door as she stepped up onto the kerb. Another key set the metal shutters rising.

She scanned the street as the grey panels wound noisily into their housing. Few pedestrians were abroad - a scattering of early-leaving office workers but nothing untoward. Seconds later, she was turning on the lights.

She knew that last bit wasn't textbook. Experienced international spies would probably use night-vision goggles or something, but that wasn't the sort of kit that most young booksellers had lying about in their handbags. Besides, she needed to see clearly if she was going to find what she'd come for. The quicker she found it, the quicker she could be away.

She hurried to her counter, expecting the rattle of glass that would tell her the door had settled shut behind her. Instead, there came a man's voice, jovial and strong.

"Hello there. Good evening."

For an instant she froze, then forced herself to turn.

The voice fitted the man. He was tall, well dressed and spreading into the roundedness of late middle age. A three-piece suit and gleaming brogues spoke of better neighbourhoods than this.

"Can I help you?" She smiled her shopkeeper's smile; an ordinary response to mask a mind contemplating extraordinary possibilities.

He returned a salesman's grin. "Miss Finn? The proprietor?"

It was a familiar overture. She saw a lot of speculative calls to the shop; offers of anything from public liability insurance to supermarket surplus.

"Yeah, hi." She turned away, feeling vainly for the precious notebook. "And you are?"

"Oh, I'm sorry. My name's Marcus. I'm a personal injury consultant."

Terrific: an ambulance-chaser. She turned back to face him. "Oh right. So that's... what? A sort of paralegal thing?"

The man chuckled, shook his head and reached into his jacket.

"You know, it's funny," he said. "A lot of people make that mistake."

He was still smiling as he took out a pistol, pointed it at her chest and fired.

We appreciate every like, tweet, facebook post and review and we love to hear from you. Please consider leaving us a review online or sending your thoughts and comments to info@mirrorworldpublishing.com

Thank you.

Lightning Source UK Ltd.
Milton Keynes UK
UKHW04f1601011018
329817UK00001B/20/P

9 781987 976489